MURDER BY SUSPICION

MURDER BY SUSPICION

An Ellie Quicke Mystery

Veronica Heley

This first world edition published 2015
in Great Britain and the USA by
SEVERN HOUSE PUBLISHERS LTD of
19 Cedar Road, Sutton, Surrey, England, SM2 5DA.
Trade paperback edition first published
in Great Britain and the USA 2015 by
SEVERN HOUSE PUBLISHERS LTD.

British Library Cataloguing in Publication Data

Heley, Veronica author.
  Murder by Suspicion. – (The Ellie Quicke mysteries)
  1. Quicke, Ellie (Fictitious character)–Fiction.
  2. Widows–Great Britain–Fiction. 3. Detective and
  mystery stories.
  I. Title II. Series
  823.9'14-dc23

ISBN-13: 978-0-7278-8524-1 (cased)
ISBN-13: 978-1-84751-624-4 (trade paper)
ISBN-13: 978-1-78010-677-9 (e-book)

All Severn House titles are printed on acid-free paper.

Severn House Publishers support the Forest Stewardship Council™ [FSC™],
the leading international forest certification organisation. All our titles that
are printed on FSC certified paper carry the FSC logo.

FSC
www.fsc.org
MIX
Paper from
responsible sources
FSC® C013056

Typeset by Palimpsest Book Production Ltd.,
Falkirk, Stirlingshire, Scotland.
Printed and bound in Great Britain by
TJ International, Padstow, Cornwall.

ONE

Whe she got there, the cupboard was bare.
In other words, the house was empty.
'Hello-o! I'm back!'
No reply.
Almost, Ellie panicked.

She'd travelled back alone. She was worn out after the long flight. She felt dizzy and sick. A headache threatened. Some people could cope with jet lag, but she couldn't. She needed to shower, get into comfortable clothes and eat something light. Then catch up with the news . . . slowly.

But, there was no one at home, and there should have been, shouldn't there?

Ellie's oldest friend, Rose, had taken it upon herself some time ago to act as housekeeper for Ellie and Thomas, but she'd become frail and hadn't stepped outside the house for months. Rose spent most of her time dozing either in her big chair in the kitchen, or in bed with the television on and the sound turned low. When Ellie had rung to say she was coming back a day early, she hadn't expected Rose to answer the phone, but she *had* expected Rose's new live-in carer to do so. The carer was supposed to listen to voicemail messages every day, and Ellie had spoken slowly and clearly, so the woman would know that Ellie was about to return.

But, Rose was nowhere to be seen. She wasn't in the kitchen, nor in her room. And neither was her carer. Had Rose been whipped off to hospital? The doctor had said that if Rose were to have another attack of bronchitis or a fall, it would be best to call an ambulance. If that had happened, surely the carer would have left a note to that effect?

What was the woman's name?

Ellie squeezed her eyes shut in an effort to remember. An

old-fashioned-looking woman, appearing older than she really was. Dumpy, bad skin, dressed in black . . . which was a bit odd these days, but beggars couldn't be choosers and she'd come highly recommended. What was more, Rose had said she didn't mind having her around, which had been the clincher.

What *was* her name? Claire? Yes, Claire.

Ellie clutched her head. She was too tired to think straight. The plane . . . ugh! And jet lag!

The house was neat and tidy, but looked different. The venerable grandfather clock in the hall had been moved from its usual place by the door to the kitchen quarters and was now standing by the door to the conservatory. Goodness! Why? And it had stopped. Well, it would, wouldn't it? Ancient clocks don't take kindly to being moved.

The house felt chilly. Almost, clammy. The central heating had been turned right down. Well, it was the end of July, though there was nothing warm about it. Ellie turned the thermostat up, and the boiler responded. Good.

There were no flowers on the chest in the hall. Ellie always liked to keep a vase of flowers there. She would do something about that soon.

Once she'd found out what had happened to Rose.

Ellie shed her coat and made herself think.

Make a cup of tea. Sit down. No, change her shoes and then sit down. Rushing around the globe had taken it out of her. She wondered how Thomas was getting on. They'd gone to Canada on holiday to see his family by his first, long-dead, wife, and then he'd gone on to take part in a seminar in Chicago, all very high powered and way above Ellie's head. She knew it had been a privilege for him to be asked. She'd said she'd go along with him to do some sightseeing and window shopping during the day and meet up with him in the evenings.

To tell the truth – and she was really rather ashamed of herself for thinking that way – she'd had enough of hanging around waiting for Thomas to stop being an important personage and return to being her very own love, which of course he always did, because he was a good man and a wonderful, caring husband. It was all right for him to be busy at home in London where she had plenty to do. More than enough to do, in fact. But this business of being at a loose end in a foreign country was, well, a teensy bit boring. And, let's face it, she'd been worried about leaving Rose for so long. So she'd decided to take the first plane home.

Actually, she'd been lucky and got an earlier flight than she'd expected . . . only to arrive jet-lagged and weary to find no one at home.

Claire, the Carer; anxious eyes, swollen ankles.

To tell the truth, Ellie's ankles weren't much better at the moment, though she'd worn the special stockings that were supposed to prevent such problems.

WHERE WAS ROSE?

Ellie went into the kitchen and opened the fridge. She wasn't quite sure why, as Rose, though tiny, could hardly have fitted in there. No Rose. Plenty of fresh milk, green veg, yogurt and salads. The fruit bowl on the table was well filled, too. At least Claire had been feeding Rose healthy food. Except, of course, that Rose didn't enjoy healthy food. She liked fish and chips, and cottage pie, and lasagne and anything that didn't put too much of a strain on her dentures. As the doctor had said, at her advanced age, why not give her whatever she fancied to eat?

Ellie checked the freezer. It was well stocked with ready meals of the vegetarian variety. Claire hadn't mentioned being a vegetarian at her interview, but there was the evidence to prove it. No roasts but nut, soya sausages instead of chicken. A couple of fish pies. All bought from the supermarket. Nothing home-cooked.

Ellie was dying for a good cup of strong, breakfast tea. It felt like the middle of the night to her but, glancing at the clock, it was only supper time back in the United Kingdom. She switched on the kettle.

Now, how could she find Rose? Who should she ring? The police, to report her missing? No, no. That would be an over-reaction. There would be, there *must* be, some explanation for her absence.

Perhaps Ellie's last phone call had not been recorded properly? She played back the messages on the phone in the hall and had the eerie experience of hearing her own voice. Yes, her message had been recorded, and Claire ought to have picked it up.

Ellie could ring her busy daughter Diana, who had originally engaged Claire to look after Diana's lively toddler. Claire hadn't been able to run fast enough to control the little imp, and so Diana had passed Claire on to Ellie rather as one passes on second-hand goods, saying: this doesn't fit me any longer, but it might do for you though it's past its sell-by date.

Or, Ellie could ring the doctor and ask if Rose had been taken to hospital. No, that was daft. If Rose had been taken to hospital, there would have been a note left for Ellie to see. Wouldn't there? She could ring the local hospital herself and ask . . .?

Diana might be able to think where Claire had taken Rose, perhaps in a wheelchair? Rose couldn't walk far nowadays.

Ellie told herself that she was not afraid of Diana. Not at all. Diana couldn't hurt her. Diana was ambitious and a career woman, and looked out for herself. It was perfectly understandable if she became somewhat terse when contacted at work.

Ellie made herself a cuppa with the last of the tea-bags, noting that they were also out of biscuits and instant coffee among other staples, and took it into the sitting room. She experienced a moment of dislocation. The room shifted around her. No, it didn't. That was nonsense. She was suffering from jet lag, that was all.

She went to the window to look out on to the garden. It was raining. The roses needed dead-heading. The lawn needed mowing, so the gardener couldn't have been that week. Or perhaps he had, but it had been raining and so he hadn't been able to cut the grass?

Don't put off ringing Diana. Ellie forced herself to sit down. Her head swam. Something was the matter, it really was. The chair, the high-backed chair that she always sat in beside the fireplace, wasn't there. She was sitting on someone else's chair, Thomas's beloved La-Z-Boy chair, which had been substituted for her own. If she sat on her own chair, which had been moved to the other side of the room, she'd be nowhere near the table with the phone on it.

How ridiculous! The agency must have sent a new cleaning team, who'd switched the chairs round. Well, they were too heavy for her to lift. She'd deal with the matter tomorrow. She moved to the edge of Thomas's chair and drew the telephone towards her. The place was neat and tidy. If Thomas had come back with her, there'd already have been newspapers strewn around and an empty coffee mug and . . . Well, he was probably addressing the delegates at this very moment. Or not, if she'd miscounted. Had she gone backwards or forwards in time? Or even lost a day? What was the time in the UK? Her watch wouldn't help. She looked at the clock on the mantelpiece. Nearly seven in the evening. What day of the week was it? Monday? Probably.

Diana must have left the office by now. Ellie keyed in Diana's home number. It bothered her that she had to sit in Thomas's chair, which didn't suit her behind. And there were no flowers in the room . . . As if that were important at the moment.

'Mother? You're back early. Something wrong?' A sharp voice, reminding Ellie that her daughter was too busy a woman to be interrupted by trivia.

'No, not really. I was worried about Rose and Thomas is tied up with work, so I decided . . . Diana, I'm home safely, but there's no sign of Rose or Claire.'

'Really? Well, I suppose they've gone for a walk.'

Ellie told herself not to shout at Diana, though she felt like it. 'Rose hasn't been out of the house for ages. You know that. That's why you passed Claire on to me, to look after her while we were away.'

'Well, you can't blame me for that!' Angry and defensive. 'She came highly recommended.'

Now what, exactly, did that mean? With an effort, Ellie made her voice calm. 'How much do you know about Claire? Could she have taken Rose to her own home? I have a feeling she was living somewhere locally, but I can't remember where.'

'How should I know? If you're so worried, you should ring the police. They might be able to . . . They know where she lives, anyway.'

Ellie had a horrid thought. 'Are you suggesting that Claire

has been in trouble with the police? Why didn't you warn me? I would never have entrusted Rose to her care if—'

'It was nothing. She had nothing whatever to do with the girl's disappearance. And it wasn't murder. The police admitted as much. A storm in a teacup.'

Murder? Ellie clutched the phone harder. 'You mean the police suspected her of—'

'No, no. It wasn't murder. They ruled that out. Honestly, Mother. Rose is perfectly safe with Claire. Anyone would think . . .! I expect she'll turn up soon. Now, if you don't mind, I have people coming in for dinner!' Down went the phone.

Ellie cradled her receiver. She was shaking. Cold. The central heating had come on, but it was raining and she still felt cold. She could ring Thomas and ask him . . . No, she couldn't interrupt him in the middle of a speech – or the middle of the night if it was night over there. He was going to ring her at his lunchtime, but she couldn't work out when that would be. She could ring the police. She was on friendly terms with someone at the local nick, and she could ask her . . .

Yes, but in the meantime, where was Rose? Perhaps she had been feeling so much stronger that she'd gone for a walk . . . but surely not in driving rain?

Ellie decided that if Rose weren't back in fifteen minutes, she'd ring the police.

Meantime, she would force herself to be practical. She would take her bag upstairs to unpack and freshen up.

She was halfway to the stairs when she heard a car draw up in the driveway and a key turn in the front door lock.

'Here we are, home again!' An over-hearty voice. Claire entered the hall, backwards, helping a large black woman to bring Rose in out of the rain. Rose was in a wheelchair. A wheelchair? Where had that come from?

'Rose!' Ellie dropped her bag and flew back down the stairs. 'Where have you been? I've been so worried about you.'

Claire started. 'Oh, Mrs Quicke. How you startled me. I didn't expect you back till tomorrow.' She didn't sound pleased about it.

'But I rang yesterday to say—'

The black woman beamed at Ellie. 'Hi, there, sister! Nice to meet you. We've been to a healing service, haven't we, Rose? We enjoyed it ever so much. And now we're all ready for a rest.' She lifted Rose out of the wheelchair and made sure she was balanced on her own two feet. Then she collapsed the wheelchair and took it away under her arm, shutting the front door behind her.

'Rose, are you all right?' Ellie got her arm around Rose's shoulders. Oh, how fragile she felt! Like a little brown sparrow. 'Where did you get the wheelchair?'

'I'm fine,' said Rose, in a tiny voice. 'Just a bit tired.'

Claire beamed at Ellie. 'She didn't want to be left out, did she, so we borrowed a wheelchair to get her to the service.'

Rose's face was a mesh of wrinkles and her eyes were weary. 'Lovely singing.' She patted Ellie's cheek. 'Glad you're back. I *am* a bit tired, yes, but it's a good tiredness. I'll sleep all right tonight.' Her voice dragged.

Ellie noted that Rose had lost weight again and her colour was worse than before. How old was she now? Eighty-eight? Or nine? 'Straight to bed, eh?'

Rose said, 'I can walk, if you give me your arm.' With Claire on one side of her and Ellie on the other, Rose tottered along the passage to her own quarters.

Some time ago, when Rose had begun to find the stairs too much, Ellie had contrived a large bed-sitting room, shower room and toilet for her off the kitchen quarters. The television was always on there, the sound turned low. It was still on now.

Claire said, 'Tck!' and turned it off. Claire gave Ellie a sharp look, which Ellie returned. Ellie opened her mouth to say something, but closed it again when Rose made a feeble movement.

Claire sounded over-hearty. 'There, there. Soon have you in bed, Rose. Mrs Quicke, why don't you let me see to Rose, while you get out of your travelling clothes? We didn't expect you back so early, did we, Rose? And, by the time we've freshened up, there'll be some supper on the table.'

Rose added her voice. 'Yes, you do look tired, Ellie.'

That did it. Telling someone they looked tired was guaranteed to make them feel a hundred and ten. Ellie decided to put Rose's welfare before having an argument about the unwisdom of taking an elderly, frail woman out of the house in the rain. Besides which, she had to admit that she herself was in no shape for a confrontation with Claire.

'Very well. I won't be long.' She dragged herself upstairs only to find her bed, the bed in which she and Thomas slept, had been moved to stand under the windows which overlooked the back garden.

Oh, really! But she was too tired to make a fuss tonight. She unpacked, showered and changed into a warm skirt and jumper. When she descended to the kitchen again, there was no sign of Claire, but some home-made soup had been heated up and left warming through on the hob, a nut roast was cooking in the oven and some vegetables were steaming on the side. A note on the table said that now Ellie had returned, Claire had gone out for the evening but would be back later.

Well, perhaps it was just as well to postpone the unpleasantness.

Ellie ladled some soup into a mug and took it through to Rose, who had drifted off to sleep but woke with a start when Ellie sat down beside her bed.

'What time is it, Ellie? It's lovely to have you back.'

'Supper time. I haven't a clue which day of the week it is. Let's sit you up so you can have your soup.'

Rose took a sip of soup. Her hand was shaking. 'Nice soup.'

'There's a nut roast for afters.'

'I'll just have the soup. I lost count of the days, kept asking Claire when you'd be back. She's been very good to me, you know.'

'She's looked after you well?' Ellie didn't mean to sound doubtful, but she could hear the reservations in her voice.

So could Rose. 'I think so.' Again, her voice dragged. Then she made an effort. She pulled herself up the pillows. 'She's done her best. She's been sleeping in my old room upstairs, so that she could hear my little bell ring if I needed her in the night. Which I haven't. Don't be too hard on her. She's had a difficult time with her family and all.' Her hand in Ellie's was warm enough. Perhaps she hadn't taken any great harm by the outing. Her eyes closed.

Ellie had forgotten that Rose had always gone to church in the old days and loved the hymns. She'd often been heard singing about the house, particularly when she was cooking. Over the years she'd gone out less and less, and her church attendance had dropped away.

Ellie was annoyed with herself. She ought to have seen to it that Rose had been able to get to church, but this and that had happened, and, well, she'd let it slide from her mind. Too much else to think about.

No, she ought to have thought of it. She winced.

The two women had met when they were both working in the charity shop in the Avenue, and they had found common cause in their efforts to deal with bossy daughters. Then Ellie's difficult, wealthy Aunt Drusilla had needed someone to look after her in her declining years and, unlikely as it had seemed at first, Rose had happily slipped into the role and made it her own. Rose and Miss Quicke had been good for one another, and when the older lady had died and left her big house to Ellie, she'd also left Rose well provided for. Instead of going off to live by herself, Rose had decided to stay on as Ellie's housekeeper and had become part of the family.

Rose had gradually – oh, so gradually – faded with the passing years. Recently she had begun to 'see' and converse with the late Miss Quicke. A harmless eccentricity.

Ellie took the mug of soup out of Rose's hand lest it fall to the floor. She let her eyes walk around the room. It was clean and dust-free. Rose's bedclothes were fresh. There was a carafe and glass on her bedside table. Plenty of water in it. Beside that was the little silver bell which Miss Quicke had been accustomed to use when she needed attention. It was ironic that Rose, who had once answered its summons, was now using it to summon others to her side. That made Ellie smile.

Ellie laid Rose's hand back on the duvet and turned the television on, low. The house was still cold. Old people need warmth. She checked the thermostat in the hall, only to find that someone – presumably Claire – had turned it down to zero.

How annoying! Ellie turned it back up again. She told

herself that she must keep calm. She was overtired, and this was such a little thing. If the woman had really been looking after Rose well – except for taking her out of the house like that – then Ellie mustn't prejudge matters. It would be easy enough to tell Claire that she liked the house to be kept warm. Anger was not helpful. She must fight it. She tried, and lost the fight.

Bother the woman!

She warmed up Rose's mug of soup in the microwave and drank it herself. It wasn't bad soup, possibly a trifle on the sweet side, but all right.

Then the phone rang, and it was Thomas, ringing to see if she'd returned safely. He was full of the welcome he'd received in Chicago and how he'd met up with two old friends, whom he hadn't seen for ages . . .

Ellie forgot about Claire for a while. Sufficient to the day, etcetera.

She ate some of the nut roast – far too dry. Unappetizing. Then bed beckoned. She was worn out, but didn't think she'd sleep. Jet lag. How long before she would feel normal again?

Tuesday morning

Ellie had set the alarm as usual. Best not to give in to jet lag. Oh dear. Was it morning already? She reached for Thomas and remembered that he was still on the other side of the Atlantic. She'd slept surprisingly well. She listened out for the grandfather clock in the hall to chime the hour, but of course it couldn't, because it had been moved.

What was the time? What day of the week was it? Thomas wasn't here. Rose, so frail. Claire, so bossy. Claire, whom Diana had indicated might be a murderess! Ouch!

Ellie sat up and nearly fell out of bed. Disorientation!

Of course, the bed had been moved from its usual position. And the room was cold. Don't say that Claire had turned the heating off again!

Now that really was annoying.

On with the day. Oh, bother! She'd just remembered she'd used the last of the tea bags the previous evening, and there was no instant coffee. She must make a list and go to the shops that morning.

The whine of a vacuum cleaner greeted her as she went down the stairs. A strange woman whisked herself across the hall and disappeared.

Ellie cried, 'Stop!' but the woman had gone. The noise of the vacuum cleaner must have drowned out Ellie's voice. The heavy door to the kitchen quarters – which was always kept open so that Ellie and Thomas could hear if Rose rang her bell – was now closed, and the door to the conservatory at the back of the hall . . . what on earth was happening there? Was that washing hanging up to dry inside? Had the tumble-drier broken?

What was going on?

Ellie clutched her arms around herself. The house was chilly, and there was a nasty draught from somewhere. Ellie's dander was well and truly up.

She marched into the sitting room, to find two young women on their knees, polishing the floorboards. Both were black and wearing black: loose T-shirts with some kind of logo on them and long, loose trousers. They were complete strangers.

Where were her usual cleaning team?

Ellie said, 'Who are you?'

The older of the two frowned. 'What?'

Ellie blinked. 'I'm Mrs Quicke. This is my house. I repeat: who are you?'

'We don't know nothing about a Mrs Quicke. We got our schedule, and we stick to it. Twice a week, two hours a time. And we don't stand no nonsense from no one.'

Ellie gaped. 'Who has given you those orders?'

'Claire did. Now if you don't mind, you're holding us up.'

Ellie swallowed hard and made her way into the kitchen. Rose wasn't up yet. Claire was nowhere to be seen. The thermostat had been turned right down on the wall. Again. Grrr!

Ellie returned it to its normal position.

She looked in on Rose, who was beginning to stir. 'Rose, are you awake?'

Rose smiled and opened her eyes. 'Lovely to have you back, dear. I had such a funny dream. I thought you'd gone away for good, and I was drifting away into the clouds.'

Ellie patted Rose's hand. 'I'm back, but I am a bit confused. We seem to have changed our cleaners.'

A look of incomprehension. Then memory stirred at the back of Rose's eyes. 'Oh, yes, dear. They were rude to Claire, so she had to tell them not to come again. Claire knew these two lovely girls from church, and they're going to look after us instead.'

Ellie clutched at her sanity. 'We've had our cleaners for ever. I can't believe they would have been rude to anyone, or not without reason.'

Rose sat upright, some vestige of animation returning to her. 'They called Claire a really bad word that I don't want to repeat. They said she ought to be in prison. Claire was so upset. She said we should pay them off, and I did it out of my own money, which was only right, dear, because as you know, Miss Quicke left me very well off, and you've been paying me a wage all along which you hadn't ought to do, especially since I've retired from being a full-time housekeeper for you, what with your getting young Vera in to act as house-keeper instead of me, and by the way, she's been popping round from her own house every other day to see if I'm all right, and so has that young limb of hers, Mikey. Mikey says his mum's working at reception in the hotel next door almost full time now. Where was I? Oh, yes. I've never had a chance to pay you back for all your care of me until now, so I was really glad to stand up for poor Claire, and I want you to tell her that her job is safe here, and that we won't allow anyone else to call her a murderess.'

Ellie tried to disguise her concern. 'May I ask who it is she's supposed to have murdered?'

'No one we know, dear. Just a silly girl who went missing, chasing after some pop star or other, but it was all a false alarm and she surfaced again later to say she was perfectly all right. Ten to one, she'll come home again when her boyfriend runs out of money.'

TWO

Ellie wanted to scream. A girl had gone missing, and Claire was accused of having murdered her? No, not murder. But . . . Claire had had something to do with a girl going AWOL? And Rose didn't seem to think this important?

Ellie wanted to hit Rose over her head – not that that would do any good.

Ellie considered a number of other options, such as taking a whip and driving the two new cleaners out of her house, but she didn't possess a whip, and even if she'd had one, she'd probably trip over it while trying to flourish it over someone's head. And suppose she actually caught one of the women with the tip of her whip and cut her?

No, that didn't bear thinking about, either.

Ellie was reduced to saying that she'd have words with the cleaning agency as soon as they opened for the day, but in the meantime she would like Rose to tell the new girls that Ellie was mistress of the house and decided what temperature it was to be at, and they were not to move the furniture around without permission.

Rose's spurt of energy drained away, and she fell back among her pillows. In a dead voice she said, 'Claire told them to, for some reason. She did explain it to me, but I can't remember why. I'm getting old, Ellie. Old and forgetful.'

Ellie was alarmed. This was the first time Rose had complained of her age. 'Well, never mind all that for the moment. Are you getting up this morning, Rose? Do you fancy some breakfast?'

'I'll be up in a little while, though I'm not really hungry nowadays.'

Ellie went back through the kitchen – no sign of Claire – and turned up the thermostat, noting that the kitchen was in a mess, with dirty plates left in the sink, and the floor needing a good seeing-to. Ellie went in search of the new cleaners. They'd finished in the sitting room, leaving the window open on a cold, wet morning. Ellie shut the window with a bang and moved on to the dining room. This was a room which nowadays was only used for the weekly meetings of the trust which Ellie administered. Here, another open window was blowing the long curtains awry, and the massive table had been dismantled, the leaves taken out and the two D-ends placed against the wall, leaving the centre of the room clear. Why? The eight dining chairs were now being polished, piece by piece.

Ellie coughed to attract the cleaners' attention. One of the women looked up, caught the other's eye and bent back to her work.

Ellie said, as pleasantly as she could, 'Good morning. I'm afraid I don't know your names.'

'I'm Dolores,' said the older one of the two. Stick thin, looked as if she could do with a good meal or two. 'She's –' indicating the younger woman – 'Liddy.'

Liddy bobbed her head up, rubbed the side of her face and returned to her work.

'Very well, Dolores,' said Ellie. 'I've had a word with Rose about employing you. I can't say that I'm happy about the situation, but I will be looking into it and I will let you know as soon as possible whether or not I shall want to have you again. Meanwhile, I'd like you to return the furniture you've moved back to its original positions and put the kitchen to rights.'

Both women stopped what they were doing. Liddy looked sideways at Dolores. The older one spoke, as before, for both of them. 'We have our schedules from Claire. Today we polish in here. Monday we do the kitchen.'

'I understand why you followed Claire's orders in my absence, but that won't do now I'm back. Where is she?'

Again, the two women glanced at one another. 'She was called in to account for herself,' said the younger woman. Ellie wondered what 'Liddy' was short for.

Dolores gave her a dark look with pursed lips, and Liddy reddened. 'We wouldn't know, would we?'

Yet it was obvious that they did know something, even if they were not prepared to say what it was.

Dolores said, 'We have to get on. Missus Rose will give us our money when we finish here, and then we'll move on to our next job.'

'Now I'm back, I'll be paying you.'

'Our contract is with Missus Rose.'

Defeated, Ellie retired to the kitchen. There was still no sign of Claire.

Rose was stirring next door. Ellie helped her to dress. Oh, how pitiful it was to see Rose fumble with her clothes in a way she'd never had to do before. Rose liked old, comfortable clothes and wore them till they were fit for nothing but the rag bag, with a button off here and the elastic loose there. Whether Rose liked it or not, Ellie was going to get some new things for her. Ellie was angry with herself for having left her old friend for so long and angry – she had to admit – with Rose for deteriorating so fast. And angry with Claire and, well, everyone.

Which wasn't like her. She set about making breakfast for herself and Rose; cereal, soft boiled eggs and toast with fruit juice, as there was neither tea nor coffee to be had. Ellie started to make a list of what was needed, doing her best to ignore the mess around her. The floor was a disgrace, and so was the oven top! As for the sink!

There was still no sign of Claire by the time breakfast had been eaten. 'Rose, dear, the new cleaners mentioned a contract. May I see your copy?'

Rose was vague. 'I don't think I had one, did I? I pay them with a cheque each time. It's almost the first time I've used a chequebook in all the years I've had it. Tell the truth, I'd almost forgotten I had one, and Claire had to show me how to fill it in.'

Ellie controlled herself with an effort. She was going to do something nasty to Claire when that conniving con woman eventually chose to show herself, if she ever did. Taking advantage of Rose like that! It was iniquitous. 'How much do you pay them each time?'

'I'm not sure. Is it ten pounds an hour each?'

That was on the high side, but just about acceptable. 'What is the length of the contract?'

Rose's gaze wandered. 'Was it three months, or six? It's all right, isn't it? I haven't done anything stupid, have I? I'm afraid I'm getting a bit forgetful.'

Ellie let out her breath slowly. Very slowly. There was no point in taking her anger out on Rose. She made herself smile. 'Thank you, Rose. You've done exactly the right thing, but now I'm back I shall be responsible for paying the cleaners, just as I used to be. Now, was there anything else?'

Rose fumbled her way into her big chair and lay back with a sigh of relief. 'I don't think so. That secretary of yours, Pat, she said she'd start work again when you got back, so to ring her when you do as she was going to take time off to visit someone in Scotland, not that I think she has relatives there, or maybe it was the Isle of Man. She'll be back by now, I think. She said she'd leave a note for you in your study.'

A pity. Correspondence would have piled up in Pat's absence. Well, it couldn't be helped. Ellie rubbed her arms. Why was the house so cold, still? She checked the thermostat. It had been turned down again. She couldn't believe it. She heard herself grinding her teeth, which is something she never, ever did, because the dentist said it set up all sorts of problems. She turned the thermostat back up. Who was it that kept turning it down? Not Rose, who felt the cold. So, the cleaners?

She looked around. She was missing something – somebody – else. 'Where's Midge?' Ellie had been adopted by a marauding ginger tom, who usually sprang into sight, demanding food, whenever she entered the kitchen. Ellie realized with a bump of dismay that she hadn't seen him since her return.

Rose sighed. 'Claire has a thing about cats. Allergies. I usually let him in when she goes out. It's all right, I leave food for him in that covered-over bit in the yard, and Mikey says he goes over the wall to the hotel next door, where they've been making a fuss of him.'

Ellie went to the back door. The cat flap had been locked.

She unlocked it. She was building up a head of steam about Claire.

The elder of the cleaners . . . Dolores? . . . sidled into the kitchen, followed by Liddy, whose eyes were half closed, and who was clutching the side of her face. Dolores said, 'We're ready to go now.'

'You haven't done the kitchen yet.'

'We can't stay no longer. Liddy's not feeling up to it. Anyway, we only does the kitchen once a week, on Mondays. Claire keeps it clean, the rest of the time.'

Oh. Ellie looked round for her handbag. 'I'll get your money.'

'It's Missus Rose that pays us.'

'Not when I'm home. I told you; this is my house, and I pay the bills.'

A weak smile. 'That's not what it says on the contract.'

'I need to see that contract. Apparently, Rose hasn't a copy.'

A wince. 'We don't have no copy, neither.'

'No copy of the contract, no need to pay,' said Ellie.

Rose cried out, 'Oh, but—'

'No, Rose,' said Ellie. 'This has gone far enough.'

'He'll sue you!' said the cleaner.

'Not without a contract. And who's "he"?'

The woman fidgeted, twisted a curly lock of hair, grimaced. 'Claire will sort it.'

Ellie nodded. 'Yes, I need a word with her.'

Rose was distressed. 'Ellie, you don't understand—'

Ellie agreed. 'No, I don't. I don't understand why the house was empty when I returned. I don't understand how they could have taken you out on such a wretched night, when you can hardly walk. I don't understand why the furniture has been moved around and why the thermostat keeps getting turned down—'

Dolores grinned. 'Claire's orders. It's bad for the furniture to have the heat on, especially in July.'

Ellie kept her voice down with an effort. 'It's my house, and if I want it warm, then that's the way it's going to be.' She made herself stop. Dolores was only obeying orders. It wasn't her fault.

'And,' said Dolores, 'your furniture was in the wrong places. Beds should always face east. What's more, the master of the house must have pride of place by the fire, and not his wife, who should submit to him in everything.'

Ellie threw up her hands. 'Beds must face east? I can't sit where I like in my own house? Whatever nonsense is this?'

'Oh, I'd forgotten about that,' said Rose, frowning. 'Claire explained it all to me. Luckily, my bed is in the right position, but yours wasn't. Tomorrow the decorator's coming to paint the downstairs in green, which is the best colour for the people of the Vision to live in. There, now! I remembered that all right, didn't I?'

'I'm going mad!' said Ellie.

Rose said, 'It's all right, Ellie. Claire will explain everything when she comes.'

'In the meantime,' said Ellie, reaching for her handbag, 'I'm going to pay these two cleaners what is owed them, plus a bonus in payment of their next two weeks' wages. I will not be requiring them again. Oh, yes, and I will require a receipt.'

'You can't! We'll get into terrible trouble!' said Dolores.

'Watch me,' said Ellie, taking out her chequebook. 'If your boss – whoever he may be – wants to make an issue of it, I'll get my solicitor to look into the matter of a non-existent contract made with an elderly person in the absence of the householder. Understand? Now, who do I make the cheque out to?'

'He'll flay us alive!'

Ellie snorted. 'Flaying went out of fashion some years ago.'

'You don't understand. If we don't work, we don't eat.'

'You should have thought of that before you decided to ignore my wishes. Shall I make it out to Cash?'

'No. We're not allowed to handle—'

'Yes,' said Liddy, holding out her hand for it. 'I'll explain it to the boss.'

'He'll be furious,' said Dolores, showing the whites of her eyes.

Liddy took the cheque. 'It's money, and we need it. As she says, be your age.'

Dolores turned on Ellie. 'You'll be left without anyone to clean for you!'

'That's my affair, not yours.'

'You won't get your old cleaners to come again. They said, didn't they, Liddy?'

The younger woman nodded. 'They said.'

'Tough,' said Ellie. 'Now, if you have any keys, I'd be glad if you'd hand them over.'

Dolores fished some keys out of her pocket and dropped them on the table. 'We'll be back.'

Ellie lifted her eyebrows. 'I'll see you out.'

Almost, she banged the front door after the two women. When she returned to the kitchen, she found Rose attempting, unsteadily, to get to her feet. 'Oh dear, whatever will Claire say? You shouldn't have done that, Ellie. They're nice girls, and they do need the work. They were only obeying orders.'

'Not my orders, and not, I think, yours,' said Ellie, feeling rather inclined to cry. 'I think this Claire must be something of a bully. Let me help you back into your chair.'

'Claire, a bully? No, really.' Rose passed her hand across her eyes in a vague fashion. 'She told me all about the right way to live. She said we must think more of others, and share what we have, so that we will be rewarded with the Blessed Vision.'

'A vision of the Blessed Virgin Mary?' Ellie knew that Catholics often found it helpful to centre their devotions around the mother of Jesus.

'No,' said Rose. 'That's not it. At least, I don't think so. I do get muddled nowadays. I remember now: it's the vision their pastor had, the one who heads up this special church of theirs. Claire says he's teaching them how to travel along the road of life.'

'She's got the right idea, but perhaps has been too enthu-siastic about putting it into practice. Now I'll make a couple of phone calls and get down to cleaning the kitchen.'

She made her way to her study to make the calls and found that the cleaners had been moving furniture around there, too. There was a pile of letters on her desk, both for Thomas and for herself. Bother. Thomas had his study in the library at the end of the corridor. Ellie's part-time secre-tary would normally have separated out the wheat from the chaff, disposed of the junk mail and placed Thomas's correspondence on his own desk. Now Ellie would have to sort them out herself. And, her computer had been disconnected for some reason. She reconnected and switched on. Nothing happened.

For two pins she'd have burst into tears. She restrained herself.

First things first. She rang the cleaning agency she'd used for years, and fortunately Maria answered the phone. Ellie and Maria were doubly connected. Not only did Ellie use the cleaners Maria's agency supplied, but Maria was married to Stewart, the General Manager of Ellie's charitable trust.

Many years ago, Stewart had been married to Ellie's ambitious daughter Diana. That marriage had not lasted, since Stewart had never been flamboyant enough for Diana, even though he was a good man, solid in every way. Diana had moved on to a man she considered a better prospect, and in due course Stewart had met and married Maria. Between them, Stewart and Maria had created a comfortable home for Stewart and Diana's son, and they'd added a trio of lively little girls to the family, who adored him and whom he, in turn, adored. Ellie was a frequent visitor to their house, where they made her feel very much at home.

'Maria, this is Ellie. I only got back last night and—'

'We wondered when you'd be back. How did the trip go?' Maria's tone was cool.

'Thomas had to go on to this seminar in Chicago, but I was worried about Rose so I got an earlier flight. Maria, what's been going on? I came back last night to find the house in chaos and Rose had been taken out to some church service or other, when she obviously wasn't fit. Today there were a couple of new cleaners who wouldn't take a blind bit of notice of anything I said, and the woman I left in charge is conspicuous by her absence. I don't want to worry Rose, but can you tell me what's going on?'

A sigh. 'Oh, Ellie. I don't know what to say. We've been working for you for ever, and know how you like things, but this Claire woman . . . We didn't know what to think when she began to change things around. My girls didn't want to do it, but Claire said she'd been left in charge and you'd be pleased when you saw what she'd done.'

Ellie said, 'Humph!'

Maria half laughed. 'Yes, I thought that too, so I asked to speak to Rose on the phone. Claire said Rose wasn't feeling up to taking calls.'

'She's not well. I'm worried about her.'

'Yes, the girls were, too. It was your usual two; Amy and Anna. I suppose they were a bit tactless, and of course it didn't help that Anna recognized Claire from when her friend's daughter disappeared—'

'I seem to have missed something here.'

'It was some time ago, maybe five months? Six? One of Anna's friends had a daughter called Gail, who disappeared after quarrelling with Claire. Gail was an almost-sixteen-year-old girl with rampant hormones, not interested in school, often played truant, got in with the wrong crowd, you know? Skirts up to here, hair and nail extensions, but that's how they all dress nowadays, isn't it?'

'Disappeared?' Ellie frowned. Had there been something in the local paper about it? 'Didn't the police decide she'd gone off with a boyfriend to a pop festival or something?'

'Well, yes, and she did phone her mother to say she was all right and living with a new boyfriend, but there's been no sign of her since.'

'So, not murdered, then? How does Claire come into it?'

'Claire and Gail lived in the same big old house, which is divided up into flats. Claire had seen the girl hanging around the Broadway late at night with a man and told her mother, who grounded the girl, forbade her to go out at night alone. Gail hated Claire for telling on her. To rub it in, Claire offered to pick Gail up from her drama club after school in the evenings, and Gail said that was treating her like a child and, well, you can imagine. They were not on good terms. Gail was seen to get into Claire's car one evening and never seen again. Claire says she dropped Gail at the front entrance of their house and then drove round to the back to park, but the girl's mobile phone was found in her car next day, and a girl like Gail doesn't leave that in someone's car by mistake, does she?'

'I think I remember seeing the girl's picture in the papers. Honestly, it looked as if she could take care of herself.'

'Agreed. Claire told the police that Gail was jailbait and had probably gone off with an older man who'd been seen hanging around the drama club at night – a man who's never been traced. Gail's school friends said she'd got a boyfriend of her own age, but apparently he was in the clear. The police put out an appeal for information, but no one came forward. After a while she rang her mother to say she was having the time of her life and had no intention of returning home, so that got Claire off the hook. Rightly or wrongly, Gail's mother is convinced that the phone call was fixed, that in some way Gail was kidnapped and induced to make the call. She thinks Claire lashed out at Gail, killed her, and has stashed her body away somewhere. She hasn't any evidence, of course, but . . . when did that ever stop someone thinking the worst?'

'The phone call was genuine?'

'The police said so.'

'So when Amy and Anna came here to work and found Claire asking them to do things which they didn't like . . .?'

'There were words. Anna went for Claire, which she shouldn't have done, of course, though perhaps it was under-standable. The upshot was that Amy and Anna left, swearing never to return. We asked Claire if she'd like us to find someone else, but she refused.'

'She's found a couple, but they've turned the house upside down, moved all the furniture around and wouldn't listen to anything I said. They've gone. So, can you get Anna and Amy back for me? Or if not them, can you find me another couple of good cleaners, to start as soon as possible?'

A sigh of relief. 'I'll do my best. I'm glad you're back, Ellie. Stewart's been worried about you too, and the children have been asking if you're going to bring them back a present from across the Pond.'

'Of course I have, or rather, the presents are in Thomas's luggage, as I came back in a hurry with only a tote bag. How is Stewart? I understand Pat's been away, and there's a pile of correspondence on my desk. I'd better schedule a meeting soonest. There must be lots to catch up on.'

'Stewart's fine. I'll get him to ring you. About Rose . . .?'

'Yes. She's very frail. I think we've got to the point where I do need someone living in to look after her. Not Claire. She was passed on to me by . . . well, never mind that now. I employed her without checking out her references, more fool me. So, can you find me someone to replace her?'

'I'll do what I can. I'll ring round and get back to you, but—'

'Thanks, Maria. Oh, I must go. That's the doorbell.'

Actually, it was someone playing a tune on the front doorbell. Or, not a tune, but a rhythm. Only one person did that. Hurray!

Ellie opened the door and hugged the young woman standing on the doorstep. 'Oh, you blessing!'

Vera had until recently been Ellie's live-in housekeeper, but had moved on, with her teen son Mikey, to complete a business degree and to marry her childhood sweetheart.

Vera hugged Ellie back. 'Am I glad to see you! I've been coming by on my way to work most days, but—'

Ellie held the girl at arm's-length. 'Let me look at you! Marriage suits you!'

'Do you think so?' Vera reddened, pleased. She was wearing a good white shirt over a black skirt, both bought from better shops than she'd been able to patronize before. Working clothes for her new job at the hotel? Her fair hair was caught back at the nape of her neck, but it had been fluffed up around her face in becoming fashion. Her complexion glowed with health and happiness. 'I wanted to check on Rose, but—'

There was a heavy tread in the driveway. Claire, looking cold and cross. She was dressed in black from head to toe and burdened with packages.

Ellie and Vera exchanged glances. Vera stepped aside while Ellie confronted the newcomer. 'Ah, Claire. I wondered where you'd got to. We need to talk.'

Claire bared her teeth in a smile. She gave Vera a sideways glance which ought to have been put in a sheath. 'Ah. Your old housekeeper. She's been round, bothering me, wanting to see Rose all the time, which is never convenient. If you think I'm late for work this morning, you've got another think coming.

I'll have you know I was finding some decent clothes for Rose to wear, her present wardrobe being fit for nothing but the dustbin.'

'We'll discuss that in a minute,' said Ellie, who had to admit that Claire had got a point. 'Vera, would you like to go through and visit with Rose for a while? Claire and I need to have a little chat.'

Vera had always been quick on the uptake. She disappeared down the corridor to the kitchen area.

'Now, Claire,' said Ellie, leading the way into the sitting room and experiencing another moment of dislocation when she realized her own comfortable chair was still not back in its usual place.

Claire followed, talking as she displayed the clothing she had brought. 'Two vests with long sleeves, white, with pants to match. Two pairs of jogging trousers, easy for her to pull up, two long-sleeved sweaters and socks to match.'

Ellie wanted to laugh. The trousers and sweatshirts were all black. Rose never wore black, and neither did Ellie. It was, perhaps, a reaction to a time when so many women went into black clothes in mourning for the loved ones they'd lost in the wars of the previous century?

'It was good of you to think of Rose,' said Ellie, 'but it's my responsibility to see to her wardrobe. I will pay you for the underclothes, but not the other things, which you can return to the shop. Rose never wears black.'

'She should do so now. We should all be in mourning for our sins.' Claire was very much in earnest, clutching the clothes to her protectively.

Ellie didn't know whether to laugh or scream with frustration. 'I'm sorry if you feel like that about it, but I don't, and neither does Rose.' She sank back in her chair, suddenly overcome by fatigue. 'Sorry . . . jet lag . . . catching up with me.' She closed her eyes for a moment. Was that the telephone she could hear ringing, or something in her head?

Claire said, 'Hold on a minute,' and clip-clopped out of the room. Ellie relaxed, but all too soon Claire was back, putting a glass of something to Ellie's mouth. 'Drink this. It will help.'

Ellie sipped. Something sweetish? Medicinal? Ellie tried to push it away, but Claire was insistent. 'Down the hatch. It will do you good.'

Ellie swallowed. It wasn't unpleasant, but there was quite a lot of it. She took a couple of deep gulps, and then another two. One more. And managed to wave the glass away. She opened her eyes. Claire's mouth was opening and shutting. She was saying something which didn't make sense. Something about a Blessed Vision.

'What?' Ellie tried to get to her feet. She could manage it, if she concentrated. Blessed Vision? Blessed Virgin? No, no. She shook her head to clear it. She must have misheard.

Ellie believed in God. She believed in prayer and reading the bible, and in trying to live as a Christian should. 'I've never heard of this Blessed Vision.'

'But you should,' said Claire, pushing Ellie back into her chair and patting her arm. 'There, there, now. There, there.'

Ellie subsided into her chair and enquired within. She did feel a bit odd. Jet lag, of course. She ought to take it easy.

Claire was saying something about a vision that transformed sinners . . . What nonsense. She crooned some words that didn't make sense. Her hand was on Ellie's forehead. '. . . must welcome the Vision into your life. Let the light of the Vision shine into the dark corners of your soul. See how your sins cower away from the light. Let it flood every particle of your being. Shed your old self . . . Let us lead you into the light . . .'

Her voice was hypnotic.

Ellie blinked. She felt light. Lighter than air. Light in her head.

'. . . as you continue to leave your old self behind and welcome the new, you will learn to grow in the light until you become part of the Vision itself . . .'

What nonsense! Ellie thought. But found it difficult to move.

'The Vision has been blocked by your sins, your idolatry, your love of money and power . . .'

What! thought Ellie. The woman's mad!

'You realize that the chains of your sin and your wealth are holding you back, speaking the words of Mammon . . . but you are slowly but definitely being drawn to the light. Even as we speak, the Vision has you in its sight . . .'

The woman was trying to hypnotize her!

THREE

'No,' said Ellie. And then, louder, 'No!' She pushed Claire's hand away and tried to stand up. Made it at the second attempt. Her balance was still not good. Jet lag. Ugh.

Claire stepped back, frowning. 'You shouldn't try to fight it.'

'Fight what?' Ellie rubbed her forehead.

'The light of the Vision, which is helping you to rid yourself of the evil powers that hold you in thrall.'

Ellie tried to laugh. Almost made it. 'Look, Claire; I don't know what you believe in, but I believe in God and in doing as much good as I can in this world.'

'We know that. I've been sent to show you the true path of—'

'Enough!' said Ellie. 'I'm sorry, but this is not working out. I think the best thing we can do is for me to give you a month's wages, and for you to leave immediately.'

The woman gaped. 'You can't do that!'

'Try me.'

'You don't understand. I have to keep this job. It's desperately important! And anyway, you can't sack me without reason.'

'Reason enough,' said Ellie, groping her way back into her chair. 'You were asked to look after an elderly, frail woman and took her out of the house when she couldn't even walk unaided. You lower the thermostat on the central heating till it's too low for an elderly woman's comfort, you've turned my house upside down, my regular cleaners have walked off in a huff, and you've brought in two women who refused to listen to what I wanted them to do, and what's more—'

'I can explain!'

'—it seems you got Rose to sign some sort of contract which she didn't understand, for an indefinite period of time. I rather think the police would be interested in hearing about that, don't you?'

'Oh, no!' Claire sank into a chair, legs awry, skirt above her knees . . . An unappetizing sight. As were the tears streaming down her cheeks. 'Not the police! They'll crucify me!'

'Hardly,' said Ellie, whose head seemed stuffed with cotton wool.

Claire slid to the floor and clutched at Ellie's hand. 'You can't, you mustn't, I beg of you!'

Ellie tried to release herself. 'Let go!'

Claire clutched all the harder, shuffling forward on her knees, kissing – actually kissing – Ellie's hand. 'They think I did it, but I didn't, honest I didn't! I'll swear on the bible, on the cross, on the Holy Vision, I did not kill that girl! But if you ring them, they'll think . . .'

Tears splashed on to Ellie's knee. She tried to pull away, but she was already at the back of the chair.

'I beg of you, see: I kiss your hands and feet!' She slobbered over Ellie's hand and made as if to duck down to kiss Ellie's feet.

Ellie said, 'If you try to kiss my feet, I shall kick you! I mean it! I shall kick you into next week, and then I'll ring the police. For heaven's sake, woman: get a grip!' Ellie fought her hand free and managed to wriggle out of her seat. She held on to the back of her chair until she felt less dizzy, then moved to the window. The sun had come out. Sort of. She wrestled the French windows open to let in the fresh air. And breathed deeply. Her head was stuffy, but now she could think more clearly.

She found a hanky and wiped her hand. Ugh. She must wash it.

Claire had stayed on her knees, an ungainly heap in stale black clothes. Her skirt had rucked up. She was wearing knee-highs instead of full-length tights. Her shoes were scuffed. Her hair was wrenched back and secured with an elastic band which was not doing its job properly. Diana had said the woman was in her thirties, but she looked fifty. Her eyes were slightly protuberant, grey, brimming over with tears. She put her palms together, as if in prayer, and held them up to Ellie. 'I beg of you! Don't ring the police!'

Ellie closed her eyes momentarily. *Dear Lord above, what a mess! What do you want me to do? She is such a poor creature that I . . . But she did try to hypnotize me. Or did she? I can't think straight.*

'If you have any Christian feeling left in your heart, you won't turn me over to the heathen.'

What heathen? The police?

That would have made Ellie laugh, if she hadn't been feeling so strange. She said, 'Oh, get up, do. I'm going to get myself a cup of coffee and some painkillers. I suggest you go and have a wash and tidy up. Then we will sit down and discuss how best to deal with the situation.'

Saying which, Ellie walked around the still-kneeling Claire and made her way to the kitchen, where, surprise!, Vera was scouring a sparklingly clean sink and Rose was sitting in her chair, looking no bigger than an eight-year-old child. The air was clean, Midge the cat was sitting on top of the fridge, and all was right with the world.

Ellie said, 'Oh, Vera: you wonder! But you shouldn't have.'

'Hah!' said Vera, drying her hands. 'You know I can't bear to see a kitchen in a mess. Five minutes' work, that's all. Now I must be on my way. I'll pop in again tomorrow.' She kissed Rose, gave Ellie a high five and banged the front door shut on her way out.

'Lovely to see her again,' said Rose. 'I told her she shouldn't bother with us now she's pregnant—'

'Is she?' Ellie was annoyed with herself for having missed that. 'I know she was thinking about having a second child with her new husband, but . . . Oh, I'm so pleased for her.' She washed her hands, reached for the kettle, remembered they were out of instant coffee . . . Well, they had some peppermint tea somewhere, didn't they? 'I could do with a cup of really strong coffee.'

'Bad for us,' said Rose. 'Claire got rid of it.'

Ellie made them both a cup of peppermint tea and sat down at the kitchen table, rubbing her forehead. Midge jumped up on to her knee, golden eyes seeking hers. He pushed his head against her hand, wanting to be rubbed behind his ears. Ellie pulled him in to her and gave him a hug. He allowed this for two seconds, and then struggled free. She was annoyed with herself for trying to hold him tightly, because Midge relished his freedom. She pulled a face at him as he jumped back up on to the fridge.

'Done it to you, has she?' said Rose. 'Did it to me, too.'

'What did she do?'

'I really don't know. I'm glad you're back. It's like I've been living in a fog. The days slid past. I went to bed and I got up and I sat in my chair, and all the time she yakked away about I don't know what. And tears! I've never seen anything like it. She told me such stories about healings and sin and repentance and how badly she's been treated, I couldn't help feeling sorry for her in a way, but I can't abide those that sit down and wail when things don't go right for them. What's more, Miss Quicke says she doesn't like her, and she doesn't like the house being turned upside down and inside out, but you'll get Amy and Anna back again, won't you?'

Claire humped herself into the kitchen. Had she overheard Rose's last words? Midge jumped down from the fridge and exited through the cat flap. Oh dear.

Claire's face still looked blotchy, but she'd tidied herself up. 'You can't get rid of my girls, you just can't. They have to live on bread and water if they don't work.'

Ellie said, 'Tough. They should have listened to me.'

'You don't understand!' Claire plonked herself down beside Ellie and would have taken her hand again if Ellie hadn't shifted herself on to the next chair. 'They're recovering addicts, you see.'

Ellie blinked. This was all too much for her to take in.

Rose was interested. 'You mean, heroin and crack cocaine? That sort of addict? No! I've never met an addict before, that I know of.'

'Yes, they are,' said Claire, earnestness leaking from every pore. 'We rescue them from their degradation and give them work. But, no work, no food – except bread and water, of course.'

'You mean,' said Ellie, clutching her head again, 'you really don't give them anything to eat or drink except bread and water? How very . . . biblical.'

'Now you're beginning to understand. If they lapse then they're out in the cold again. But very often, it works.' Claire reached for Ellie's hand again, and again Ellie evaded her.

Ellie tried to think straight. 'And you? Are you going to go back on bread and water if you don't keep this job here?'

Claire reddened. 'Something like that.'

'Yet you said you were innocent.'

Claire seemed to shrink in size. 'I am, I am! Totally innocent of killing that silly little girl.' Her eyes implored Ellie to understand. 'Of course, I sinned. Before she disappeared, I told that girl exactly what I thought of her. You may say, "Who was I to judge?" And yet I did. I was proud of my own integrity. I was not like other women, refusing to speak when I could see she was heading for damnation. I spoke out to admonish her and point out where she was sinning, but I did it the wrong way. I did it because I was proud of not being like her. I did not do it in love. And so the girl went astray. Of that I am guilty and must pay the price.'

Ellie desperately tried to think clearly. 'You gave her an earful, and she went off in a huff? Is that what happened?'

'They tried to make out I killed her. It's true she scratched me, the little cat, when I spoke my mind, and yes, I admit that I was consumed with anger and would have slapped the young . . . girl, when she called me . . . what she did call me. But when she banged out of the car, when I'd been so good as to give her a lift, and kicked the door panel, when she had no right to harm my poor little car . . . well, that was it, as far as I was concerned. Good riddance to bad rubbish.' She nodded, bridling.

'I see,' said Ellie. 'At least, I think I do. But no one saw her after that?'

Claire flicked her fingers. 'She phoned to say she'd gone off with a new boyfriend and was perfectly all right. I told them that I'd seen her chatting with an older man outside the drama club, but they said it couldn't be him, and that I was making it up.'

'What older man?'

A shrug. 'How should I know? They said, her mother said, that I lied. I don't lie. I speak the truth as I find it. I saw her

with an older man the night before she went off. He had
his hand down the back of her jeans, and she was tickling his
neck. The hussy!'

Ellie could believe this. It wasn't the sort of tale which a
woman like Claire would make up. Or would she? Was it just
a fantasy, because she herself was unlikely to attract a man?
Had Claire, without realizing it, been jealous of a young,
flighty girl? 'But the girl did phone later on to say she was
all right?'

'She did, and the police stopped looking for her. As I told
them, she was off enjoying herself and didn't want to be found.
If you point the police in my direction now, they'll start on
me again. I mustn't bear her ill will,' said Claire in saintly
fashion, clearly lying through her teeth. 'If anyone's to blame
it's the mother for not controlling the girl. Is it surprising that
she went off with a man, as stupid girls of that age do, without
any thought for the consequences? The mother had no call to
tell the police that I'd had words with her. I deny absolutely
that I enjoyed getting the girl into trouble. It was my duty to
report what I had seen, and I have never flunked my duty.

'The police took the mother's part, of course. Well, they
would, wouldn't they? I was out of work and had debts to pay
. . . Well, never mind that. Then I had to go to work for a
demanding old bitch who . . . No, I don't mean . . . She
couldn't help wanting . . . And I had to do everything for her,
put on her socks and shoes, make her cocoa in the night, see
she took her linctus, and listen to her boring . . . No, I mustn't
say that, because she did see the light before she died, and
that was good, wasn't it? A soul saved for eternal life in the
sun.'

'After which,' said Ellie, trying to get the time frame straight,
'you went to work for my daughter?'

The woman tossed her head. 'It wasn't my fault that it didn't
work out with Diana. At my age, I can't be expected to cook
and wash up and run around after a toddler as well.'

That was fair comment. 'Diana passed you on to me?'

'I saw that the Lord had directed me to the right house,
where I could ease the passage of a strayed lamb into the
Vision of the end of the world . . .'

Did she mean Rose? Ellie shot a glance in Rose's direction, only to see that her old friend had drifted off to sleep, thank goodness.

'. . . and then it was sheer providence that caused those two nasty cleaners of yours to disobey my orders and call me names, so I got rid of them, which allowed me to bring in two of our black sheep to work here and provide them with food and drink. Now you have returned, and –' with a brilliant smile – 'we will be able to work together to bring the Vision a step nearer to reality.'

Ellie blinked. 'I'm not so sure about that. I like the house as it was, and I'll have no truck with furniture being moved around, central heating being turned down and elderly ladies being made to overexert themselves.'

Claire leaned forward to try to take Ellie's hand again. Again Ellie avoided her.

Claire said, 'I see I must teach you how to live your life so as to move to a higher level. Wealth is not to be squandered on bursaries and institutions, but directed to help the deserving poor . . .'

Ellie recalled a Victorian philanthropist who'd said that the Deserving Poor generally didn't deserve it and were never grateful, anyway. That had been the conclusion she'd reached too, in the years she'd been administering her charitable trust. You needed to be really, really sure about someone before you gave them money. You never gave to alcoholics or gamblers. The best use of the trust money was to give to organizations with a proven track record: schools, clubs helping a particular section of the community, and so on. Yes, the trust had given to individuals now and then, but the results had not always been satisfactory.

Ellie thought, *I'm hysterical. I want to laugh, and it's no laughing matter.*

Claire continued, 'We must never allow our eyes to fall away from the Vision at the end of the world. We must deny ourselves in little ways to strengthen our moral fibre. We must wear black to show that we repent of our sins. We must always look to the east first thing every morning, so our beds must be oriented that way, and of course we must eschew meat and wine and stimulants such as tea and coffee. Where man and woman are joined in matrimony, they must sleep apart, to—'

Ellie had had enough. 'Stop!' And, with relief, 'That's the doorbell.'

It was indeed the doorbell. Ellie opened the door to find no fewer than four people outside, none of whom looked pleased to be in the company of the others.

'Decorator,' said a fiftyish man in paint-stained overalls. 'As arranged.' He had a beak of a nose and bold eyes which assessed Ellie's figure and dismissed her as being of no importance.

Behind him, sniffing, stood a thin boy dressed in black T-shirt and jeans, who was trying – and failing – to manoeuvre a step-ladder into the porch. A refugee from the drugs programme?

Ellie gaped.

The decorator tried to push the door wide open so that he might move forward into the hall. 'Come on. Let us in. We're painting your dining room today.'

Ellie stood her ground. 'Thank you, but no thank you. There seems to have been some sort of mistake and—'

'Oh, for heaven's sake, stop arguing and let me in!' Ellie's daughter, Diana, eeled her way past the decorator into the hall. She was also clad in black, but that was her regular office gear and nothing to do with repentance. Diana didn't 'do' repentance.

'Maria said you were back,' said the fourth person, stepping in after Diana, but keeping a wary distance from her. Diana wasn't looking at him, and he wasn't looking at her. That was par for the course, as they'd once been man and wife. A long time ago. The contrast between them had grown rather than lessened over the years. Stewart's substantial figure spoke of a contented life, whereas Diana was still as thin as a whippet and constitutionally discontented with her lot.

The decorator flourished a piece of paper at Ellie, his eyes going beyond her to look round the hall. 'I suppose you're the old housekeeper. See? It says. This morning to start. I shoulda been here earlier, but the boy here –' he sent 'the boy' a darkling look – 'wasn't out of bed in time. So if you'll stand back to let us in, we'll make a start.'

'Claire? You?' Diana advanced on the shrinking figure. 'I might have known you'd be at the bottom of this talk about decorating my mother's house. What nonsense!'

Claire wrung her hands. 'Oh, no! How can you say that!'

'Easily.' Diana swung round on Ellie. 'We have to talk. Now!'

'What, now?' said Ellie, knowing that was an inadequate response.

Stewart was also looking anxious. 'Ellie, yes; I know you're only just back, but—'

A little voice piped up. 'Such a lot of people. Shall I make coffee?' A tiny brown wren of a woman stood in the door to the kitchen quarters.

Ellie experienced another moment of dislocation. Had her formidable Aunt Drusilla really come back to life? No, of course not. It was Rose, who seemed to be shrinking with every day that passed.

'Thank you, Rose. But I don't think so, especially since we haven't got any. Diana, I was just about to go to the shops. I can't—'

'Ten minutes. You can surely give me ten minutes. I'm due back at the office in—'

'Mind your backs, there!' The decorator wrenched the step-ladder off his lad and tried to insinuate himself past Stewart into the hall.

Ellie had had enough. 'Out! No decorating today. Stewart –' she turned to her general manager – 'would you be so kind as to get this man to go away? I have not ordered any decorating and—'

'This paper here says—'

'I don't care if it's signed by the Prime Minister, the Queen of England and the Archbishop of Canterbury. I didn't authorize any decorating. Stewart: get him out of here!'

Stewart placed his substantial body between Ellie and the decorator. 'Let me see that piece of paper.'

Diana seized her mother by the arm and led her into the sitting room. Once there, Diana stopped short. 'What's going on here?'

'Claire is what's going on,' said Ellie. 'And, before you

start, Diana: no, I didn't ask her to do it. She got my own cleaners to leave and substituted hers, whom I've sacked. I'm in the process of sacking her, too. Whatever possessed you to recommend her to me?'

'That's what I wanted to speak to you about. It wasn't my fault. I didn't know anything about the murder or disappearance or whatever it was when you asked me if I knew anyone who could look after Rose while you were away, and I didn't know she was a member of this silly sect that believes in poverty for others but loadsa money for themselves.'

'Is that what they believe? She said—'

'Oh, she'll say anything to worm her way into the house and get control. That's what she does, you know. It wasn't till after you'd gone that I heard what she's been getting up to, her and her like. They've formed a "church" of their own, which is nothing but a cult. She goes out working for people who have money and are on their last legs, and then the people they're looking after die and they inherit. I needed someone to look after little Evan, and when she said she was desperate for work, well, I didn't think anything of it – at the time.'

'You think she came here to get her hands on Rose's—?'

'Rose inherited quite a bit from my great aunt, didn't she? Also, you've been paying her to look after you all these years, and she's never spent a penny on herself, so, yes, she must have a nice little nest egg. No wonder Claire jumped at the chance of looking after her.'

'Would she have known that Rose had money when she took the job?'

'Oh, this cult, or whatever it is, does their homework all right. They select their targets with care. They pretend to do a lot of good, looking after waifs and strays, taking people off the street – drug addicts and I don't know what; nobody you should trust with a key to your house – and then their victims die, and who gets the money? They do, of course.'

'That's a serious accusation, Diana. Where did you get this information?'

Diana looked uncomfortable, but only for a moment. 'Well, that's what I wanted to tell you. A wealthy widow died locally, and this Claire said she was going to inherit and asked us to put her house on the market for her. Only, then we got a letter from a solicitor saying that the will had been challenged by the woman's children who live in Australia or New Zealand, somewhere far away, and we would be best advised to take it off our books. So we had Claire in, and she admitted that there was a hitch. She was in tears. She said she'd worked for the widow for ages, doing everything for her, and that when she died, she'd left only a few thousands to her children and the rest, including the house, to this church of the Vision that Claire acts for, but the children were contesting the will. They'd got a solicitor on the job, and Claire had been turned out of the house and had nowhere to live.'

Ellie put her hand to her head, which was aching in earnest. 'The children think their mother made a will giving the best part of her estate to Claire because . . . Are they claiming undue influence? I'd better warn Rose.'

'Rose is small time. Once they'd got a foothold in this house, they'd have realized who you were and how much money you've inherited. So now they'll be after you and everything you own. That's why I came round to warn you. You've got to throw them out before they trap you into making a personal will in their favour.'

'Give me credit for some common sense, Diana. You know perfectly well that I've put the money I've inherited into a trust. It's not mine to keep or to spend. It's for people who need it more than I do.'

'So you say, but if Claire can extract money from people she works for once, she can do it again. I want you to promise that you'll let me have a look at any proposal they make so that you don't get taken for a ride.'

'Nothing of that sort has been suggested, and if and when it happens, I shall deal with it as I would deal with any other business matter.'

Diana was not appeased. 'These are not just any other business people. They don't play by the rules.'

Stewart appeared in the doorway, waving a piece of paper, with the decorator frowning at his side and Claire close behind them. 'Ellie, a word. This paper. It looks as if you signed and dated it last week. As I've told them, you weren't here, so you can't have signed it.'

The decorator folded his arms at them. 'I'll swear it on the bible. That paper's gospel true.'

Stewart repeated, 'I'm sorry, but this signature is a fake.'

Diana was triumphant. 'Told you! Fraud!'

The decorator coloured up and flashed a look of dislike at Diana. 'The old lady signed it herself. For the Quicke person.'

'Rose signed it?' said Ellie. 'She had no authority to sign for me.'

The decorator grinned, showing a gap in stained teeth. 'Tell that to the lawyers.'

'Yes, I will,' said Ellie, thinking that perhaps Diana was in the right for once.

The decorator wasn't taking 'no' for an answer. 'So, I'll start on the dining room, shall I? It was supposed to be cleared this morning, ready for me.'

Was that why the new cleaners had dismantled the table?

Claire nodded. 'That's right. I told Rose all about it, and she signed on your behalf.'

Diana sniffed. 'Unless you can produce an authority signed by my mother for Rose to deal with her affairs, that idea is a non-starter.'

Tears started in Claire's eyes. She wailed, 'I was told, I was assured on the best authority that it's legal.'

'Well, it isn't,' said Ellie, who'd had more than enough of this conversation. 'Look, I need to do some shopping, and I want you all out of here before I leave.'

Claire wrung her hands. 'I don't have anywhere else to go! What am I going to do?'

Ellie felt herself weakening. 'Well, I suppose we can discuss that when I get back. Meantime, you can start by returning the furniture to its usual places.'

The decorator was getting angry. 'I know my rights. I ain't moving.'

Stewart took out his mobile phone. 'I'll get the police to remove him and his mate, shall I?'

'Do that,' said Ellie. 'And Stewart, could you stick around till I get back? I won't be long, but I must get tea, coffee and some meat before I do anything else. Diana, can I trouble you for a lift to the shops?'

'A pleasure.' Diana shot a look at her diamond-encrusted watch. 'If we hurry.' She walked around Stewart as if he didn't exist.

Ellie kissed his cheek as she passed him by. 'I leave you in charge, Stewart. Just don't enter into conversation with Claire, because she doesn't play fair.'

'What do you mean by that?'

'Trust me. You don't want to find out. Whatever you do, don't promise her anything.'

Collecting her handbag and a jacket, Ellie wondered if Claire really had tried to hypnotize her. Or had she imagined it? Possibly. Mind you, she still felt strange. Her wits had gone a-wandering. Her mind was dull. Odd, very.

She shook her head, trying to pop her wits back into their usual slots.

Had she made a shopping list? Well, she'd started to do so . . . Oh, there it was.

Tucking the list in her handbag, Ellie reflected that she couldn't be sure whether or not Claire was a wrong 'un, but she did feel that by warning Stewart against Claire, she was doing the right thing. Better to be safe than sorry. Stewart was a man too decent to believe ill of a woman without proof positive that she was Lucrezia Borgia. Or Mata Hari. Or Cruella de Vil?

No, none of them. They had all majored in sex appeal, but Claire had none.

So who was she like? Ellie couldn't think.

Some meek little woman who poisoned everyone she came into contact with? Ellie presumed there must be such people, although she'd never heard of them. Perhaps a female Dr Crippen?

Enough of that. She could rest easy, leaving Stewart in charge. She trusted him. But, murderess or no, Claire was not to be trusted.

FOUR

Ellie staggered back into the house laden with shopping, in time to see Stewart in his shirtsleeves manoeuvring the grandfather clock back into its old position. He stood back, looking pleased. The clock struck one.

Ellie's watch said it was after two.

Claire was hovering, looking damper than ever. 'Oh, Mrs Quicke! I was beginning to worry. Are you all right?'

Stewart grinned at Ellie as he fiddled with the clock's mechanism. 'Just a mo. There!'

The clock struck two. Splendid. All must be well if the clock was now on time.

Ellie took her shopping bags into the kitchen and dumped them there. She still felt dizzy at times, but had convinced herself the sensation was wearing off. But, oh, she was worn out! Jet lag, jet lag. If she didn't lie down soon, she'd fall down . . . and then where would they all be?

'Thanks, Stewart. I wish I could be more coherent. I'm not sure I'm making sense at the moment. I'm going to make myself a mug of tea and have a little lie down for a few minutes. I'll be all right after that.'

In other words, Stewart: don't try to make me attend to Claire, or to business, or the weather forecast till I've recovered.

'Suppose I bring a cuppa up to you?' Stewart the reliable.

She thanked him and hauled herself up the stairs to totter into her bedroom. The bed was still in the wrong place. She let herself down on to it, shucking off her shoes. There.

Stewart came up with a mug of tea for her. 'Strong enough for you?'

She made herself smile. Sipped. Aaaah. 'You blessing!' She leaned back against the pillows. He found her dressing gown and draped it over her feet. He was a nice man, and she was very fond of him. What's more, she trusted him.

He didn't leave, but sat on a chair nearby, big hands clasping and unclasping, a frown mark between his eyes.

She summoned enough strength to say, 'Out with it.'

'Maria rang. She'll get you another couple of cleaners, starting tomorrow morning, though they may not be the ones you had before. She'll see what can be done to switch the rosters round.'

'I suppose Amy and Anna won't return if Claire is still in the house?'

'Probably not. The woman keeps saying she's got nowhere else to go. Not sure I believe her.'

It was unlike Stewart to be suspicious. Well, he was probably right.

He said, 'Maria's still trying to find someone to live in here and look after Rose. No luck yet, but she'll keep trying. You may have to advertise.'

Ellie felt her limbs grow heavy. Ah, sleep . . .

Stewart shifted. 'Vera rang. Worried about you. Said she'd pop in after work today. She's a gem, isn't she?'

Ellie smiled. Yes, Vera was a gem.

He cleared his throat. 'While you were away the trust was approached to fund the purchase of a large house locally, which is run partly as a hostel with community accommodation and partly as flats let out to people on the council's housing list.'

Ellie's attention was wandering. She tried to concentrate. 'For the deserving poor? Mostly, they aren't. Deserving, I mean. And certainly not grateful. We've found that out, running the charity for so many years, haven't we?' Then she closed her eyes and said, 'Uh-oh. So that's it. Claire's lot? Holy rollers, or something.'

'Vision. Claire's a foot soldier, not the captain of the crew. They rescue those who slip through society's net: the widows and orphans; the recovering alcoholics and drug addicts. Their application to the trust ticked all the boxes. Our esteemed financial director, Kate, was all in favour, and so was I, at first.'

'You did all the usual checks?'

'Of course. The organization has been renting this house locally for quite a while and has had some success in getting the down-and-outers back on their feet. All very commendable. The house is owned by the council, but they have recently been approached by a developer with an offer to buy. He wants to tear the building down and put up a block of flats, thus throwing the Vision project out on to the street . . . unless they can come up with money to buy the place for themselves. Again, we were sympathetic to them. The sum required is large but not impossible. Kate and I were both in favour and, provisionally, I told them so. We said we'd be presenting their case to you on your return.'

He took a deep breath. 'Maria doesn't usually carry work home with her, but she knew I'd be interested in anything to do with you, and so—'

'She told you that either Amy or Anna had had a spat with Claire and accused her of murder?'

'I don't think it was murder, but yes; it made me think.'

'I suppose the organization is pressing for an early reply? We normally meet to discuss trust business on Thursday mornings. Are you on for that this week? And our wonderful finance director, Kate?' She squinched her eyes shut. 'I don't know if my secretary Pat will be around – I think she took a holiday while I was away – but I suppose the rest of us could meet.'

'I'm sorry to burden you with this, the moment you're back.'

'That's what I'm here for.'

He pressed her arm. 'You have a nice rest. I'll see what I can do to get downstairs back into shape, and then I'll have to get back to the office for a while. Ring me when you're up to dealing with business.'

Ellie surfaced. She felt rested and warm.

She was warm because a large ginger tom was nestling by her side and purring. Midge, who could climb anything. A late-Victorian house was no sort of challenge to him. Ellie's headache had gone, but she was aware that dark clouds loomed on the horizon. Hiding under the duvet was not the answer to her problems, and she ought to get up and face the day.

Or, rather, the afternoon. The sun was still high in the sky, but it had lost its intensity. Her bedside clock was . . . somewhere else. The bed was still in the wrong place. She sat up, slowly, gingerly. No, it was fine. No headache, no dizziness.

She would make it downstairs and see what was going on.

Dear Lord, I'm in such a muddle here. Is Claire really a murderess, because if so, I am not going to let her stay . . . and, anyway, she's such an annoying drip of a woman that . . .

That was not nice. I shouldn't judge her just because she's unattractive and a cry-baby. I ought to give her the benefit of the doubt.

No, I don't. She doesn't deserve it.

Oh well, I suppose I ought to try to see her point of view . . .

Ellie shook her head at herself, said, 'Ouch!' Her neck was stiff. She massaged it, washed and brushed herself down, and descended the stairs.

The hall looked its usual self. Light music seeped through the open door to the kitchen quarters, and someone was moving furniture around in the sitting room. Someone had also put a vase of flowers on the hall chest.

Vera appeared in the doorway to the sitting room. 'Ellie, are you feeling better?' Vera, smiling, rosy and sane.

'Bless you, my dear.' Behind her was the lanky figure of Vera's son, Mikey. 'Gracious, Mikey! I've only been away five minutes, and you've grown again!' And behind Mikey was the tall figure of Vera's very new husband, Dan, deputy head at a local secondary school.

'Welcome back, Mrs Quicke!' said Dan. 'Vera thought we should come straight from work to get things straight for you. Now, she says I've got to shift the table in the window to the left a bit. Is that right?'

Vera was holding a small vase of flowers cut from the garden. 'Yes, Dan: six inches to the left. And this vase goes on a mat, so as not to mark the surface.'

Ellie's chair was back in its usual place and, when Vera placed the vase of flowers on the table nearby, the room looked its old self. 'That's wonderful. Thank you. But Vera—'

Vera said, 'It's quite all right, Ellie. They wouldn't let me lift a thing.'

So she *was* pregnant? Good.

'She speaks and we obey,' said Dan, putting his arm around his wife with a tenderness that warmed Ellie's heart.

Thirteen-year-old Mikey jigged from one foot to the other. 'Mrs Quicke, did you bring me back a present from—'

'Mikey!' Dan and Vera spoke as one.

'Of course I did,' said Ellie. All this kindness. Unexpected. She sought for a hankie and, predictably, didn't find one. 'I had to come back in a hurry, and it's in the big case which Thomas has got with him. Which reminds me that I haven't unpacked my own bag yet.'

Vera pushed her gently into her own chair. 'We've brought enough supper over for all of us, because you must be tired and Claire only cooks vegetarian so we thought there probably wasn't anything you'd fancy for supper. We can catch up on all the news, and then we'll go home so the men can get on with their homework.'

'Am I not to be included in your plans?' Claire, standing four-square in the doorway. 'Am I not the official carer here?' She spoiled the effect by bursting into tears.

She is such a drama queen! Ellie didn't feel she could cope with Claire's tears. 'Bless you, Vera. Supper, by all means. Thank you, and thank you, Dan, too. Claire, can you find something for yourself to eat?'

Mikey shot off, saying it was his job to lay the table, while Vera and Dan flanked Ellie as she made her way past Claire and into the kitchen. Mikey had eased Rose into a chair at the table and was tying a large bib round her neck. He was chattering away. Mikey either talked a blue streak or withdrew into silence. '. . . so I got this new saddle for my bike, and it felt a bit strange at first, and I tried some panniers, but it's better to wear a satchel on my back . . .'

Vera made for the oven and started to dish up from a large casserole. 'His father gave him this bike, which can't be left out in the rain and has to be polished every day—'

Dan handed Ellie into her chair. 'It gives him freedom. He's been popping in to see Rose on his way back from school most days and at weekends—'

'I bring her crisps and smoothies,' said Mikey, throwing

knives and forks on to the table. 'We both like them. And sucky sweets.'

'And chocolate chip biscuits for us to dunk in our tea,' said Rose, cackling. She had perked up wonderfully and now looked as lively as ever. No need to call the doctor in yet?

'And,' said Mikey, 'we sit and eat them together. Claire wouldn't let me have a key, so Rose gave me hers—'

Claire had followed them in. 'You little imp! So that's how you've been getting in!'

'It wouldn't matter if I hadn't a key,' said Mikey. 'I'd still have got in.'

He would have, too. Like Midge the cat, Mikey could climb anything and knew which windows were always left open at the top in summertime.

Of course, Ellie thought, aiming for a frown at Mikey and failing, it was all very reprehensible that the boy should think he could enter a house in which he no longer lived as and when he wished to do so, but understandable in the circumstances. She noted that Dan looked as if he were trying not to grin. Vera bit her lip, exchanged a glance with Ellie and said, 'Now, Mikey . . .' Without heat.

Ellie looked for the cat, but he was nowhere to be seen. Perhaps he was still on her bed?

Rose said, 'Mikey waits till Claire's back is turned, and up he pops. He gave me such a jump the other day that I was all of a fluster. Ellie, I'm making a new will, now you're back. I'm leaving a bit to my daughter that never comes to see me and everything else to you and Mikey.'

Sensation. Vera ceased to ladle out bowls of stew. Dan stopped sawing up chunks of crusty bread. Claire let out a squawk.

Ellie didn't know what to think. Rose had actually gone ahead and made a will? Should she pinch herself? Rose had always refused to consider making a will before.

Claire had seated herself at the end of the table, isolated from the others. She suspended operations on her piece of her cold nut roast . . . no beef stew for her! . . . and sat there with her mouth open.

The news had also taken Vera and Dan by surprise. They looked at one another for a lead.

Mikey seemed to have heard about this before. 'Yackie yackie doo-da. I told you, Rose, I don't need it.'

Vera recovered sufficiently to say, 'Rose, your daughter will expect—'

'Much she cares about me,' said Rose, whose spoon was already at work. 'I'll give her something, of course. As for the rest, I was going to give it to Ellie to use for her charity, but now I'm giving a bit to Mikey so's he can buy a racing bike.'

Dan frowned. 'But Rose, we can afford to—'

Claire bared her teeth. 'Rose, you've already made a will.'

'Yes, dear,' said Rose, 'but I don't know these people you said needed my money so badly, and I know Mikey because he takes care of me.'

Claire dabbled at her mouth. 'Rose, you can't change your mind!'

'Of course I can,' said Rose, tearing the soft dough out of her bread and smashing it into the stew. 'I can make a new will any time I want. You said so yourself. You said my daughter would rather have the money go to a good cause than buy her a conservatory or a new car or whatever it is she fancies.'

Claire put both hands over her face and rocked to and fro. 'You're going to spoil everything!'

Rose dropped her spoon and leant back in her chair, looking her age and more. 'I'm a bit tired. Nice stew that, Vera. Well up to your usual standards. Now, Mikey; can you help me to my room? I could do with a lie down.'

Mikey sprang to help Rose to her feet. Dan's mobile phone rang. He answered it, listened and said, 'I'll check the diary and get back to you.' He disconnected. 'Sorry, Ellie. Sorry, Vera. I have to go home and attend to this tonight.'

'Understood.'

'I'll come with you.' Vera collected plates and put them in the sink. 'Fresh fruit for afters, Ellie, with ice cream or yogurt. I'll be round tomorrow for an hour before I go in to work.'

Ellie watched Mikey help Rose out of the room. Mikey was growing up. Rose was so fragile . . . Ellie felt she ought never to have left her. Even if Rose were looking better since Ellie had returned, it would be best to have her checked over by the doctor.

Dan helped Vera clear the table and stack the dishwasher. Good for Dan.

Claire was back to chewing on her nut roast, her beady eyes on Ellie. Claire was going to start on her the moment the others had gone.

Dan stooped over Ellie. 'Sorry, have to dash. Will you be all right?'

'Thank you, Dan. For everything.'

'I owe you big time, Mrs Quicke. I'd never have met up with Vera again if it hadn't been for you. We'll be round tomorrow again. At least—'

'No, you won't,' said Vera, her hand pressing Dan's shoulder. She explained to Ellie, 'He's got a meeting after school tomorrow, but I expect Mikey will pop in some time.'

Mikey emerged from Rose's room, saying, 'She says she's off to the land of Nod.'

Dan looked at his watch. 'We have to go, Mikey. Do you want to come with us?'

'I'll get on my bike and be there before you.'

They waved goodbye and departed. And then there was silence.

Ellie decided to have a healthy, non-fat pudding. She helped herself to some yogurt.

Claire scraped her plate along the table to get closer to Ellie. 'I have never, ever, pushed Rose to make a will. I wouldn't! Yes, I told her all about our plans for the future, and said how the Way had been eased when another old lady had left us a share of her house, but I didn't put any pressure on her to do the same thing.'

Ellie thought that she was too tired to argue. She added some fresh strawberries to her yogurt.

Claire moved up a gear. 'Rose must leave her money as she thinks best. Her daughter doesn't need it. She told me that herself. Got a good job: bank manager, or something? Married to a man who provides well for her. Never comes to see Rose. So, why give the tax man more of the same?'

Bother the diet. Ellie got out a carton of double cream and stirred some into the mixture.

Claire clasped her hands together. 'You employed me to look after Rose, and I have done so. I have looked after her as if she were my own mother. I have prepared good, wholesome food for her and changed her bed linen and seen that she has clean clothes to wear, though they're a total disgrace, if you ask me . . . which is why I spent some of my own money on buying some new ones for her.'

Ellie pulled the sugar bowl towards her. The strawberries were a trifle on the tart side, and she had a sweet tooth.

At least Claire wasn't in tears for the moment.

'Yes,' said Claire, 'we did discuss the matter of her making her will, and I did say I'd arrange everything if she decided she wanted to do it. And she did. So I arranged it. All legal and above-board. As for moving the furniture around, that was me thinking how much more comfortable you would be when the spirits could move around the house without meeting a sharp corner. Everything in our lives must be channelled into the forces of good. We must look always to the Vision. We must live the Vision. We must clear the dross from our lives. Beds must face to the east so that the first thing we see when we wake is the morning sun and—'

Ellie sighed. 'False pretences.'

'What?' Claire didn't like being interrupted mid-flow.

'You got this job under false pretences.'

Claire flushed. 'No, I didn't.'

'Your references were, shall we say, incomplete? If you had told me what happened in the past, would I have taken you on? No.'

A toss of the head. 'I don't know what you mean.' Her bulging eyes told a different story. In a moment, they'd fill with tears. Again.

'A girl who went missing.'

Out came the tears. 'It wasn't my fault, it wasn't! The police cleared me, they did! She ran away to be with her boyfriend.'

'Crocodile tears.' Ellie wouldn't have thought she had it in her to be so hard. But then, this woman had taken advantage of Rose in the most appalling way.

Claire sobbed, 'You have no idea what I've been through. I've suffered so much. I've been thrown out of the house I grew up in, I lost my job and my little flat and my car, and now you want to turn me out into the cold!'

Ellie pushed herself up from her seat. 'In the morning I'm going to ring the police and find out exactly what's been going on.'

'No, don't do that! They'll kill me!' The woman actually went down on her knees again, with hands upraised and tears on her cheeks.

'Oh, get up, do!' Ellie was in no mood for histrionics. 'If you'd been straight with me from the beginning, this would never have happened.'

'Are you going to tell them I trapped Rose into making a will in our favour?'

'Are you admitting it?'

Claire gulped. 'I know it looks bad, but really . . . I beg of you—'

'Enough! It's getting late, and I won't turn you out tonight if you really don't have anywhere else to go. We'll talk again in the morning.'

Claire scrambled to her feet, all eager beaver. 'No, you wouldn't turn me out, of course you wouldn't. Everyone says how kind you are. I promise I won't say another word to Rose about the will, and of course I'll be listening out for her in the night though she hasn't rung for me at all. She's still able to get to the toilet in the night by herself.'

Ellie knew she was too tired to make a fair judgement about what to do with the woman tonight. She shivered. She had a mental picture of Claire as a slug, crawling around Rose, leaving slimy traces everywhere she went. Ugh.

'Look, I'll do the dishes, though it's not my place to do so!' Claire started to wash up the supper things in the sink, even though Dan and Vera had put almost everything else into the dishwasher. Ellie decided not to speak of it.

She tapped on the door to Rose's room and went in. The door had been ajar. Mikey had left it that way. Deliberately? Probably. Rose must have heard every word. She hadn't even turned the television on, which confirmed Ellie's guess that Rose had been listening. She was sitting up in bed, bright eyed and bushy tailed. Ellie shut the door behind her and went to sit beside Rose.

Rose said, 'I couldn't understand what was happening to me, why I was sleeping all the time. I prayed every night for you to come back. Mikey prayed with me. Well, just the once, he did. I thought I was going gaga. Claire said I'd done things that I couldn't remember doing. Like signing those papers. Mikey said I wasn't going round the twist, but that I was drifting off somewhere every now and then. I was going to tell you that I wasn't responsible for my actions any more, Ellie, and that you must put me in a home.'

'You seem all right to me. Claire has a way of confusing people.'

Rose nodded. 'With that stuff in a bottle, yes. Mikey got worried about it, because he caught her putting some of it into my food and she was furious with him and said he was a little sneak, which he wasn't. He saw her by accident, coming in when she hadn't known he was there. So then he got worried that she might be doping me, but of course it wasn't that. It was all the fault of my coughing in the night that was making me feel so tired, so it was the linctus she was giving me which he saw her putting into my food, and that did seem to cure it because I slept better than ever.'

'I didn't know you had a bad cough.'

'Claire said I woke her up in the night with it, and I suppose it worked, even if it did make me feel a bit as if I were floating on the ceiling sometimes.'

If Rose had had a cough, Claire had been right to give her something for it. But it did sound as if Rose had been given too much. Straight from the bottle?

Is that what she'd given Ellie, too? Claire seemed to be acting for the best, but was she always correct in her judgements?

Ellie stroked Rose's hand. 'She's sort of pushy, isn't she?'

Rose leaned back and closed her eyes. She looked exhausted.

'You signed things you don't remember reading?'

A tiny nod. 'She said I'd agreed to things, and I wasn't sure if I had or not. So I went along with it. Ellie, you won't believe this, but I was frightened of what she might do if I crossed her.'

'I believe you. Did you really want to go to church with her?'

'She told me I'd said I wanted to go, so I suppose I did. When Thomas comes back, he'll deal with her.'

Ellie kissed Rose's thin cheek, folded her hands one over the other, dimmed the light, adjusted the television sound to low and left the room.

Claire was still noisily clearing up in the kitchen. Ellie passed her by without comment. And the phone rang in the hall. She picked it up and, oh, blessing . . . it was Thomas, worrying about her.

She had so much to tell him. Where should she start?

He sounded full of beans. 'Are you all right, Ellie? I'm in a bit of a rush, been asked to meet up with someone in five minutes for a chat before we settle in for the afternoon, but I wanted to make sure you were all right.'

'Yes, of course I am.' There simply wasn't time to tell him about Claire and Rose and the Vision and all. 'Will you be able to ring me again later?'

'No, I don't think so. We've been invited out tonight. Everyone's so friendly, and there's some really interesting people around. I'd been asked to attend this conference before, but hadn't realized . . . What? Oh. Ellie, I'm sorry to cut it short. Ring you tomorrow, right?' And he cut the call.

Ellie sagged against the wall. For two pins, she'd have wept.

She thought of Claire's tears, and didn't. In fact, she almost managed a smile. She would take herself off to bed, and in the morning she'd feel better able to cope. Up the stairs to beddy-byes.

Bother. Her bed was still in the wrong place. Well, *she* couldn't shift it.

She heard the 'ping' of the phone being placed back on its receiver downstairs. Someone else ringing her? Rose never used the phone. It must be Claire, ringing out. Ellie shrugged. Did it matter? Claire would have a mobile phone of her own, of course she would. But then, it would cost her nothing to use Ellie's phone instead.

A slug. Hm. If Claire were a slug, then Thomas, that great-hearted, wise man, would be . . . what? She clicked her fingers. An ox. The ox stood for one of the four evangelists, but she couldn't remember which one for the moment. Luke, possibly?

She reached out her hand for her bible – and it wasn't there. She looked around. It must be there. Her bible was always kept on the table on this side of the bed, and Thomas's on the other . . . only, he'd taken his with him, and she had taken a book of the psalms instead. Which meant that her own bible ought to be here. And wasn't. Claire must have put it somewhere, though why . . . Well, not to bother now.

She forced herself to unpack, thinking about Thomas as an ox. He was big and strong like an ox. And gentle. And couldn't be moved if he'd taken up a certain position. And wise.

She wondered what she herself might be like as an animal. An old sheepdog, perhaps? And Rose . . . a tired little grey cat, gradually sleeping more and more.

What she didn't expect to confront next morning was a fully-grown, charismatic leopard.

FIVE

Someone rang the front doorbell. Ellie opened the door and took a step back, wondering if she were still asleep. All night long she'd been dreaming about animals, about slugs and oxen and collie dogs, and here was a full-grown leopard. Or was he a cheetah?

Black, anyway. Lithe. Handsome. Charismatic. All of those.

A children's rhyme popped into her head. 'He who is born on a Sabbath day is bonny and blithe and good and gay.' Not that you could use the term 'gay' in its original sense nowadays, and in any case this man almost certainly wasn't gay.

It wasn't even Sunday. So what had brought that rhyme to mind? He was certainly 'bonny', but that wasn't enough, was it?

Power, that's what. This man leaked power like a damaged electric cable. Now, why should 'Sunday' mean 'power'? It didn't, did it?

Late thirties? Forceful. Clever. Self-absorbed. Yes.

Evil? Mmmm. Not sure. But possibly not good.

She knew good when she saw it. Thomas was good, and so was Rose. Stewart was good, as were Vera and Dan; even Mikey was, when he was on form.

'Mrs Quicke. Our benefactor.' He reached out with both hands to clasp hers. His hands were warm. He had a splendid figure. Close-cropped black hair, flashing eyes and perfect teeth, expensive casual clothes. 'I am so glad you're back. Claire said you might have time to see me this morning, even though you've only just returned from, ah, the States, was it? Without your dear husband, I believe.'

He made it sound as if Thomas had not returned because he'd left her.

Ellie thought it was too early in the morning for her to cope with this man.

'And you are?' Though she'd guessed.

'Pastor Ambrose, of the Blessed Vision church. You were expecting me, weren't you?'

No, she wasn't. Maybe she ought to have been, but . . . She felt punch drunk. She hadn't even had her breakfast yet, or roused Rose, or even begun to work out what she was supposed to be doing that day. It occurred to her that this man was pushing her off balance in order to work his wicked way with her, his object being to obtain funds from her trust to purchase the building he was currently renting. She was pleased with herself for working that out. Her brain might be slow, but it did still seem to be limping along.

'I'm afraid it's too early to—'

'It's never too early to be about God's work, is it? Early to bed and early to rise? I'm sure you must have heard that.'

'Yes, but . . .' He was sapping her energy. She resented that.

He looked around him with sparkling eyes. 'Delightful old house. Big. Just as it was described to me. Well maintained. There's just the two of you living here now, is that right? And Rose, of course. But we know all about Rose, don't we?'

Ellie stood there like a dummy, holding on to the front door while he stepped past her and prowled around the hall, looking into the dining and sitting rooms. Without being invited to do so.

She'd lost the initiative. If only Thomas had been able to return with her! He would have been able to deal with this intruder.

She shut the front door, with care. 'I'm afraid you have assumed too much. I have not yet had time to look at the paperwork which has been piling up during my absence. When I have done so there will no doubt be questions which will need answering—'

He held out his arms. 'Ask away. What do you wish to know? Our affairs are totally transparent. We toil in the depths of humanity to bring forth the fruits of the spirit, and—'

She held up her hands. 'Stop! Stop right there. You are being most unbusinesslike. I have just told you that I can't—'

'Oh, but you can, you can! What is to stop you listening to the voice of truth! God has laid on me a heavy task, to work with the dregs of society. He has told me that you are the one who will rescue us in our hour of need. You are to bring hope to the despairing and balm to the wounded.' His voice rose to a clarion call. 'You will provide shelter for the homeless and work for those wearing the rags of poverty. You will—'

Ellie had both her hands to her head. She was getting another headache. 'Just go, will you!'

'But you invited me to—'

'No, I didn't.'

A movement at the back of the hall. Claire crept into sight, washing her hands in apology.

Ellie said, 'Claire, did you invite this man?'

He said, smiling, 'Yes, of course. She said to be prompt, and so I am.'

Ellie took a deep breath. She opened the front door again. 'Out. Both of you. Yes, I can see it's raining, but as far as I'm concerned it is far too early in the morning for me to attend to business. Pastor Ambrose, or is it Reverend?'

'Whichever you wish, gracious lady.'

'I don't care which title it is, but—'

'That shows a certain lack of respect.'

'If you'd behaved with respect to me, I might show some for you. Out! Both of you!'

He turned on Claire. 'What have you done! I asked you to arrange this meeting. Can't you even manage the simplest—'

Claire started to cry. Of course. 'I've just prepared a lovely breakfast for us all.'

Pastor Ambrose took a turn around the hall, breathing hard before coming to a halt, eyes closed and face uplifted. He swept his hands outward. 'So be it. God has spoken to his servant. We will forgive one another and eat the bread of reconciliation. We will forgive our sister Claire, who sometimes oversteps the mark in her eagerness to be of service . . .' And here he shot the woman a glance which Ellie couldn't interpret. A frown, yes. But also – or was she reading too much into it – an order to keep her mouth shut?

'This way,' said Claire, opening the door to the kitchen, the door which Ellie kept propped open so that if Rose rang her bell it could be heard throughout the house: a door which seemed mysteriously to shut whenever Claire was around. And, yes, the temperature had dropped again.

What was that? Rose, weakly calling Ellie's name. Ellie had no choice. She shut the front door and followed Claire and Ambrose down the corridor into the kitchen. Rose was already in her big chair, trying to fasten her bib around her neck. Claire had laid the table for four, which proved she'd planned that Ambrose should join them for breakfast.

Claire was all smiles. 'Freshly squeezed orange juice in the glasses, scrambled eggs, chicken sausage, mushrooms, fried bread, tomatoes and baked beans. Toast and fresh fruit to follow.'

Altogether it was a sight to tempt the pickiest of appetites, and Ellie was hungry enough to eat the lot. But.

If she broke bread with them, they would assume she had accepted their intrusion into her life. Which she hadn't.

She thought about upending a plateful of the cooked food over Claire's head. It was a thought that gave her pleasure. She could just imagine the baked beans slithering down the woman's pasty cheeks. She'd do the same to the pastor. That would wipe the grin off his face.

Ambrose had seated himself at the head of the table. He glanced up at Ellie. 'When you are seated, I will say the grace.'

Ellie took a deep breath. This was going to be difficult. 'I fear you have been misled. I see that Claire has invited you to have breakfast with her, but I have not. You must excuse me from eating with you. It would be unethical until I have come to a decision about your application for funds. To do that I have to study the papers you have sent in, after which I may well need clarification on certain points. Only then will I convene a meeting with the other members of the trust to discuss the matter. I suppose that may take a week or so. I understand you are in some haste. I cannot prejudge the issue, but I promise I will get back to you as soon as I can.'

'You haven't understood—'

'Oh, I think I have. Claire, you and I will have a talk after breakfast. I will take mine in the sitting room.'

Her pulse was too fast. She was breathing like a grampus. But she'd left them in no doubt as to her position, hadn't she?

Claire bridled. Yes, she really did. Her shoulders moved up and down, and her head wagged from side to side, while her mouth looked as if she'd tasted something sour. 'I was not employed to be your maid of all work. I have prepared this meal out of the goodness of my heart because it is a great honour for the pastor to eat with us, but—'

That was it! Ellie marched round the table, picked up the heavy frying pan with all its luscious contents and tipped it into the waste food bucket.

Claire cried out in horror. Ambrose half rose from his seat, but Ellie was too quick for him. She seized the toast rack and flicked the slices in, one by one, on top of the fry-up. Then she reached for the jug of orange juice.

'No, you shan't!' cried Claire, reaching for it at the same moment as Ellie. An undignified tug of war took place till Ellie suddenly let go . . .

. . . which meant that Claire took an undignified dive backwards, slipping from chair to floor . . .

. . . and the juice went all over her.

Claire screamed, throwing the jug on to the floor and clawing at her T-shirt.

'Bravo, Ellie!' Rose fell back in her chair, laughing so much that she had to hold herself together.

Ambrose didn't go pale with rage. A dusky skin doesn't allow for that. He thrust back his chair and thundered, 'Woman! What do you think you are doing!'

Ellie didn't feel ashamed of herself. Not one bit! Well, perhaps a little bit. She'd behaved like a spoilt child, and one part of her mind informed her that she was going to regret her hasty actions when she'd calmed down. But she hadn't calmed down yet.

Hands on hips, she said, 'I did *not* invite you into my house. That was *my* food, bought with my money, which Claire prepared. I had every right to dispose of it in any way I wish. I can't imagine why you think I'd enjoy being browbeaten. I have already asked you both once to leave this house, and now I ask you to do so again.'

'Look at what you've done to me!' wailed Claire, sitting up and holding her T-shirt away from her.

Ellie's better self tried for contrition, and failed. Normally, she'd have sprung to the rescue of someone who'd spilt juice down herself with offers of help to get them into clean clothes. Now, she folded her arms at Claire.

Ambrose raised his hands in the air, to bring down a curse upon her? 'Woman, you are piling up a mountain of sin—'

'Oh, don't be ridiculous,' said Ellie, losing patience. 'You can't just barge in on people and take over their household, no matter how good your project may be. Now pick Claire up off the floor and take her to wherever it is you live.'

Claire wasn't giving up that easily. 'You can't manage on your own, you know you can't.'

Rose, who had crept out of her chair and was now at the sink, said, 'Oh, yes, we can. Shall I make us boiled eggs and soldiers for breakfast, Ellie? And a nice cup of strong tea to follow.'

'Come!' The pastor seized Claire by one fleshy arm and lifted her to her feet.

Claire wailed, 'I can't go out like this! I've got to change! My things are all upstairs! Mrs Quicke, you can't be so hard of heart as to throw me out without letting me even change my clothes.'

Ellie hesitated, then nodded. 'All right. Go upstairs, change and pack. Perhaps your pastor will be so good as to wait for you. Outside.'

A look passed between Claire and the pastor. He let go of her and nodded. 'I'll wait for you in the car.'

'One moment,' said Ellie. 'Before you go, I need your keys, Claire.'

Sniff, sniff. A bunch of keys was produced and laid on the table.

The pastor said, 'I speak to you, Mrs Quicke, more in sorrow than in anger. I pray you will see the error of your ways. Meanwhile, I'll consult my solicitor. You cannot expect to get away with assaulting someone as you have done, or to dismiss them from their job without giving them notice.'

Ellie grinned. 'Do make sure I get a copy of the contracts which Rose or I am supposed to have signed, and I'll give them to my solicitor as well.'

He didn't ask what she meant, but he did send a glance of barely-contained fury in Claire's direction as she stumbled to the back stairs and disappeared. Ellie led the way to the front door, hoping Ambrose would take the hint. She couldn't think what she'd do if he refused to budge. Would she have to call the police to remove him?

Fortunately, he took his dismissal calmly and followed her to the hall. She opened the front door for him. A good-looking silver car was standing outside. His, presumably? He must be getting a good stipend to run a Lexus . . . At least, she thought it was a Lexus. She'd heard it said a Lexus was the cream of cars at the moment, but what did she know about cars? It was raining, not much, but enough to deter further conversation. She saw him get into his car, and she closed the front door on the outside world.

Now, breakfast. Rose might or might not have achieved boiled eggs, and she might well have poured boiling water into the pot without first putting in any tea bags, but Ellie could sort out what needed to be done, and they could eat in peace.

It was early yet, and she could be at her desk by nine – with luck. After she'd sorted out her washing . . .

By ten past nine Ellie was indeed at her desk, sorting the pile of mail into His and Hers. Thomas edited a quarterly Christian magazine. He'd put the last issue to bed and made a good start on the next before he left for Canada, and meanwhile the follow-ups were being handled by his part-time assistant, who would work from home while Thomas was away. But still some correspondence had landed up on Ellie's desk. Also bills. She dealt with those, collected all the envelopes addressed to him and left them on his desk.

When she got back, she found Midge had taken over her chair and was pretending to be asleep. She lifted him up and placed him on her lap, which meant she couldn't access her computer properly . . . but then, it hadn't come on when she'd tried it the day before. Bother. She tried it again, and this time it decided to obey her instructions. Oh, good. There were over a hundred emails. Oh dear.

Someone tapped on her door and entered.

Pastor Ambrose. Smiling. Not at all hesitant.

Ellie was not amused. In fact, she was annoyed, with an undercurrent of fear. This man had invaded her space once too often. Midge sat up on her lap and stretched, with his eyes on the intruder. Was he going to leave her to face the man alone? How ridiculous, to depend on a cat's presence to protect her!

She said, 'I suppose Claire let you in? Which tells me that neither of you can be trusted to carry out your promises.'

He held up his hands in a gesture of surrender. 'Forgive me. I was misled into thinking you were a godly woman who worshipped the light. Claire thought she was helping you on your way and did not realize how far you still have to travel. That was very wrong of her. I fear she frequently mistakes her role in life. In a sense, I have made myself responsible for her, so I asked her to let me in, to apologize to you most profoundly for offending you. She means well, but she is not always wise.'

Ellie stilled her heartbeat. He did not mean her any harm. Probably.

So, Claire's role in life was to be the fall guy? Anything Ambrose did which turned out badly could be blamed on Claire? The perfect scapegoat with a spotty past?

She stroked Midge, who refused to settle down again but didn't leave her. 'I think I've made my position clear. I cannot enter into any discussion with you until—'

He took a seat, unasked, and leaned forward, clasping his hands in a praying position. 'I realize we have got off to a bad start, and I want to correct that. Let me tell you about our organization.'

Ellie indicated the pile of papers at her side. 'I am sure your application is here, and I will get round to it shortly. Now, if you don't mind . . . You can see how busy I am.'

Another tap on the door; this time a timid one. Claire sidled in.

Midge jumped from Ellie's lap to the top of the filing cabinet, where he fluffed himself out to twice his normal size and growled.

Claire gave a little scream. 'Oh, save me!'

Ellie would have laughed if she hadn't been so annoyed. 'Midge won't hurt you.'

Claire cringed into a corner, as far away from Midge as she could get, hands over her mouth. 'Help! Oh, save me!'

Ambrose said, 'Pull yourself together, woman!'

Ellie knew it was no good telling people to pull themselves together if they were as distressed as Claire was. And Claire really did seem to be distressed. She wasn't making it up.

Ellie opened the door and, risking Midge's claws, removed him from his perch and put him down in the corridor. He was the type of cat who believed himself to be hard done by if he were picked up and ejected from the room he'd chosen to grace with his presence. He turned his back on Ellie and proceeded to attend to his toilet.

'Now,' said Ellie, returning to her seat, 'if you will kindly leave, I really do need to get on.' She swung round to her computer, hoping they'd take the hint.

Pastor Ambrose put his large, warm hand over hers as it rested on the mouse. He said, 'A woman's first duty is to her church, and then to her family and friends. She should leave financial affairs to those who understand them.'

'Make up your own mind. You can't have it both ways,' said Ellie, who secretly agreed with him and left all financial dealings to those she considered better equipped to deal with them . . . except, of course, that Kate, their financial wizard, did also happen to be a woman. 'Either you are talking to me as the head of a charitable trust, in which case I have already informed you of my position, or you aren't . . . in which case we have nothing to say to one another.'

'We need you!' Claire was in tears. Again. 'You've got to help us! They said you were a good, kind person who went to church and helped people who are in trouble, and we're in desperate trouble!'

'Hush, woman!'

'But we are! And I am! Pastor, you did believe me when I said I hadn't killed that girl, didn't you? You said, before the whole congregation, that I was blameless in that matter—'

'You were foolish in other ways.'

'I admit it! I was spiteful. I carried tales. I was uncharitable and envious, but I didn't deserve to lose my job, my flat and my car!'

'How did you lose all of them?' asked Ellie, who was, reluctantly, becoming curious about this.

'I . . .' The woman stopped. Her face flooded red with embarrassment and, possibly, with shame.

'She assaulted one of the pupils at the school where she was working,' said Ambrose, shooting Claire an unfriendly glance.

'He provoked me beyond bearing!'

The pastor wagged his finger at her. 'Your loss of self-control could have landed you in prison. You were fortunate indeed to be let off with the loss of your job and a hefty fine.'

Ellie sat back in her chair. 'Is that how she came to work for your organization? You help people who've been through the courts by giving them work?'

'Not everyone comes to us through the courts. We do take those addicted to drugs and drink, but Claire came to us long ago because she believed in the Vision, and it only later transpired that she nursed a secret sin. Claire is an addict to anger. She has to learn—'

'I have, I really have! I was happy to give up my car and my flat and move into the community rooms to prove that I am on the right path—'

'You were rebellious and ungrateful when we found you another job—'

'Helping an old lady dress and feed herself! I'm worth more than that!'

'There speaks your pride. You convict yourself out of your own mouth. You promised us much good would come of that job, and what happened? Nothing but trouble. Not a single penny has come to the Vision, for all your boasting. Then you failed to inform me that our young neighbour was behaving wantonly in—'

'I hoped that if I warned her—'

'Too late! She was steeped in sin and rebellious. You should have spoken out earlier, either to her mother, or to me.' Ambrose displayed a nasty temper. 'You did nothing to stop her descent—'

'I did, I did! I spoke to her. I warned her! And I did tell you, you know I did!'

'Too late, too late! You thought you knew best, didn't you? In your pride, and envy of someone much younger and far more attractive, you let her drift down the path to destruction. And now she is a lost soul!'

Claire ducked her head. 'I know I did wrong!'

Ambrose put his hand to his brow. 'It has just occurred to me. Perhaps you struck her, as you struck that boy?'

'No, I didn't! I wouldn't! Oh, Mrs Quicke, can't you help me? I haven't any money now, only what I earn, and I know you're about to turn me out of doors and I don't blame you really, though I was only following instructions, but I can't get another job while everyone thinks that I killed that girl, though they can't prove anything, can they, because I didn't? You believe me, don't you? Say you do!'

Ellie felt like Alice in Wonderland, drowning in tears. She looked into Claire's eyes and saw something move in their depths . . . Some knowledge that she wasn't sharing? No, no. She was mistaken. Claire radiated sincerity.

Claire clasped her hands in despair and hope. 'I'll work for you for nothing!'

Ellie didn't want that, either. 'No, that's not necessary.'

Claire was radiant. 'Oh, I will, I will! Just till everyone's forgotten about those stupid girls and I can get a better job. I'll be for ever grateful!'

'I don't want your gratitude—'

'Oh, thank you! Thank you!'

'I'm not promising anything, mind.'

'But you've believed in me, and that's everything! You are an angel in disguise!'

SIX

Ellie thought, What have I done?

Claire was a happy bunny. 'Now I can get on with my work. I'll just pop into the kitchen and see that Rose is all right. Then I'll work out what we should have to eat this evening. Something wholesome and good for the bowels . . .'

Ellie let her go, thinking that it had probably been a mistake to let the woman stay, but not at all sure how to deal with the situation.

Ambrose was not happy, either. 'Mrs Quicke, you have more important things to do with your time than to run around after that sinful woman.' Did he mean that she ought to be concentrating on his application for funds? Probably.

Ellie felt she'd been driven into a corner. What Ambrose said was quite true; she did have more important things than Claire to think about.

Or did she? If there had been a miscarriage of justice . . .? Well, of course, Claire hadn't been convicted of anything, if you overlooked her attack on a child who had probably taunted her into slapping her or something . . . Yes, but she only had Claire's word for it, and that needed to be checked.

Ambrose was still talking, saying something about vines bearing no fruit and having to be cut down. Ellie was pretty sure he'd misquoted, but tuned him out. She definitely had more to worry about than that. Perhaps she'd have a word with her contact at the police station, see what she had to say. Meanwhile: 'Mr Ambrose, you can see I have much to do. Now, if you'd like to get on with your work, I'll be able to get on with mine.'

Amazingly, this time he accepted his dismissal.

As Ellie saw the pastor out, up the drive came two welcome figures: Amy and Anna, her old cleaners. Ellie welcomed them with open arms. 'Am I glad to see you two!'

Anna was a bulky forty-year-old with dyed fair hair. Amy

was younger and slimmer, but had also dyed her dark hair yellow. They were hard-working, opinionated, tea-drinking, biscuit-devouring gossips. They criticized their menfolk, adored their children, smoked when they knew they shouldn't and never let anyone down. The salt of the earth.

Both looked pleased to see Ellie. 'It's safe to come back? You got rid of that old cow?' That was Anna.

Ellie winced. 'Yes and no. Come in, come in. Problems. Look, I've agreed to keep Claire on for a bit—'

'Then we're off. We can't work with her in the house.' That was Amy.

'I know. I understand. But I'm desperate. I'm letting her stay on for a bit to look after Rose till I can find someone else. Meantime, you take your orders from me and not from her. If she asks you to do anything, you say you have to ask me. Can you manage that?'

'I'd rather not,' said Amy, bunching her formidable forearm muscles. 'Not after what she done.'

Ellie sympathized. She'd rather not have had to keep Claire about the place, too. But here came the cavalry, in the form of Vera, flying in to the rescue. 'Dear Amy, dear Anna; how lovely to see you again. I'm not really here, just passing on my way to work. Oh, but I'm so glad you've been big-hearted enough to come back. I've been so worried about Ellie and Rose being left alone in the house with Claire.'

What could Amy and Anna do but laugh and agree that Yes, they thought they could manage if that woman was going to make herself scarce while they went about their work.

Vera kissed Amy. Vera kissed Anna. Vera also gave Ellie a hug and a kiss, saying she was late for work, but would try to drop in later, or Mikey would, and was that all right?

Then she was off, and the day seemed less bright with her departure.

'Well,' said Anna. 'Let's get down to it, shall we?'

Ellie said she'd leave them to it, as they knew what needed to be done better than she did. She went off to ring her friend Lesley – or DC Milburn, to use her full name – who worked at the local police station. After which Ellie made a list of people she needed to talk to, and she started on that . . .

Wednesday afternoon

Ellie surfaced from work in her study at lunchtime when Amy and Anna knocked on the door to say they'd finished and would see her as usual next week. They had restored all the furniture to its usual places and left the kitchen spotless. They said they'd not seen Claire all morning, and that she was probably holed up in her own room, which they had no intention of going in to, not on yours!

Ellie thanked them most sincerely and went to check on Rose, who woke long enough to take a mug of soup and nibble at a sandwich, saying she was perfectly all right. Rose said she'd seen no sign of Claire, either. Ellie wondered if the woman was still in the house, or if she'd popped out for some reason. Claire was supposed to be staying on to look after Rose, but her promises were not to be relied on, were they?

Ellie told herself she was too busy to bother chasing Claire up. She could only be thankful the woman had made herself scarce. Ellie made herself a sandwich and took that back to her desk. Some of her phone calls were being returned and needed to be followed up, and those emails . . .

Stewart rang, anxious to know how she was getting on with Claire, confirming he and Kate would be turning up on the morrow for their usual Thursday morning meeting.

Diana rang, to make sure Claire had been thrown out of the house; Ellie equivocated. She found it hard to explain why the woman was still hanging around. Diana also wanted Ellie to babysit little Evan that weekend, but Ellie cried off. She loved her grandson dearly, but he could be a little tartar, and now that he was walking he was into everything, and if he didn't get what he wanted that instant, he'd roar the house down. Ellie didn't feel up to coping with him at the moment.

There were still sixty-odd emails to deal with. Not all the business for her charitable trust empire was done on email, but a great deal was, and Ellie was always copied in on anything out of the ordinary. Most of the work was routine, but there were queries about appointing a new electrical contractor, as the old one had moved out of London, and some tycoon or other wanting to buy a block of flats down by the river, which might bring them a nice return on their investment, but if he wanted vacant possession would create lots of other problems such as rehousing the tenants. And so on . . .

Ellie phoned Pat, her part-time secretary. Pat was pleased to hear Ellie had returned and said that she'd be in the following morning to take notes for the trust meeting.

Maria rang from the agency to say Amy and Anna had agreed to continue working for Ellie on the strict understanding that Claire was leaving forthwith. Maria confessed she hadn't had any luck yet with finding someone suitable to look after Rose. Ellie herself tried a couple of other agencies without luck.

At four the doorbell rang, and there was Lesley Milburn, Ellie's friend, the plain clothes policewoman. In her late thirties and with a pleasing appearance and personality, Lesley had a reputation for hard work. Her upward climb in the force had been prevented by her immediate boss, who feared and disliked her ability, but surely some day soon she'd break through the glass ceiling he'd imposed on her.

Ellie had found Lesley to be a good friend as well as a good detective, and she ushered her in, saying, 'Am I glad to see you! Tea and a biscuit? I've only just got back home, so there's no cake yet.'

They had known one another long enough not to stand on ceremony, so went straight through to the kitchen. Bright voices emanated from Rose's room where she was probably dozing on her bed with the television on. There was no sign of Claire, but Midge was curled up, asleep, in Rose's big chair . . . which was another sign that Claire couldn't be anywhere nearby.

Lesley said, 'When does Thomas get back?'

'Early next week, with luck. I could do with him now. What do you know about a cult called the Vision, who are supposed to be doing good works all over the place?'

Lesley knew where the biscuit tin was kept, and she hoicked it out. 'The Vision? Um, yes. I've heard about them. A good thing, no?'

'I believe they're supposed to rescue drug addicts and alcoholics and cure them by giving them a job and a place to live under strict supervision. Is that what you've heard?'

A bland look. 'Sounds just what our broken society needs. Why? Are you looking for dirt on them?'

'Is that what I'm doing?' Ellie made her voice as sweet as sugar.

'Knowing you, yes.'

'Let's take our tea into the sitting room. You bring the biscuits. I honestly don't think there'll be anything in the police files to their detriment, although . . . No, I don't suppose there is.'

'You asked me for the low-down on someone called Claire Bonner. Why?'

'She's latched on to Rose, and she introduced me to someone from their group. They want my charitable trust to stump up the money to buy the house which they're currently renting. I'm looking for a good reason to turn them down.'

'Sorry, I haven't heard anything which would help you there, but I have sorted out some background on Claire.' Lesley seated herself on the settee, allowing Midge to jump up on to her lap. She pushed him aside to rummage in her bag for a notebook.

'We had a look at her at the beginning of the year, when a young girl disappeared locally. The boss headed up the investigation. I was only involved in background checks, sitting with the mother, that sort of thing. Basically, when this girl Gail was reported missing by her mother – no father in sight; they said he'd died in an accident, but it was a drug overdose – we homed in on the girl's boyfriend. He had an alibi. He'd gone away for the weekend. We checked, and he was definitely not in London that evening. We interviewed Claire because she'd given the girl a lift home in her car on the evening she disappeared.'

'Gail's mobile phone was subsequently found in her car?'

'There was that. Also, no one seems to have seen hair or hide of her after she got into Claire's car. We interviewed Claire up hill and down dale—'

'Did she have hysterics?'

'Every five minutes. Her capacity for tears was quite astonishing. The boss got nowhere with her, though he tried hard enough. I was present some of the time, and I don't think I could have done any better. She stuck to her story like glue.

Hard though it was to accept, we came to the conclusion that, even if she had done away with the girl, we couldn't prove diddly-squat. There was no forensic in her car, in her garage, nor in her flat. Then Gail rang to say she was perfectly all right and enjoying herself in the arms of a new boyfriend. She was technically under-age, but only by a month . . .' A shrug. 'So we kept on looking for that month . . .'

'But without any great urgency?'

'As you say. It let Claire off the hook. We had looked at her very hard in the first place because she'd been involved in an earlier incident—'

'Ah, a problem at a school? Claire lost her temper and smacked a kid?'

'Not half, she did! I interviewed both him and his mother. Mind you, he's a nasty little tyke, likes to wind people up and then step out of harm's way just before retribution descends. His mother thinks he's an angel. The teaching staff think that the sooner he's locked up, the longer he'll live. Like all bullies, he'd homed in on the weakest of the flock. Claire was support staff; helped out in the art classes, ran errands—'

'Not in the office?'

A stare. 'No. Support staff in the classroom. She wasn't a trained teacher. Why?'

'Why did I get the impression that she worked in an office?'

Lesley shifted, looked down at her notes. 'I think she had worked in an office before. Yes, sometime before she moved to her present address, she'd been working as office manageress in the accounts section of one of the big supermarkets in the northern part of the borough. Not that that's relevant.'

'Claire's career seems to have been a downhill progression from a peak as the manageress of an accounts section, to living on bread and water at the beck and call of the Vision people. Why did she leave the supermarket?'

'Family reasons. She'd been living at home – I've got the address somewhere – Perivale? The other side of the A40. She'd been attending this cult or sect, or whatever they are, in the evenings. Then her mother died—'

'Leaving her money to the Vision?'

'No, I don't think so. I suppose Claire felt that when her mother died, it was time to grow up and move on. So she upped sticks and moved down here. She rented a nice flat, ran a car, looked around for another job, but only managed some temporary, part-time work which always petered out. She didn't get beyond the interview stage for a full-time job anywhere, and I suppose you can see why. So, to keep her hand in, she went to work for the school while continuing to go to interviews.'

Lesley tapped her teeth with her pen. 'She was on edge when we questioned her about Gail, but in a way I can understand it, because she had the assault charge on the schoolboy hanging over her at that time. That had happened at the end of the Christmas term, but the case didn't come up in court—'

'It was actually taken to court? For such a minor offence?'

'The child's parents didn't think it was minor. They insisted on prosecution, but the case didn't come to court till February. It was a foregone conclusion that Claire was going to be found guilty, although, being a first offence and not having any previous convictions, she was pretty well bound to get a suspended sentence. Meanwhile, she couldn't work at the school any more and went to look after some old lady or other.'

'How did she come across Gail?'

'Claire had a nice flat in the house rented by the Vision people. It's a big house, divided into flats. It's actually owned by the council and administered by Housing and Social Services. The people of the Vision rent the ground floor and some rooms at the side, while the rest of the building is occupied by tenants, some of whom have been living there for a long time, though some are transient. Gail and her mother occupied one of the top flats in the main building, but they all used a common staircase and front door. That's how Claire came into contact with Gail and her mother. According to Claire, Gail was rude to her from the start. Perhaps she was. Anyway, there was no love lost between them. I can imagine Gail having fun at Claire's expense when it came out that she'd slapped a schoolboy, and Claire getting back at Gail by telling tales on her. An unhappy situation, though not uncommon.

'Anyway, as expected, Claire was given a suspended sentence and fined for the assault on the boy, which put her out of the running for the sort of office job she'd had earlier. The Vision paid her fine. They took and sold her car to pay for it. She had got herself a new job, but it only paid peanuts so she moved into cheaper accommodation.'

'A stiff sentence, perhaps more than she deserved?'

A shrug from Lesley. 'We checked with the elderly lady Claire went to work for. She was a bit confused about dates, but insisted that Claire was a real treasure and that she'd never been so well looked after in her life. She said this included her no-good son and daughter who lived on the other side of the world and never visited her. She said that when she died she intended to leave half the value of the house to people who deserved it. I don't know if she did or not, but that's what she said she was going to do.'

Ellie helped herself to a couple of biscuits and passed the tin over. 'Then you don't know whether or not she did leave her house to the Vision . . . or to Claire?'

Lesley shrugged. 'She was still alive when we were investigating the case.'

Ellie wondered how long a disputed will would take to go through the courts. Months, presumably. 'There's nothing in Claire's previous life to indicate she was interested in young girls, was there?'

'What? What do you mean "interested in"? If you're asking about evidence of short temper, well . . . yes. I could see her sloshing Gail all right. I could even see Claire killing her by mistake. Knocking her down so that she hit her head on a kerbstone, something like that.'

'Gail was an annoying teenager?'

'Grade One. Sulky, not interested in anything but make-up and hair. Bursting out of her blouse. Her mother showed me some photos. She's probably shacked up with an indulgent "protector" somewhere.'

Ellie was amused. 'Even if Claire had killed the girl—'

'Which she didn't. I've told you, Gail contacted her mother later on, saying she was fine and dandy. Yes, we did suspect Claire at first, but she had a pretty good alibi for the rest of the evening after Gail disappeared, attending some service or other run by these Vision people. No, Claire is in the clear.'

'And anyway,' said Ellie, 'even if she had clocked the girl one, what would she have done with the body? You say there was no forensic evidence in the car or . . . Don't take any notice of me. I'm rambling. But I can't help thinking . . . No, nobody at the Vision would have helped her. They keep on the right side of the law. Even when Claire was convicted of an offence in court, they were holier than thou about it. They paid her fine, but made her reimburse them by taking away her car. So now she has no car, no future and must work for demanding old ladies . . . and, finally, for me. I suppose I ought to feel sorry for her.'

Lesley grinned. 'You don't, do you?'

'How can I? She's such a poor creature. The only thing about her is . . .' Ellie frowned. 'I think she tried to drug me.'

Lesley almost dropped her mug of tea. 'What?'

'Can't be sure, but I think she tried. She's perhaps not as helpless as she seems? Oh, I don't know. I want her out of the house. You may say she's looked after Rose well while I've been away, but I'm not convinced about that. She fed Rose some linctus that made her so sleepy that she didn't know which end of the day she was at. She took Rose out of the house in a borrowed wheelchair to go to a meeting of the Vision. Another thing: although she's been pleading with me to keep her on, she's never here when she should be. As of now, this very minute, I haven't a clue where she is. She's certainly not taking care of Rose. Then again, she got two of the Vision girls to move all our furniture around, and she tried to bring in a decorator to paint everything green, and . . .' She threw up her hands. 'You'll laugh, but the clincher is that she's a vegetarian and we aren't.'

Lesley said, 'You think she's been brainwashed by the Vision people?'

'I think she's in thrall to their pastor, a man called Ambrose. He's been leaning on me to give him the money to buy their house. He's charismatic. I can see how he'd appeal to someone looking for an authority figure to obey. I get the feeling he knows all about Claire's spotty past and is prepared to use her as a scapegoat whenever it suits him to do so. Blame Claire for everything. Why not? She's not going to fly off the handle with him.'

Lesley put her empty mug down. 'Can't you get Vera back to look after Rose?'

'She's got a full-time job at the hotel working in reception, and a new husband, and Mikey, the young limb. Also, she's pregnant. I gather the men in her life have demanded a baby girl. She's dropping in here when she can, and so is Mikey, but she's got her hands full.'

'Have you tried agencies?'

'Yes. No luck so far. I feel I'm going to regret it, but I sort of promised Claire I'd look into what happened when Gail left home. She feels she's still under suspicion, even though the girl surfaced later.'

Lesley shook her head. 'The case is dead in the water. Tell her to get on with her life and forget about Gail.'

Ellie leaned back in her chair. Oh, how good it was to be able to sit back in her own chair and look at the flowers Vera had placed on the small table in the window . . . and past them to the garden. The sun had come out. The grass needed cutting. The roses needed dead-heading. Soon she'd be able to get out into the garden and attend to it. But, sufficient to the day.

Lesley got to her feet. 'Must go. Let me know if there's anything else I can do for you.'

'Mm. Could you find out – it's probably nothing – but when you looked into Claire's past life in Perivale . . . There wasn't another incident of a girl going missing at that time, was there? Someone she could have been in contact with?'

'What!'

Ellie rubbed her forehead. 'Now, what made me say that? I think . . . Did Claire speak once about girls in the plural, or was it a slip of the tongue?'

'What makes you think of . . .? There wasn't the slightest hint of anything like that. I spoke to the people in personnel at the supermarket. They said she'd wanted a clean break after her mother died. I suspect she moved down here following her vision of the Vision, if you get me.'

'Yes, of course. I can't think why I—'

'Young girls who have grown up too fast go missing all the time. You know that. They run off with the boyfriends, or chase after a rock star, or get out to escape from Mum and Dad.'

'And most of them end up in care. Yes, I know that. But, could you run it through the computer for me?'

'Claire didn't smack another school boy, I can tell you that.'

'Yes, but did another girl go missing from the supermarket where she worked?'

Lesley stared into space. 'I am an idiot. I ought to have checked. It never occurred to me, and it ought to have done so. No, no. That's ridiculous. Claire's been formally cleared of involvement with Gail's disappearance. What makes you think . . .?'

'It's just an idea that floated into my mind.'

Lesley said, 'How do you do it, Ellie? I bet you're right. And I'm not a betting woman.'

'I hope I'm wrong,' said Ellie, 'but somehow, it feels right.'

SEVEN

When Lesley had gone, Ellie felt restless. Where was Claire? Had she left the house, and if so, why had she done so when the sole reason she'd been allowed to stay was because she was supposed to be looking after Rose? Ellie checked on Rose, who was sleeping on top of her bed with the telly on.

A light summer rain shower had cleared the air, so Ellie went out into the garden to do a little dead-heading before she started to cook supper. And no, it wouldn't be vegetarian. Claire had said she was going to look out something for supper, but there was nothing to show that she'd done so. How about sausages and mash? The butcher had a wonderful array of pork sausages. Ellie had bought some with a leek and mustard flavour and some of the old-fashioned Cumberland variety. With lots of veg, they should make a really tasty meal. At least Claire had kept the fridge well stocked with fruit, so they'd have a summer pudding for afters.

Ellie had hardly made a start on the dead-heading before another rain shower drove her indoors. Resignedly, she went into her study and found that even more emails had arrived. She was in no mood to deal with them. The room felt airless. She opened a sash window at the top to air the room. She wished Thomas were on a plane coming home at this very minute.

She decided to drop into their Quiet Room, into which Thomas went every day to meditate, to study and to pray. It was always peaceful in there, and she needed a spot of peace and quiet. She opened the door and couldn't believe her eyes, for there was a body lying on the floor in front of her.

Correction: Claire was lying face down on the floor, arms outstretched, shoes off and neatly placed to one side.

Was she dead?

No, she seemed to be breathing.

'Claire? Are you ill? Whatever's the matter?'

Claire raised a tear-stained face. Her hair was all over the place.

Ellie bent over her. 'Shall I get an ambulance?'

Claire pushed herself up to a sitting position. 'I have seen a vision of hell, and you are in it!'

Ellie ironed out a smile. 'Yes, yes. Are you all right?'

Claire raised both hands in supplication. 'Lord, forgive her. She knows not what she says.'

Ellie felt and sounded sharp. 'I know very well what I'm saying. Oh, get up: do!'

Claire tried to get up. She groaned. 'Give me a minute . . .'

Ellie helped Claire to a chair. Not the big chair which Thomas used, but one of the smaller ones. 'There, now. Of course you'll be stiff if you've been lying on the floor. Whatever possessed you to—'

Up went Claire's arms. 'I have seen a vision of hell, and—'

'Yes, and I'm in it. So you said. Now, are your arms and legs working? Good, good.'

Claire repeated herself, louder. 'I have seen a vision of—'

'I dare say.' Ellie raised her own voice to drown out Claire. 'I've been looking for you everywhere. I thought you were supposed to be staying on to look after Rose, but instead—'

'I have been wrestling with the Lord. I have implored him to overlook my many imperfections and show me the way to soften your hard heart. I have been—'

'That's enough of that!' Ellie cut her off. 'You leave my soul alone.'

Claire began to rock to and fro. 'I saw your soul in hell, twisting and turning in the flames, screaming for help to—'

'That,' said Ellie, 'is *more* than enough. If God wants me to alter my ways, he'll tell me so himself.'

'You aren't listening to him, I can tell. Otherwise you wouldn't—'

'Have you packed, as I asked you to?'

'It was more important to spend time in prayer and—'

'Have you eaten?' Ellie was beginning to think Claire was round the twist.

'Eaten? No, no. I fasted, and I prayed. Not a drop of water, not a crumb has passed my lips, and I have vowed that I will not break my fast till the Lord has vouchsafed me an answer to my prayers and—'

'That's it,' said Ellie, pushing the woman's shoes into her hands. 'Put those on. Now! Don't argue! Just do it. Then go and sit in the hall. I will fetch your belongings.'

Ellie didn't wait for a reply, but banged out of the room, stamped up the stairs and opened the door of the room in which Claire had been sleeping. It was a large, comfortable bed-sitter, en suite, which had once been occupied by Rose.

It stank of some joss stick, or perfume. Ugh.

Ellie hammered the window open.

The room was neat and tidy. A large tote bag lay beside the wardrobe. Ellie emptied the contents of wardrobe and chest of drawers into the bag, swept everything off the bedside table and added Claire's nightdress and dressing gown. And slippers. And a bedtime book – of prayers? A couple of tracts?

The bathroom contained very little . . . some medication, herbal. A large bottle of linctus. Toothbrush, etc.

Altogether, a small enough collection of belongings.

Ellie threw back the bed coverings to air the bed – ugh, that scent! Or whatever it was. Yes, a scented candle, thankfully not alight.

One last look around, and Ellie made her way down the stairs with the tote bag, which she dumped on the floor by the front door.

Claire was sitting in the hall, looking as if she were going to start crying at any minute. 'You're not going to throw me out now, are you? I haven't anywhere to go.'

'Ring your friends at the Vision house, or whatever it calls itself—'

'Don't blaspheme!'

'Claire! I'm trying not to lose my temper with you, but frankly, if you're not out of here in ten seconds, I shall not be responsible for my actions. Out! Sleep in the road, for all I care. So long as I never see you again.'

'But you can't—' Here came the tears. 'I'm going to cook supper!'

Ellie opened the front door and threw the tote bag out into the drive.

Claire shrieked, hands to mouth.

Ellie spotted a black coat which had been left on the chair by the clock. It certainly wasn't one of hers. 'Is this your coat?' Ellie threw that outside, too.

Claire tottered out after her belongings, tears streaming down her face. 'You are a wicked, wicked woman!'

'Sure!' Ellie slammed the door, double-locked and bolted it. She realized that she was as high as a kite, and didn't care.

Yes, she did. She cared a lot. She was going to have to sit down and have a good cry. Or lie on the floor and scream.

Like Claire.

Which thought made her laugh. A bit. No, she wasn't going to go down that road. But, she did need to shut herself away and be quiet for a while, which meant using Thomas's Quiet Room.

Only, Claire had been using that recently. Fancy lying down on the floor and weeping like that . . .!

All right, Ellie had been thinking of doing the same thing. Well, not exactly, no.

She looked around the Quiet Room. Thomas's chair was still there; also the two smaller chairs that she and Rose used. The table with the bible on it had been pushed to one side. Ellie returned it to its usual place. The rather absurd Victorian wool-work picture of the Good Shepherd bearing a sheep on his shoulder was still in its usual place. Thomas liked that picture. He didn't need statues, or even pictures, to help him to pray.

She didn't, either.

She let herself down into her usual chair and pressed her hands to her eyes. Was she going mad? Was Claire right?

A vision of hell . . .?

She tried to pray, but her brain had become scrambled. Odd words came through, but didn't make any sense.

Please, Lord. Your humble servant . . . Please . . . A picture of hell? Am I so . . .? I'm crying out for help, but . . . She's such a poor creature, but . . . What was she trying to do to me?

Ellie was exhausted. Finally, she stopped trying to pray. She let her hands fall to her lap. The words whizzing around in her head began to slow down.

Almost, she could feel the peace of the room. Almost. But not quite.

Because someone else had come in and seated himself, cross-legged, on the floor. Looking at her, but waiting, patiently, for her to notice him.

Mikey. Serious. Tranquil.

He was only a child.

She must pull herself together, not let him see how distressed she'd been.

He waited.

She blew her nose. Tried to smile.

He nodded. He was waiting for her to say something?

She didn't know what to say. So said nothing. It didn't seem to matter.

He went on sitting there, still as a mouse. Not a mouse. A cat. Usually, Midge was with him. It occurred to her that Midge didn't often come into the Quiet Room. She wondered why not.

He said, 'Mum wants to move back in here, but Dan says "no". He's right, I think. She shouldn't.'

Ellie agreed. 'No, she shouldn't. She's got enough on already.'

'And we don't want her getting across Claire more than she has done.'

'Dan thinks Claire's dangerous?'

'*He* thinks she's just tiresome. It's *me* that thinks she's dangerous. I heard her, you see, talking to Rose, making her feel bad, slagging me and Mum off.' He eased his shoulders under his shirt. 'I've sort of been spying on her, watching her when she thinks I'm not looking. I didn't like it that she kept putting some stuff from a bottle in Rose's food, as well as giving it on a spoon.'

'Rose had a cough.'

'Not that I noticed.' Mikey would have noticed, wouldn't he?

'Do you know if Claire is on medication herself?'

He shook his head. 'She keeps a bottle of something in her

handbag, but I've never seen her take it. She said it was ordinary stuff that you can buy over the counter. The thing is, it made Rose so sleepy, she didn't know what day it was. I don't know why Claire didn't take any for herself. It might have calmed her down. I was thinking she might try to put some of it in the food she was making for you, and I didn't think she should, so this morning I rang Thomas.'

Ellie started. Thirteen-year-old boys didn't interfere in adult matters, did they? All right, Mikey was no average schoolboy. 'Mikey, I didn't want to worry him. He's got enough on his plate. And wouldn't it have been in the middle of the night for him?'

'No, he'd been out late, had just got back to the hotel. I was pretty sure you hadn't told him, but I thought he'd want to know. And he did.'

Ellie was amazed. 'But . . . how did you get his number?'

'He left it for you in his study, so I made a note of it, easy-peasy.' Scornful. 'But, like, I'd have yanked him out of a meeting if I'd had to. He said to tell you he'd come back early if you really needed him, but he thought you ought to be able to manage. He said he'd ring you this evening, usual time, dunno what that is, but he said you'd know. Oh, yes, and he gave me a message for you . . .' A heavy frown as he tried to remember the exact words. He recited, 'I'm to tell you that nothing can separate you from his love.' He cancelled out a grin. 'I thought you'd take that for granted, being married and all. But that's what he said.'

Ellie almost laughed. 'What he really said was that nothing bad can separate me from the love of God. In other words, God loves me, no matter what.'

Of course Thomas loves me, but God loves me even more. I'd forgotten that. Even if I do something silly, even if I make the wrong decision about supporting the Vision people, God will still love me. And support me. And be ready to advise me, as soon as I turn to him in prayer. Which I have failed to do.

Mikey hadn't finished. 'He said he'd pray about it. He said I'd got to pray, too. So I did.'

Ellie tried for a light touch. 'Did God tell you to bunk off school?'

'No. I decided that myself. I wanted to be sure Claire wasn't worrying you. I saw what she did to Rose. If you'd been all right when I popped in, I'd have gone back to school. But I could see you weren't, so I stayed.'

Ellie knew she ought to give him a right telling off and send him straight back to school. Instead, she said, 'Thank you.'

He relaxed, taking his eyes off her, letting his gaze rove around the room. 'I suppose I'm a bit like a guardian angel today, though I'm not sure I believe in guardian angels. Or not all the time, anyway. What do guardian angels do, anyway? If you were in the road and going to be run over, would they pick you up and fly you over the road to the other side, do you think?'

'Perhaps they'd just remind you to look both ways before you cross?'

He grinned. 'Will you write me a note for school, to say you were ill or you fell or something?'

'I'll ring them and say I was poorly and asked you to sit with me till I felt better. Which is true.'

He nodded. 'Have you noticed that Rose is "seeing" Miss Quicke more and more? It used to be only now and then, but she "sees" her more or less every day now.'

Ellie felt a stab of grief. 'How do you feel about that?'

He put his chin on his hand. 'I think Miss Quicke's like a guardian angel to Rose, because Rose was like a guardian angel to Miss Quicke when *she* was alive. They sort of pair off, in my mind.' He narrowed his eyes at Ellie. 'Rose is coming to the end of this life, isn't she?'

Ellie felt her heart thump. Should she prevaricate? 'What makes you think that?'

'The thought came into my mind one day. I don't *want* to think it, but I find I can't send it back.' He gave a long, long sigh, and stood up in one lithe movement, without touching the floor or reaching for a chair. Ah, the fluidity of youth! 'Cup of tea? Claire threw away our old tea-bags, but I see you've got some more. I've missed double art at school, but that's no skin off my nose. If it had been double maths, now . . . I don't think I'd have wanted to miss that.'

Wednesday, early evening

Supper time had been and gone. Vera had rung to say she couldn't make it that evening, as Dan wanted her to do something or other, and was that all right? Vera didn't seem to know that Mikey had missed a couple of lessons at school, and Ellie didn't enlighten her.

There'd been no sign of Claire. Hurray.

Rose picked at her supper, but was in good spirits. 'Now, Ellie; I don't want you bothering the doctor about me. I'm just fine. Aches and pains not nearly as bad as usual, and the bowel's working all right. What I don't want is being pushed and pulled about and being given dozens of pills to take every day which aren't going to make a mite of difference. I don't want to be sent for hospital appointments and wait around for hours on uncomfortable chairs only to be told what we all know, which is that the old heart is worn out. I want you to promise me that you won't ring the doctor.'

Ellie sighed. The doctor had indeed told her that there was nothing more they could do for Rose. 'So long as you don't have any pain.'

'I shall go into a home the moment I become a nuisance.'

'You'll never be a nuisance. You're family.'

'You can't cope on your own. We need someone living in to look after you, as well as keep an eye on me.'

'I've asked Maria to find someone.'

'I trust her. I don't trust Claire. Can you get that nice solicitor friend of yours who likes my Victoria sponges to come round one day soon, so that I can make another will?'

'I'll ask him.'

'Good.' Rose nodded off.

As Ellie got to her feet to clear the table, Rose started back into consciousness, saying, 'You be careful now, Ellie. Miss Quicke's been watching that Claire and says you mustn't trust her an inch.'

'I'll remember.'

The phone rang. Ellie went to answer it, trying to work out if this might or might not be Thomas. He rang whenever he could, but Ellie didn't think this was one of his free times. It wasn't Thomas.

It was Lesley, her friend in the police. 'You were right, Ellie. I can't think how you do it. Though it may mean nothing.'

Ellie took a moment to realize what Lesley was talking about. 'Ah. Another schoolgirl went missing about the time Claire left her job at the supermarket?'

'I'm not sure there's any connection. Claire left the supermarket in May, and it was well into June before a local girl disappeared. She wasn't like Gail. Pretty but pale, if you know what I mean. Just turned sixteen. She was still at school and didn't work at the supermarket, so there was no call to connect her with Claire. In fact, nobody has ever linked her to the supermarket or to Claire, and I can't see any reason why they should do so. The girl was still at school and planned to go on to do her A levels. The only possible link was that she sometimes waited at the bus stop near the supermarket. She left school one day in the company of one of her friends. They separated at the bus stop. Jenna – that was her name, Jenna – said she needed to buy a new biro before she got on the bus home, because hers had run out that day. She didn't need to go into the supermarket to buy it. There is a small parade of shops not far off, but none of the shopkeepers remember serving her. She didn't arrive home. She just disappeared.'

'The police were called in?'

'Of course. Not our lot. Different part of the borough. No trace. Eight months ago, last November, her body turned up in some scrub at the side of a canal bridge.'

Ellie sat down, with care. 'Dead?'

'Dead. Now this was some time after Claire left the area. I can't think there can be any tie-in. One strange thing: the body was found wearing a niqab.'

'A what?'

'She was naked except for the full black robe which Muslim women sometimes wear. Head to toe. Complete with headscarf and face mask. You can't see anything except the hands and the eyes when they wear the lot. It made it difficult to identify her at first.'

'You mean that Jenna had converted to Islam and this was why she disappeared? That she went undercover, so to speak?'

'It's a working hypothesis, but no one locally would confess to having had any contact with her, and that includes the people at the mosque. So it can't have been an official conversion.'

Here was a turn up for the books. 'How long had she been dead when she was found?'

'Not long. About a day. She was alive and living somewhere, probably in a Muslim household, until the day before she died.'

'Natural causes? Was she pregnant?'

'Strangled. And yes, she was four months pregnant. We have the DNA of the foetus; father unknown.'

So she'd been impregnated almost as soon as she disappeared. 'You say she was naked under the niqab?'

'The current theory is that she went off willingly enough with some bold spark of a Muslim, lived secretly as his woman, and then there was a quarrel about something – possibly the pregnancy? Possibly he didn't want a girl whom he'd picked off the streets to bear his child? For whatever reason, instead of divorcing her or turning her out into the world again, he killed her.'

'It could be that his family let her live with them, but objected to the pregnancy?'

'It could, but the police couldn't find any Muslim family who admitted to knowing her, or hearing about her.'

'Naked,' said Ellie, not quite sure why this was important, but thinking that it was. 'Ah, to avoid your being able to trace her by her clothing?'

'Possibly. The police up there were thorough. They contacted everyone they could think of, put up posters, the lot. Nothing. Eventually, they had to move on to other cases. I repeat, I can't see how Claire can have been involved. How have you been getting on with her, anyway?'

'I threw her out of the house this afternoon. I suppose she'll go back to the Vision people, wherever they may happen to be. I'm sorry if you wanted me to keep her here for you, but I couldn't take her trying to convert me any longer.'

'Convert you? Her?'

'She tried. The woman's barking mad!'

Lesley laughed. 'Clinically mad?'

'How should I know? Yes, I imagine she might well . . . No, I shouldn't say that. But she's been brainwashed by these people and believes . . . But that isn't a crime, is it? Brain-washing people? Or is it?'

'Oh, you . . .!' Lesley wasn't taking Ellie seriously. 'Anyway, there's nothing to suggest that—'

'Lesley, it may be me who's going round the twist, but would you do something else for me? Would you check to see if any other girl's body has turned up recently, naked except for a niqab?'

'What!'

'Yes, I know. It sounds ridiculous. But would you?'

'You're thinking that Gail might have gone the same route?'

'I don't know. But, as someone said, the thought popped into my head, and I can't get rid of it.'

Lesley was quiet for a moment. 'Ellie, if you're right, it doesn't bear thinking about. You're pointing the finger at the Muslim community, who are on the whole pretty law-abiding. Yes, they sometimes flout immigration or food hygiene regulations, or get caught up in the drugs trade, but where their womenfolk are concerned, many of them are still bound by cultural ties to Islam. I know that if they choose to live here, they should abide by our laws, but I don't think it's practical to think that their attitude to women is going to change overnight, because it isn't. The older people in particular still think in terms of their family's laws and customs. Suggesting that one of their young bucks has been going round kidnapping white girls and forcing them to wear the niqab is not going to go down well.'

'Even if that is what's been happening?'

'If we asked around, they'd deny it. Possibly, they might investigate for themselves, but they wouldn't necessarily share their findings with the police.'

'Is that what you think happened after the body was discovered? That police enquiries caused them to search for a family who might have been harbouring the girl? And, even if they found out where she'd been living, they didn't inform the authorities?'

'It's a theory.'

Ellie wasn't happy about it. 'It still doesn't make sense. Surely, they wouldn't want to cover up for someone who killed a pregnant woman? And why would any man want to do that? I don't understand.'

'Perhaps . . .' Lesley was hesitant. 'Perhaps if she was his bit on the side, and he was already married to someone his family approved of . . . and his legitimate wife found out . . . but in that case, he could just have turned her out on the streets. Oh, I don't know.'

'Neither do I. It's a can of worms.'

Lesley sighed. 'It's not our case to worry about. There really is nothing to link your Claire with Jenna's disappearance, and my boss is hardly likely to go looking for a connection. He's keen on race relations, has been on all the courses. He turns out for all the multicultural activities and gets his picture in the paper. He supports integration, and he goes on and on about not upsetting anyone who doesn't think exactly the same way in the indigenous population. He knows the Race Relations Act by heart. He's a bleeding heart when it comes to poor, oppressed immigrants—'

Ellie didn't care for Lesley's boss. 'It's only skin deep, isn't it? For public consumption.'

'Ellie, sometimes you're so sharp that—'

'I'll cut myself. I know. What you mean is that he'll soft pedal anything which looks as if it might reflect badly on the Muslim community.'

Silence. A reluctant: 'Yes.'

'Jenna's death did not occur in his territory, so he doesn't have to think about it.'

'That's right. And he's not the only one.'

'You think enquiries about Jenna's death were not pursued as stringently as they would have been if she weren't wearing a niqab?'

'I can't answer that.'

'Coming back to our own particular mystery, if Gail was killed soon after she disappeared, would her body have been found by now?'

'Yes, of course. If an unclaimed body is found anywhere

in the country, we check to see if they're on the Missing Persons list.'

'Gail hasn't turned up though.'

'Why should she? A couple of days after she disappeared, she rang to say she was off enjoying herself. I interviewed the mother, remember, and I'm not at all surprised the girl wanted some excitement in her life. Television mad, that one. With beer and cigarettes on the side.'

'I know, but . . . Jenna was kept alive for five months after she disappeared. It's five months since Gail went missing. No, I do realize she disappeared of her own accord and . . . No, I agree that there's absolutely nothing to indicate that the two cases are linked, but I have a horrid itchy feeling at the back of my mind about this. You really haven't any Jane Does – corpses without identification – who might turn out to be Gail? Do you think you could check for me one last time?'

Lesley sighed and put the phone down. So did Ellie.

The phone rang again. This time it *was* Thomas, and they had a most satisfactory conversation.

EIGHT

Thursday morning

Ellie woke to a fresh-looking morning. She had found her bible – which had dropped down under the bed – and she managed to read a few verses before she made herself get up. She tended to skip the 'Oh, Woe is Me!' bits and look for the 'Don't be Afraid!' words, but what was wrong with that, especially if it helped her to face whatever the day had in store?

It had rained again in the night, but not too much. Her fingers itched to get out into the garden, to weed and dead-head and tie up the sweet peas, which she'd planted around some trellis, and which had fallen away from their support.

It was Thursday, and this morning she would have to sit through the usual business meeting, but as soon as that was over, she'd be out there. How pleasant it was to look out on green grass and a deep herbaceous border and shrubs, almost all of which she'd planted herself. She was tempted to don an old T-shirt and cotton skirt suitable for gardening, but with a sigh pulled on a formal blouse and a tailored skirt. As she was the head of the trust fund, she felt she ought to dress accordingly. Kate, her finance director, and Stewart would undoubtedly be wearing suits, and so would her secretary.

Breakfast was a bit of a rush because she'd slept late, but there was still time to settle Rose into her big chair in the kitchen, to make coffee and break open a packet of biscuits before the meeting. She checked the dining room to make sure Anna and Amy had put the big table back together again, which they had. A bluebottle buzzed. She fetched the fly spray and zizzed it. Or, had it escaped? Annoying. She'd have another go at it later.

She wondered why the dining table had ever been taken apart by . . . what were their names? Dolores and something.

Ah, it was because the Vision people had planned to redecorate the room, wasn't it? Oh well. A shrug. Stewart had seen them off, hadn't he?

The sun was shining. If they whizzed through the agenda at the business meeting, they could probably be through in an hour. She had no intention of making up her mind about a grant to the Vision people in a hurry. She'd hear what Kate had to advise and suggest they make some more enquiries before coming to any decision. And probably let it slide . . .

Vera popped in for a moment, looking very smart in her work outfit of black and white. She'd brought a punnet of ripe cherries for Ellie and Rose, picked that morning from her garden. She was in a hurry, saying she'd try to get back later that day as Ellie would probably want to place an order for a delivery of food on the computer, and she'd do it for her.

Then there was peace and quiet.

Ellie hesitated. Could she slip out to the garden for ten minutes . . .? But no, here came her secretary, Pat, voluble about her holiday, wanting to show Ellie some pictures of her nephew, and not all that keen to settle down to work . . .

And Stewart, frowning, looking at his watch, saying there was an awful lot on the agenda . . .

Kate whizzed in last of all, still talking on her smartphone, getting her laptop up and running even before she'd finished her phone call.

Ellie brought in the coffee while Stewart and Pat dealt out paperwork and turned on their own laptops. Ellie had forgotten the sugar, and by the time she got back from the kitchen with it, the other three were already eyes down and muttering to one another.

Ellie seated herself. 'Lovely to be back. Now, how's things?'

Kate flicked through papers. 'Why can't we have the agenda on our laptops? I'm in a hurry today . . .'

She always was. Kate was financial adviser to a growing number of important clients.

'. . . so I'd like to take the application from the Vision church first.'

Stewart frowned. 'There may be a problem. I've come across some information which may influence our—'

'What information?' asked Kate, flicking through her papers. 'I don't have anything here which—'

'My wife tells me that one of her cleaners believes that—'

'Hearsay.' Ellie had to say it. 'Kate, it's only hearsay, but it's caused me to ask my friend in the police to enquire whether or not there may be something in it.'

The doorbell rang. Insistently. Someone was leaning on it. Only one person rang the bell like that. Mistress Impatience. Ellie's daughter, Diana.

'What?' Stewart recognized the way the bell had been rung, too. 'Why . . .?'

Ellie said, 'I'll go.' And did. Knowing exactly what had brought Diana to their house that morning. Thursday mornings were always kept for trust business. The agenda this morning was bound to include the Vision's application for funds, and Diana would want it turned down.

'Mother, you took your time!' Diana swept through the hall, in a hurry, also on her smartphone, also carrying her laptop. 'I hope you haven't started yet.'

Ellie didn't even bother to ask what Diana wanted. In any case, her daughter was already marching into the dining room. They really ought to stop calling it 'the dining room', since it was rarely used for the purpose of eating.

Diana pulled out a chair, without being asked to take a seat. 'Before you start, yes, I am here on business pertaining to the trust, and it is vitally important that I tell you the sort of people who are trying to get you to give them—'

The doorbell rang again. One sharp burst of sound. Before Ellie could attend to it, she heard the sound of a key being turned in the lock. In marched Pastor Ambrose with Claire the Tearful close behind him. After them came the cleaners, Dolores and Liddy, looking as if they wished themselves elsewhere. Liddy had her hand pressed to the side of her face, which looked swollen. Toothache? Poor child.

Ellie took a step back. 'How on earth did you get in?'

Ambrose smiled, the forgiving smile of an adult explaining what ought to be obvious to a somewhat backward child. 'Claire always has a copy made of her house keys, in case she mislays one. In this case, we felt it important that we attend the meeting which is to set the Vision on its way into the future.'

Ellie ground her teeth. Claire had been made the scapegoat, as usual. 'I regret, the meeting is not an open one.'

'Ah, but for us . . .' He smiled, widely.

Rose appeared, hesitating in the doorway to the kitchen quarters.

Ellie wondered if Rose had told Claire about their weekly business meetings. Was that how Ambrose had come to hear about it? She said, trying to be polite, 'Forgive me, but the meetings of our trust are private. None of you have been invited to join us, and I don't think—'

The pastor waved her objection away. 'Ah, but we were invited. Rose invited us.'

That took Ellie's breath away. The effrontery of the man! She looked at Rose, who shook her head, worried, grimacing. 'I don't think I did, did I?'

Ambrose wasn't listening. 'This is the way to the boardroom, isn't it?' He gestured to the dining room. 'I asked that it be cleared specially for us . . .' He stepped inside and halted. 'Oh. The table has been put back again, although I thought the room was to be redecorated . . . Well, I can rise above that. We will sit around it and confer. Claire, you may sit here on my right. Dolores, Liddy: sit on either side of us. Mrs Quicke, I see you are serving coffee, which is poison to our systems. We of the Vision do not take stimulants, and I trust you will soon see the sense of that.'

Rose sent a helpless look in Ellie's direction and vanished.

Diana half rose from her chair. 'How dare you force your way into a private house!'

'It is not just a private house, is it? This is where you hold the meetings of the trust. That is why I am here and why I have brought witnesses to the good work which we do.'

Kate looked from one to the other. 'I don't understand. I have here an application from the people calling themselves the Vision for funds, but—'

'That is us. Continue.' Pastor Ambrose waved his hand, giving permission.

Ellie stood behind her chair. 'Pastor Ambrose, we cannot

be bullied into varying our procedures. It is true that we have received an application for funds from you, but we have not yet had an opportunity to discuss it among ourselves, and when we have done that, there will no doubt be questions which—'

A radiant smile. 'Which is why I am here, to remove all possible objections to our application.'

Diana said, 'Shall I ring for the police to remove these people?'

Ellie shook her head. 'No need. I suggest that, due to unforeseen circumstances, we adjourn this meeting to a more convenient time. All those in favour?'

'Seconded,' said Stewart.

'Agreed,' said Diana, rising from her seat. 'And now, I really must get back to work.'

Pat hesitated, halfway out of her chair. 'I don't understand why these people are here. We've never invited visitors to these meetings before, have we?'

'I feel,' said Kate, frowning, 'that I have been inadequately briefed. Ellie, there is obviously a lot more going on with this application than we have been told. I agree we should adjourn until we have all the information we need.' She closed her laptop and picked up her smartphone, checking for new messages.

'But,' said Pastor Ambrose, 'there are five of you, and only four of us, which makes for uneven voting.'

'You are not trustees,' said Pat, who liked to follow rules and regulations. 'This is not a situation in which you are eligible to vote.'

'A trivial objection. Let me put you in the picture.' He laid an A4 photograph on the table. 'The original house was built a hundred years ago for a large family, with servants' quarters in the attics, capacious outhouses and a large garden. Some forty years ago, the house was sold to a business man who divided it into flats of various sizes. Later, a developer added a block of flats to one side, thinking to rent the place out for student accommodation. The building was eventually sold to the council and used for social housing, and that is how it came to our attention.'

He pushed back his chair and began to stride about the room, gesturing widely. His followers tracked him with adoring eyes. 'Two years ago we, the people of the Vision, were looking for a large house with some rooms which could be used for communal living while we pursued our aim of rescuing those cast out of society for various reasons: the recovering addicts who were under the spell of Evil Alcohol and Killer Drugs and bound for hell till we rescued them and placed them on the road to recovery.'

'Not Claire, I think,' muttered Diana.

He swept on, disregarding her. 'Dolores, stand up! Tell these good people in what degrading condition you were found in, selling yourself for drugs and alienated from your family, your children taken into care and—'

Ellie said, 'This is irrelevant—'

He ploughed straight over her. '—you forbidden to see them. And now, tell them! That you are clean and free of drugs and being helped to see how you were dragged down to—'

'Yes, yes! It's all true!' cried Dolores, arms and eyes uplifted.

'Soon, very soon, you will be able to see your children again—'

'Alleluia!'

Ellie saw that everyone but her was watching the pastor. Mesmerized. Ellie wasn't mesmerized. In fact, she was more than slightly annoyed. Yes, if all this was true, the pastor was doing good work in the community . . . though she would like to consult a doctor or two, *and* Social Services, before she was totally convinced.

'Now, Liddy; tell them how you were found in a squat, with the needle still sticking in your arm. How you are willing now to wash and clean and—'

He's their lord and master, and they are his slaves. They've exchanged one dependency for another. It's as if he's removed their power of independent thinking as neatly as a surgeon might remove an appendix. If he told one of them to jump in the river, they'd do so. Which, knowing how much toxic waste flows into the River Brent hereabouts, would be the cue for having one's stomach pumped out and a course of antibiotics.

I do understand that if he had not taken them in, they might by now be very very dead, and that I should applaud him for turning their lives around, but I can't help feeling that there's some snag here I'm not seeing.

'Truly, God is great!' cried Liddy, with tears in her eyes. One side of her face seemed swollen. Had Ambrose hit her? No, she was back to rubbing it again. Definitely, toothache.

Claire, down on her knees, was holding on to the Pastor's legs. 'Alleluia!' she screamed, her eyes rolling up in her head. She threw herself backwards on to the carpet and writhed.

'Oh dear, oh dear,' said Ellie. 'Should I call for an ambulance?'

Ambrose caught himself up, caught mid-sentence. Seeing Claire lying at his feet, he held up his arms, closed his eyes and shouted, 'Alleluia!' And then, 'Get up, woman!'

Which Claire did.

Stewart half rose from his chair, but subsided when he saw that Claire had regained her feet.

The others looked on, stunned. Speechless.

Except for Ambrose. He resumed his chair and said in his normal voice, 'Our work in the anterooms of hell flourished from the start. We raised funds and, supported by Social Services, and with the help of some private donations, managed to rent our new home. We had to accept that there were some tenants already in place, but on the whole they have given us very little trouble. Our success rate has been phenomenal. It has not been easy. No. But worthwhile. No one can dispute that. Only, now we are faced with a crisis of truly desperate dimensions. A developer has made an offer to the council for the site and we, who have spent our all on caring for the poor and neglected of this world, are unable to raise the amount needed.

'That was when I had one of my visions. I saw the name of Ellie Quicke, as clear as the day is true. A voice from heaven told me that she will be the angel to rescue us in our hour of need. She will assist us in our crusade against the forces of evil—'

'Praise the Lord!' cried Claire, raising her eyes and her hands high to heaven.

Ambrose was hitting his stride. Fist in the air, he thundered,

'We have rescued our brothers and sisters from the very pit of hell!'

'Hallelujah!' screamed Claire, jumping up and down.

'We have beaten back the powers of darkness, we have grappled with the fiends from the pit! We fought and we won! Alas, the enemy has not been defeated for good! No! He returns, trying to destroy all the good we do. He threatens to throw us out of our home, to make us homeless! Are we cast down? No! I have prayed and I have fasted. I have wrestled with God, and he has assured me that he will not let us fail!' The cords were standing out on his neck. He was working himself up into a right royal tantrum.

'No, no!' chanted Claire. 'He will not let us fail! O blessed Vision, fly swiftly to our aid!'

Diana had had enough. She pushed back her chair and stood, leaning forward with both hands on the table. 'What a load of rubbish! I can see through you, if no one else can. You are a fake, a charlatan! I am not taken in by your claims to save people. You may pretend to be oh so holy, but you are nothing but a con man, who has surrounded himself with poor creatures who don't know the difference between day and night!'

Bravo! Diana's actually got it right for once.

Ambrose tore open his shirt. 'You dare to attack me, the saviour and prophet of the Vision? How dare you, woman! I see you for what you are! A servant of Mammon! Spawn of Satan!'

Diana was not to be faced down. 'Oh, for heaven's sake! It's as clear as the nose on your face that you're after my mother's money, just as you've conned other elderly women into handing over everything they own. As for these poor creatures you're talking about, if Claire's an example, they stink!'

Claire cried, 'Shame! Oh, alleluia! Our leader will trample his enemies underfoot!'

Ambrose shook his fist at Diana. 'I see you . . . I see you . . . I have this vision . . . Aaargh!' His eyes rolled up in his head. He staggered, hands outstretched. 'I see you writhing in the torments of hell. I hear you cry out for relief, and relief there will be none for such as you! You are a child of Satan.

I look into your black heart, and I see how you want the money for yourself. And so I lay a curse upon you! I curse you for coming between us and the money which is meant for us! Coming and going, sleeping and waking, at home or abroad, I curse you for—'

Ellie looked around the room, thinking it was time someone stopped the man.

No one moved.

Everyone, bar Ellie, was horrified, hanging on his every word.

She'd sometimes wondered why she was the chair of this committee, because Stewart was a brilliant administrator, Kate could read a balance sheet in a blink of an eye and Pat knew her way round everything a computer could do. Ellie had none of these skills. She'd often sat through these meetings, thinking the most she could bring to the table was the ability to serve coffee on demand.

The other trustees didn't seem to know what to do now, though.

Ellie did. She picked up the fly spray and aimed it at the centre of Ambrose's chest. Accurately. 'Oops,' she said. 'A wasp!'

'A wasp? What? Aargh!' He flailed at his shirt. 'Get it off me!'

'Stand still,' said Ellie. And aimed again, a little lower.

'What!' He shook himself, glaring down at his crotch, fumbling with his belt, pulling his shirt away from his chest. 'Help me!'

Claire cried, 'Let me! Oh, let me see!'

Ellie squirted once more, this time to his left shoulder, but he was on edge, dancing around . . . and the spray got him on the chin. Perhaps a few drops got as far as his mouth?

'Gerrough!' he said and choked.

Coughed.

Oh dear. Ellie tried to read the label on the can. Was this stuff poisonous? Possibly.

Claire gaped, crying, 'I can't see any wasp! Where is it?'

All eyes were on Ambrose. No one but Ellie seemed able to move. Once she was sure he'd been neutralized – if that was the right word? Possibly not, but – she put the spray down and handed him her almost empty cup of coffee. 'Here, drink this.'

He swilled it round his mouth and spat.

Claire wailed, 'The wasp! Has he been stung? Shouldn't we get the doctor?'

'No need,' said Ellie.

Ambrose gasped, eyes bulging. A shaking hand reached out to her, forefinger pointing. She struck it aside. He gobbled something. Another curse?

She said, 'Shut . . . up!'

Amazingly, he did.

The atmosphere in the room was so tense, they could hear the clock tick in the hall.

Ellie thought, This is all too funny for words. And she giggled.

There was an appalled silence.

Everyone's eyes switched to Ellie. Except for Ambrose, who was still wheezing.

Ellie giggled again. 'Too ridiculous! Dear me! All this fuss over a wasp.'

Kate sank back into her chair. 'You're right.' And she began to laugh, too.

Stewart thumped the table and joined them. 'Oh my . . .!'

Diana didn't laugh. There were white patches either side of her nose. She grabbed her bag and pushed her chair back. 'I've had more than enough of this. This . . . this . . .! I don't know what to call him . . . but he's gone too far. Mother, you should hand him over to the police!'

Ellie sighed. 'Well, I would if I had any proof that he'd done anything against the law of the land. Oh, I suppose I could claim trespass, since he has forced himself into our meeting, but he'll only say he was invited, and it's not worth it, is it?'

Diana snapped back, 'What about what he's doing against the law of God!' She rushed out to the hall and left the house, slamming the front door behind her.

Ellie's eyes opened wide. This, from Diana, who had said religion was all nonsense, and who never went to church except for funerals and weddings! This, from Diana, who'd said she wouldn't bother to have little Evan christened! Did this outburst mean that Diana did, at bottom, believe?

Ambrose was, for once, without words. He was alternately spitting saliva – oh dear! – and pulling his shirt away from his body. Ellie was, slightly, alarmed. Did the man have asthma? It had been an accident. She hadn't intended the stuff to go into his face, but he'd moved into the target area, instead of stepping away from it.

Claire, needless to say, was in tears, hands upraised to heaven, whispering to God to help them.

Ellie was inclined to think that, yes, God was in heaven all right, but he could be everywhere else, as well. Only, of course, most people couldn't see him nowadays. Prophets could, perhaps? Ambrose was not, in her opinion, much of a prophet. She wondered what sort of brain might produce illusions which could be passed off as visions. She thought it more likely that his were produced by hysteria rather than religious fervour. In this particular case, the line between religious fervour and madness seemed to her to be very thin indeed.

Ambrose held on to the table. His breathing slowed and became normal. His shirt was drying on him, sticking to him. As were his trousers. He passed a trembling hand across his forehead and flicked away moisture. He might, also, be perspiring. It was hard to tell.

Stewart pushed back his chair. 'Are you all right?' Stewart *would* want to help, wouldn't he!

Kate leaned back in her chair, preparing to withhold judgement till she'd ascertained the facts of the matter.

Pat was smiling nervously as she fiddled with her laptop.

Ambrose opened his mouth and pointed at Ellie. About to curse her, too?

'I wouldn't if I were you,' said Ellie. 'You don't kill the goose which lays the golden eggs.'

He wasn't prepared to give up yet. In a hoarse voice he said, 'You assaulted me!'

'You,' said Ellie, 'disrespected me. You have abused the laws of hospitality not once but several times.' She'd never used the term 'disrespected' before and was pleased to see that she'd understood it correctly and that it worked, for

Ambrose staggered back, clearly wanting to say that you couldn't 'disrespect' a woman and that he wished her dead. Some remnant of common sense made him refrain.

His hands shook as he twitched his shirt away from his body. 'You are . . .'

'Yes, indeed,' said Ellie. 'I own this house, I head up this charitable trust and, in spite of your behaviour today, I will study your application papers and give them the attention they deserve. Now I suggest that you take your witnesses and depart. Claire, leave your unauthorized set of keys on the table, please.'

'Oh, but—' Claire wept.

'Keys!' Ellie pointed to the table, which had some flecks of saliva on it. Bother: water stained mahogany. She must remember to give the table a polish as soon as the uninvited visitors had gone.

Claire sought in her handbag. She shot a despairing glance at Ambrose. Looking for support? Which plea he refused to see. Claire dropped the keys on to the table. As her hands were slimy with tears, Ellie made a mental note not to touch the bunch without first gloving up.

Ambrose made his way a trifle unsteadily to the door, followed by Claire and the two women. Ellie opened the front door for them and shut it with a firm hand after they'd left the house.

Kate followed her into the hall. 'Is that man mentally unbalanced? Is he a con man, or a misguided fanatic?'

'I suspect a personality disorder of some kind,' said Ellie. 'As to whether he does some good in the world or not, I really cannot say.'

Kate frowned. 'I suppose that if he's really doing the work he claims . . .? No, I don't think the trust should back someone who's mentally unbalanced.'

'It may be worse than that,' said Ellie, feeling rather limp. 'There's a murder in his background somewhere. Or in Claire's. I can't be sure yet, but I think that, if she did kill someone, he might feel it his duty to protect her from harm provided she devoted her life to raising money for his needs.'

'You appal me,' said Stewart, joining them.

Pat dithered in the doorway. 'What do we do now?'

Ellie took a deep breath. 'We always meet on Thursday mornings to consider business matters. I vote we have a fresh cup of proper coffee – freshly ground coffee with cream and sugar – in the sitting room, and catch up on what we've been doing lately, holidays and such. Then we go back into the dining room and get down to business, with the proviso that we leave the Vision application on one side, pending further enquiries.'

'Carried,' said Kate.

Stewart nodded. 'Agreed. There's a lot to discuss.'

Just wait, thought Ellie, till I tell Thomas what's been happening today. Whatever will he say? He'll want to be on the next plane back, but . . . No. It's not often that he gets the recognition that he deserves and can mix with people who are on his wavelength. I mustn't bring him back just because I don't quite know how to manage the problem of the Vision project. Those poor people that Ambrose is helping . . . He's doing a lot of good there, isn't he? He's right about that. But his brand of 'religion' isn't like anything I've ever heard of . . . well, apart from some bits of the Old Testament where there's an awful lot of cursing going on . . . I'll have to give this some thought, won't I?

NINE

Ellie had a little nap after lunch. She was feeling much more like herself, but at her age, and after that long journey, she was allowed to lie down on her bed for a bit, wasn't she? After that, she decided not to deal with any more paperwork and managed to get out into the garden. She was wrestling with a sycamore seedling which had somehow managed to grow up unseen behind a rhododendron bush, and which would cause no end of trouble if allowed to grow any taller, when Rose tapped on the window of the conservatory to attract her attention.

'Ellie, I think it's Diana, trying to get in!'

Oh. Ah. Ellie tried not to grin. Diana had been really upset when Ambrose had cursed her, hadn't she? Despite swearing she didn't believe in God or indeed in an afterlife of any sort.

Shucking off her gardening gloves, and leaving her clogs in the conservatory, Ellie got to the front door before Diana broke it down.

'Where have you been! Where. Have. You. Been? I've been ringing the bell for hours . . .!' Diana, in a temper, wheeling a sleeping toddler in a buggy before her.

No, she hadn't been ringing the bell for hours. Three minutes, max? 'I was in the garden.'

'I had to bring Evan. I didn't think you'd mind since you must be pleasing yourself this afternoon, after working so hard this morning.' Heavily sarcastic.

Was it Diana's new nanny's afternoon off? Ellie did not feel up to coping with the boy. The last time she'd had him for the afternoon, he'd broken a side table with a rather good Coalport vase on it, spread the flowers and the water around on a silk rug, fallen over and roared his displeasure for ten solid minutes, upset his milk all over himself, lost a shoe in the garden (and how he'd got out there was a mystery), terror-ized Midge (and that took some doing), pulled all the saucepans out of the cupboard while Ellie was washing out his T-shirt, causing Rose to trip over them and hurt herself and, oh, yes! He'd peed in his pants not once but three times. He was supposed to be out of nappies, but refused to use his potty.

She really couldn't face that again. She sought for her indoor shoes. Where had she left them?

Diana was in a right state. 'Those people, this morning! Out of order! They ought to be excommunicated, or something. They oughtn't to go around cursing people. It's . . . it's . . . not right!'

Ellie sighed. No, it wasn't the most pleasant way of commu-nicating with your neighbours. She must have left her shoes in the conservatory somewhere, because that's where she kept her clogs and trowel . . . She went to look for them. Ah, yes. There they were.

'Mother! You are not paying attention.'

'I am, indeed I am. I find this all very upsetting, too.'

Diana prowled around, hitting one hand against the other. 'What he said . . . What nonsense! Of course, he was just spitting in the wind!'

'Um. He does seem to have upset you.' Ellie eased her feet into her shoes and looked at her watch. 'Time for a cuppa? You've left the office early today?'

'Yes. No. It's the nanny's afternoon off. Mother, I'm serious! He shouldn't be allowed to—'

'Lots of people go around doing things they ought not to do. They tell lies, cheat on their income tax and sleep with other women's husbands.' All of which Diana had done in the past. 'I'm making a cuppa, anyway.' She set off for the kitchen.

Diana followed. 'There's absolutely no question of your funding this project of theirs, of course. Is there?'

'Probably not,' said Ellie. 'But, it's a dilemma. He seems to be having more success in rescuing druggies and alkies than most people do. I agree that his take on religion is not the usual one, and that he personally is way over the top.' She put the kettle on and found the biscuit tin.

Diana exploded. 'Over the top? He's stark raving mad. He should be locked up!'

'Because he cursed you? Because he invoked the name of God? I don't see why you're so worried, Diana. You've always claimed that God doesn't exist.'

'Well, I . . . One has to keep an open mind about . . . It was the venom with which he attacked me! If Thomas were here—'

'He would protect you?' Ever so slightly sarcastic.

'What? Well, I suppose he'd have stopped the man, somehow.'

'I'm sorry, Diana. You're right. You need protection as much as anyone.'

Diana flushed and was silent. She accepted a mug of break-fast tea and a biscuit, forgetting that she usually insisted on having Earl Grey in a china cup. 'You should have stopped him earlier.'

'Perhaps I should.' Ellie was prepared to concede that. There was no point in quarrelling with Diana, who did seem genu-inely distressed. 'Do you think you could talk to God about it, ask him to look after you? After all, if he does exist, he might be pleased to hear from you.'

An attempt at a smile. 'Oh well, I suppose there'd be no harm in it. Covering all bases, as you might say.'

Ellie thought that this could be a very interesting develop-ment for Diana. Lots of people had doubts about the existence of God. Some lived with doubt all their lives. Even she, occa-sionally . . . and Thomas had once confessed to her that when his first wife had been dying, he'd gone through a bad patch.

'Why not try it and see?'

Diana was rapidly regaining her composure. 'I'll leave it in your hands, then. I'm sure you'll do your best for me.'

'I'll do what I can. Tell me something. How exactly did you come to take Claire on?'

Diana fidgeted. She didn't like that question. 'I thought I'd told you. She'd been working for this widow, who died and left the house to the lot that Claire hangs around with, the people of the Vision. Claire came to see us, to ask us to sell it for her. We got a buyer within the week. Only, then we got this letter from a solicitor, saying that the will was being contested. I rang Claire, and she came in, saying the house had been left half to her and half to the widow's children and that they'd asked her to sell it for them, which meant we could go ahead, but the solicitor said we couldn't. What a can of worms! We had to tell the buyer. He was so angry . . . I can't tell you! Look, we acted in good faith. It wasn't our fault! We weren't to know that the will was going to be contested. Undue influence, the family said, and they've got their old GP to back them up.'

'I do see that you're out of pocket over the deal. The Vision people, too. They must be furious. So how come you took Claire on, after all that?'

'She came to see me in tears, saying that if only we'd acted faster, the sale would have gone through, which was nonsense and I told her so. Then she asked if we had a job for her in the office, which we hadn't. She went on and on about needing a job, and Nanny was due for her holiday, and Claire begged me to let her look after Evan, so . . .'

'And she was cheap. She didn't tell you that she'd been convicted of an assault on a schoolboy a while back?'

'No.' Horrified. 'Well, as it happens, she wasn't up to looking after Evan, and you needed someone to look after Rose. It seemed like it was meant.'

'You wanted to get rid of her so passed her on to me, without warning.'

Diana didn't want to answer that. She looked at her watch. 'I must go. We're out for supper. I suppose it's all right for me to leave Evan with you for a couple of hours?'

Ellie summoned up all her energy to refuse. 'If you're going out this evening, you'll probably not be back till midnight, if then. You'd better get a babysitter for him. I'm in bed by eight at the moment – jet lag – and wouldn't hear him if he woke and cried. Sorry.'

That put Diana into a bad temper, but she made the best of it, knowing which side her bread was buttered. 'Oh well. I suppose I'll see you tomorrow. Perhaps you'll have some good news for me by then?'

'About the curse which Ambrose laid on you?'

Diana blanched and hastened away, taking little Evan with her.

That was a bit naughty of me, but if it's made her think about something other than making and spending money . . . Perhaps . . .?

No, I ought not to have said it. Please, God. Look after her?

And all of us? Amen.

Friday morning and afternoon

Another fine day. Ellie got Rose up, made them breakfast without any more appearances by Claire. That was a blessing. Vera popped in to help Ellie order some more food online, and Pat arrived to assist Ellie in dealing with the mountain of emails and paperwork that had accumulated. After lunch Ellie had a very short nap – she seemed to be getting over the jet lag nicely – and escaped into the garden. She had only just started pruning a rambler rose which had finished flowering for the year, when Rose tapped on the window and mouthed, 'Phone!'

Bother. Ellie went to the phone, struggling to get out of her gardening gloves and dropping the secateurs on the floor.

Lesley. 'How did you know? Are you in? Silly question: of course you are. I'll be round in ten minutes.' She cut the call.

That didn't sound like good news, did it?

The biscuit tin was almost empty. Ellie decided to do something about that.

Lesley arrived just as Ellie was putting some scones in the oven to cook. Rose was sitting in her big chair, talking to Midge as if the cat would understand what she was saying. Perhaps he did, as he was intelligent and aware that if he looked as if he were paying attention, Rose might reward him with a titbit.

Ellie let Lesley in. As they were old friends, she said, 'I can offer tea, but the scones won't be ready for fifteen minutes.'

'I want more than scones.' Lesley led the way into the sitting room, but instead of sitting down, she went to stand by the French windows which were open on to the garden. She didn't compliment Ellie on the roses. She probably wasn't even seeing them.

Ellie shucked off her apron and sat down. 'Tell me.'

'How did you know? How ever did you know?'

Ellie wondered if she'd put the timer on before she left the kitchen. If she hadn't, the scones would be burnt. Perhaps she really ought to have a modern oven with all the timing gadgets on it? Except that she'd never be able to work out what they all did. 'I imagine you've found Gail's body. Where was it?'

Lesley stiffened her shoulders. 'Last week they were dredging the canal in Perivale – not far away from where Jenna's body was discovered under the bridge – and found the body of a young woman in a black plastic bag weighed down with stones. She wouldn't have been found for ages, if they hadn't been dredging that part by the lock.'

'Was she wearing a niqab?'

'No. You got that wrong, anyway. She was naked and three months pregnant.'

'There must have been some means of identification or you wouldn't be so tense.'

'They checked against their register of missing girls, found a possibility and asked Gail's dentist for her records. The result came in last night. The girl had had an accident with a Frisbee last year, and her two front teeth had been crowned. They're doing the DNA tests, which should give us a clue as to the father of her child, but that all takes time. There's no doubt that it's Gail. Her mother has been informed.'

'Cause of death?'

'The hyoid bone was broken. Probably strangulation.'

'Jenna was strangled, too, wasn't she? How long had Gail been in the water?'

A shrug. 'The pathologist can't say exactly. Best estimate is about a month.'

'Dumped soon after death?'

'Hard to say. But yes, probably.'

'So the case has boomeranged back into your territory.'

Lesley ground her teeth.

Ellie checked her watch. Those scones . . . She wondered

how she could think about scones when Gail's mother must be grieving. 'You say her mother's been told?'

Lesley nodded. She paced from the window to the door and back again.

Ellie said, 'You are assuming the same person was responsible for both girls' deaths?'

'Two young schoolgirls disappear. Granted, they are sixteen plus, but the school leaving age is now eighteen . . . Mind you, how you keep a sixteen-year-old in school when she doesn't want to be there is something the powers that be haven't worked out. Locking up the parents because they haven't made sure the children are in school is a no-no. The age of consent for sex is sixteen, so . . . To get back to these two; after some months they turn up, pregnant, in the same canal, within fifty yards of one another. Both strangled. There has to be a connection. There's all hell to pay.'

'Because you've now got a serial killer on your hands?'

'It's a reasonable assumption.'

'Jenna disappeared in Perivale and was found there. Gail disappeared from this part of the borough, but has been found in the same place. The A40 road creates a barrier between Ealing and Perivale. One is a London borough but, if I remember it rightly, the other comes under Uxbridge, so they must have different police forces. Which has priority?'

'Neither. Hands off. Murder takes precedence. Experts move in. Eyebrows are lifted. Aspersions are cast. Files are requested. Who was responsible for looking into Jenna's disappearance and investigating the subsequent discovery of her body? Who was responsible for looking into Gail's disappearance, mmhm?'

Ah. Now Ellie began to understand Lesley's problem. 'It was your beloved inspector, "Ears", who took charge of Gail's disappearance, wasn't it? I seem to remember you were also involved.' She got to her feet. 'Excuse me a minute. The scones are calling.'

Lesley followed her out to the kitchen.

'Ears' was the commonly-used nickname for Lesley's boss, coined by Ellie in a 'senior' moment, since those appendages of his turned bright red when his blood pressure rose. He was a middling-good policeman who'd reached his potential and would probably go no further. He resented Lesley's flair and gave her routine tasks rather than encouraging her to climb the ladder. He hated Ellie for having given him a nickname and had been heard to wish her to the devil. He lacked Ambrose's powers of invective, but his sentiments were similar.

Ellie rescued the scones just in time. Rose had fallen asleep in her chair. Midge was sitting plumply in the middle of the kitchen table, so Ellie shooed him off. As quietly as she could, Ellie made some tea and put mugs and milk, scones, butter and jam on a tray. Lesley helped by following Ellie back into the sitting room with the teapot.

Ellie poured tea, and they helped themselves to scones without speaking.

Only when they'd finished eating, Lesley said, 'Rose . . .?'

'I gave Claire the Tearful the sack. I'm trying to find someone else to look after Rose. I don't like to leave her alone in the house. She's happy here, and there's nothing more the doctors can do for her. She'd be miserable if she were put in a home, and the hospital would only push and pull her about and fill her with drugs in an effort to fend off the inevitable.'

Lesley licked a trace of jam off her fingers. 'If Ears knew I'd asked you for help, he'd have my guts for garters.'

'*Are* you asking for my help? Surely the man responsible for the murders should be looked for in Perivale, and in any case the matter has been taken out of your jurisdiction.'

'True. But. Ears has been hauled over the coals because he didn't take Gail's disappearance seriously. Actually, no one did. Dozens of young girls like her disappear every year. Most of them turn up when the boyfriend's money runs out. Nobody fusses much unless they're under-age.' Lesley took a turn around the room. 'Everything's changed now that the girl has turned up dead. Ears is in the frame for blame. He's mad as fire. Black mark on his record. So he's taking it out on me. If he possibly can, he'll make out that I disobeyed his instructions to keep working on the case.'

'Nonsense,' said Ellie. 'He's the senior officer. It's his responsibility.'

Lesley fiddled with the full-length curtain at the French windows. 'Ellie, I want you to do something for me, if you will. I've been told it's hands off the case "while people who know what they're doing solve the mystery of the two deaths". But, you know Claire and could talk to her about it, couldn't you?'

Uh-oh. Here it comes.

Lesley was going to persuade her to do something she did not want to do. The less Ellie had to do with Claire the Tearful, the better. Ellie said, 'No.'

'Oh, come on! You know you have a way of getting people to talk to you. It's clear that Claire was involved in some way. She must have been. Perhaps she saw something, heard something . . . Ellie, I'm desperate.'

'No,' said Ellie.

Lesley wasn't giving up. 'Look, she used to live in Perivale, as did the first girl, Jenna, when *she* disappeared. I know there's no obvious connection, and I know that Claire moved down here before Jenna's body was found. What I can't ignore is the fact that in due course Claire has words with another girl, who is living in the same house as her, who turns up dead back in Perivale. It's too much of a coincidence.'

'Are you trying to say that Claire killed them, because I don't think that's sensible. For a start, both girls were pregnant, which would indicate a man's involvement, but . . .' Ellie's voice tailed away.

'Yes? You've thought of something.'

Ellie hesitated. 'It seems to me that Claire makes a perfect scapegoat for anything that goes wrong in her circle. She blotted her copybook at the school, which brought her to the attention of the Courts. The Vision people paid her fine, but are making her reimburse them. Once upon a time she had her own flat, her own car and a good job. Now she's reduced to babysitting elderly ladies and living on the charity of the Vision. Yes, she has exhibited a hasty temper in the past, but I think that nowadays she's so beaten down that she bursts into tears rather than raise her voice even to defend herself.'

'You are thinking that a man connected with the Vision might be the murderer, and that he's using Claire as a cover for him? Yes, why not? Why didn't I think of that? What do you know about them?'

'Very little, and I wish I knew less. The head of this cult – I really think they are a cult, as they don't belong to any recognized church that I've ever heard of, and they appear to owe allegiance to no one but themselves – anyway, the leader is one Pastor Ambrose. They have applied to the trust for funds to purchase the house they are currently occupying here in Ealing. They rescue alcoholics and drug addicts from the streets and rehabilitate them with the application of a carrot and a stick. Yes, Claire is a member of this cult, and Gail lived in a flat in the same house, but you can't do much with that.'

Lesley said, 'Claire moved to this area from Perivale after her mother died, and we thought it might have been because she'd fallen under the influence of the Vision. Was Gail a member? Was Jenna? It's worth looking into.'

Ellie was following her own line of thought. 'You might also see if there was ever anything reported about Claire in her job at the supermarket. I can't quite get my head around her leaving the place just because her mother died. Maybe it's perfectly all right, but if she had such a good job and wanted to fly the nest, why didn't she find herself some more accommodation locally and stick with it? Good jobs aren't ten a penny. She must have taken a big pay cut when she moved down this way. On the other hand, if Ambrose had inspired her with a vision of living simply and giving a percentage of her earnings to them . . . No, that doesn't work. Surely, they would have got more money out of her if she were in a well-paid job than they would have done when she was working at the school.'

Lesley nodded. 'I'll see if I can find out.'

Ellie sat back in her chair, wondering if Pastor Ambrose himself might have fancied a fling with a young and pretty girl like Gail. Neither Dolores nor Liddy could be described as young and pretty, and Claire . . .? No, definitely not. Ambrose didn't seem the sort to go for boys. So, who did he take to his bed at night?

'He might be married, of course,' said Ellie, to herself rather than Lesley.

'You've thought of someone?'

'For five seconds, yes. Then common sense prevailed.

Ambrose, the Vision's leader, is surrounded by adoring women. If he so much as winked at a young girl, his followers would know. I can't see that being kept a secret. As for putting a girl in a niqab . . . No, he wouldn't do that. He likes his women to wear black, apparently to show that they are in mourning for their sins. Besides which, he's no follower of Islam, and they're the only ones who put their women into niqabs, aren't they?'

'Ambrose. What's his second name?'

Ellie pursued her own line of thought. 'Even if he were to fancy a series of secret lovers, where would he keep them hidden? You say that Jenna was alive for some months after she disappeared and Gail for . . . how long? Four or five months? Were they kept in a cellar at the big house? Locked away in a private room? Without anyone knowing?' She shook her head. 'Ridiculous. The practicalities would defeat him. He couldn't keep them fed and watered, or visit them, without someone in the house tumbling to the truth. Besides which, why would he need to hide them away? He's their leader, the One Who. He wouldn't wish to hide his prowess. He'd boast of having womenfolk at his beck and call, because they would be a living testament to his virility. And, if he isn't married, there's absolutely no reason why he shouldn't be having a bit on the side. I can imagine that Gail's mother might object to the age gap, but . . . Is she a follower of this cult, too? It doesn't sound as if Gail was herself, but . . . who knows? She might well have been attracted by his charisma. Power, they say, is an aphrodisiac. I really don't know if that's true or not, but it sounds right. Look at the way beautiful women flock around rich and powerful men. No, Ambrose doesn't fit the profile.'

'Ellie! I asked you: what's this Ambrose's second name?'

Ellie said, 'Then again, if he did take a young lover, why would he want to kill her? Because she was pregnant? Surely he'd think that helpful to his image. No, it won't do. He may or may not be married, but he's definitely Holier than Thou. He lives in the public eye. He boasts of his success with his project. He rescues damaged women from the streets. He has the backing, or so he says – and I think I believe him, though I'd need to check – of people in Social Services. Why would he risk his reputation for the sake of a bit on the side? He wouldn't.'

Lesley's patience had run out. 'Why haven't I heard of this man before?'

'Why would you need to, if Gail wasn't a member? I agree there must be some sort of connection if Claire knew about him when she was living in Perivale, but he doesn't live there now. He lives in a sort of commune near here, and altogether, no, I don't think it's him.'

Lesley lit up with excitement. 'He might have a separate place, a hideout, where he could keep the women. If he's married, and they get pregnant and start to make trouble for him, then he'd want to get rid of them.'

Ellie shook her head. 'I don't think so.'

'It's a valid line of enquiry, and it's got to be followed up. You're the obvious person to do it.'

Ellie leant back in her chair. 'You're really worried about this, aren't you?'

'I am. Ears visited the girl's mother originally, and the boyfriend. He heard there was an older man in the picture, and he lost interest. From what I'd seen myself, I agreed with him that the girl had gone off with a man of her own accord, especially after she rang to say she was fine and off enjoying herself. And then we let the case slide out of sight.'

Ellie could understand that.

'So.' Lesley pressed her hands to her cheeks. 'I feel now that I messed up, that the girl wouldn't have died if I'd kept on the case. That's why I'm asking you, Ellie, to help me.'

'How?'

'You could go to see Claire and get her to give you some background information about this hostel or whatever it is. Find out if there's a hidey-hole anywhere. Then, when you've found it, I could tell Ears. He'd tell the Murder Squad, and they'd get a search warrant, and Bob's your uncle.'

'I've heard it's a pretty big place. I suppose I could make an excuse to visit it and . . . No, I can't, Lesley. I can't leave Rose.'

A calculating look. 'What if I find someone to look after Rose?'

Ellie grimaced. 'Chance would be a fine thing. I've got Maria looking for someone, and I've contacted all the agencies I can think of, but there's no one suitable who's free at the moment. Summer holidays, you know? They say there may be someone in a couple of weeks' time. And, it would have to be someone better than Claire, someone both Rose and I can get along with.'

Lesley nodded. 'I wasn't going to mention it if you'd got yourself fixed up but, well, I do know someone, my niece, who's at a loose end. You'd be doing me a favour if you could give her a room and a job for a couple of weeks. That's all. Just a couple of weeks. She's a student at West London University, doing all right, sensible enough girl, house-trained. She drives me crazy, but that's my fault, not hers.'

Ellie was amused. Lesley didn't usually blush and become incoherent. 'Start at the beginning. What's the girl's name?'

'Susan. Nice girl. Studying food technology, wants to be a chef. She was in a house share locally, but at the end of term they had to move out. The students have all scattered to the four winds, returning home, going away on holiday, waiting for the results from their exams. Susan didn't want to go back home for the summer because she's not getting on with my sister, for which I can't actually blame her, menopause and hot flushes and all that. So she landed up on my doorstep a couple of nights ago with a couple of kit bags, begging to sleep on my settee.'

Lesley had got herself engaged to a very pleasant young man some time back, and though they didn't plan to get married till the end of the year, he had actually moved into her one-bedroom flat. Ellie could well imagine they wouldn't want a student under foot.

'I mean, I thought we could manage at first,' said Lesley, 'because she's a nice enough kid, but it's getting on our nerves. Both of us work long hours and . . .'

'Send her round,' said Ellie. 'Which doesn't mean that I'm going to poke into affairs at the Vision.'

'Bless you. She'll be no trouble, I assure you. She can cook, too.'

TEN

Susan was everything that Lesley had said. She was no beauty queen, being solid-looking with capable hands and frizzy ginger hair drawn back and up into a pony-tail. But she had a no-nonsense approach to life which was appealing. She liked Rose, and Rose liked her. Also, she was ready to move in straight away.

Only after they'd agreed terms and conditions, and Susan had been shown the bed-sitting-room and bathroom directly above Rose's quarters, did Ellie begin to be suspicious.

Susan was too good to be true, which meant that there was a catch somewhere.

Ellie said, 'How much is Lesley paying you to move in here?'

Susan blushed. 'Oh. No, not really. Honest.'

'You could have got a live-in job anywhere, couldn't you? Did you really not want to move back in with your mother?'

Susan fidgeted. 'We-ell, I wasn't looking forward to it much, but—'

'Lesley made you an offer you couldn't refuse?'

'Something like that.' More fidgeting. 'Do you not want me to come, then?'

'My dear, I'd be delighted. Move in as soon as you like.'

'My stuff is all in the back of my old banger outside. If that's all right . . .?'

Ellie smiled grimly. 'I suppose Lesley wants me to get straight on to the case this evening?'

'She says you're ever so clever.' The girl actually seemed to mean it.

With Susan settling herself in, Ellie rummaged around in her study till she found the paperwork relating to the Vision project. She would ring up and make an appointment.

No telephone number given. That was odd? Why ever not?

She consulted the A to Z. It wasn't far, as the crow flies, but it was uphill all the way. Oh well. The sky was light and bright. No showers forecast. She could have a quick look at the place before the supper which Susan had promised to cook.

At the top of the hill Ellie came to a T-junction, on the far side of which stood the house she was looking for. When it had been built, it had stood in splendid isolation at the junction of two country lanes. Much, much later a row of small, terraced 'town' houses had grown up around the original house and its garden, while the original lanes had been widened and covered with tarmac.

The house had been built sideways on to the road, so that there would be a good view down the hill from the reception rooms. It was larger than she'd expected and twice as ugly. Correction; the original Edwardian mansion was well enough in its way, but the bleak apartment block which had been built on to the back quarters was about as ugly as the sixties and a cheese-paring developer could make it. Ellie wondered how the builder had managed to get permission for such an eyesore.

The original house was four storeys high, gabled though not turreted. It had been built in the pleasant dull ochre London brick which used to be standard for houses built thereabouts. It had large sash windows, hinting at nicely-proportioned, high-ceilinged rooms within. It had been built by someone with money and status, to show off. It was the Edwardian equivalent of bling.

A carriage drive led off the road, past a front door sheltered from the elements under one of those massive wooden porches with a gable roof beloved of that bygone age. The driveway was flanked by laurel bushes – what else! – and curved out of sight, presumably ending up at a garage and some outhouses. A tradesman's van was parked in the driveway, but there was no sign of Ambrose's Lexus.

Skylights had been inserted in the roof of the original building, turning what had once been servants' quarters into rentable accommodation.

The apartment block to the right was in a lighter, yellow brick. It didn't attempt to match its neighbour in any way although it was built flush with it. It had a flat roof, and the small windows screamed 'utilitarian' and 'built to maximize space on a small budget'. It didn't exactly advertise itself as a prison, but there was a hint of the institution about it. There were four small windows on each of the three floors, none of them open, even on this warm summer's day.

Ellie was puzzled. Why did that block look so forbidding? There were no bars on the windows. Ah, she had it. There were no curtains at the windows, just blinds, and the blinds were all of the same sandy colour. Was this where Ambrose housed the people he rescued from the streets? Losers like Claire, ex-junkies like Dolores and Liddy? And, possibly, the boy who'd been acting as the decorator's mate? Was the decorator himself one of Ambrose's followers? She shivered, remembering that she'd thought him a bit creepy, though she couldn't quite put her finger on why he should have struck her that way. He hadn't been subservient like the members of the cult that she'd met so far.

Perhaps he was one of the original tenants of the house? That would make sense.

She crossed the junction and walked along the front of the new extension, looking for a front door. There was none. Instead, a high wall at the end of the block continued along the roadside, probably enclosing what remained of the garden of the house. Yes, she could see the tops of trees inside. She came to a halt as the wall took a turn away from the road, presumably marking the end of the property. Beyond that there was the landscaped garden belonging to a newer, better-designed block of flats.

There was no access to the extension from the road. No front door, no gate into the garden, even. Access must be through the main house, which would be convenient if you were monitoring the comings and goings of the people who lived there.

She told herself not to jump to conclusions. This place was not a prison, and Ambrose was not a jailer.

He was way over the top, yes. His view of heaven and earth seemed somewhat skewed, but in all probability his heart was as pure as driven snow.

Ellie scolded herself. There was nothing whatever to be worried about. She wasn't entering the lions' den, and even if she were, Daniel & Co had managed all right in the Old Testament when they were thrown into the lions' den, hadn't they? And, she told herself firmly, God was everywhere, even in the darkest and dirtiest of places.

She turned into the driveway and pressed the old-fashioned bell-push in the porch. There was no reply. She peered at the bell-push. The name tag read: Pastor Ambrose. She couldn't see any other name. She rang the bell again. Still no reply.

The house had a dead feel to it. Not empty, exactly, but lifeless. Waiting for people to come back and let themselves in and bring it back to life? Presumably, it had been swarming with police from the Murder Squad earlier that day. They must have visited Gail's mother – no, wait a minute, hadn't Amy and Anna said the woman didn't live here any more?

Ellie stepped back into the sunshine, crunching gravel underfoot. She scanned the windows on this side of the house. Blinds were drawn behind the large windows on the ground floor. On the first floor some curtains were partly drawn to protect the furniture within from the sun. Some of those windows had been left open a crack at the top. Well, it was a warm day.

Curtains flapped on the top floor where a window had been left wide open . . . and was that a drift of TV noise? So there was someone at home at the top of the house. How to make them hear her?

The house was between her and the sun. It was almost chilly in the shade. There wasn't much garden on this side of the house. Shrubs lined the driveway, and then there was a high wall which shut off the view of the neighbouring 'town' houses.

The van. Perhaps there was someone in the van whom she could ask about how to contact Ambrose? She walked right round it. No keys in the ignition. No paperwork on the passenger seat. An empty bottle of Coca Cola. There was no heat coming from the engine so it must have been standing there for some time. A tradesman's van? No logo on the sides. Dark blue. She'd never remember the licence number . . . and why should she?

A van meant a workman doing something to the electricity or the plumbing inside the big house. But then, he'd not be likely to answer the doorbell, would he?

She went back to the porch, deciding to leave a note asking Ambrose to ring her. She tore a page from her diary and looked round for somewhere to sit while she wrote the note. Only then did she notice that there was a row of modern bell-pushes right behind where she'd been standing before. How could she have missed them? She switched her eyes to and fro. The house's original bell-push had only one name on it, and that was for Ambrose. This other lot – six bells in all – would be for the tenants who occupied the flats in the big house. Ambrose was obviously out, but one of the others might well be in.

She would try them, one after the other. First bell . . . Flat Number One? No reply.

Flat Number Two. No reply.

'What do you think you're doing!' A sharp, angry voice. A voice she'd heard before?

Dolores, the elder of the two cleaners whom Claire had imported to disarrange Ellie's house, and whom Ellie had thrown out.

Ellie fixed a smile on her face. 'I am trying to reach Pastor Ambrose. I have to find out more about this venture of his before we can discuss it in committee.'

Dolores hesitated. Weighing the risks of letting Ellie in? Did Ambrose forbid visitors?

'Well, at least you're not the police. We've had them crawling all over the place, as if we knew anything, which we don't.' She took a key out of her pocket. 'He's out till late on Fridays. He said not to let anyone in, but I suppose you're different.'

'The Murder Squad has been here?'

'Interviewed all of us, all over again. Took for ever. Gail's mother moved away a while back, so it was all a big waste of everybody's time.'

She swung open the door and ushered Ellie into a large hall with a tiled floor. The walls had been painted green. An impressive staircase curled up past a stained-glass window and disappeared into the gloom above. A chandelier had once lit this space; the iron framework for it still hung in place, but the original bulbs had long since gone, and neon strip lights had been installed on either side of it instead. Presumably, large pictures of hunting dogs, or stags at bay in the mountains had once adorned the walls, but these were now bare except for two cork boards covered with notices for the residents. Rules and regulations? Last one to turn out the lights is a sissy?

Panelled doors led off in different directions, one of which had not one but two locks on it. Was that where Ambrose lived?

'This way.' Dolores crossed the hall and opened a door on to a dining room, complete with serving hatch into a modern kitchen beyond. Where there had once been a mahogany dining suite, there were now ranks of fold-down tables with washable surfaces and piles of stackable chairs. The floorboards had been covered with vinyl. There were no pictures on the walls and no padding on the chairs. Walls, floor and furniture were all green.

Institutionalism replaces fine living.

'This is the communal room where we have our meals and meet for the evening services,' said Dolores. She collected a couple of chairs for them to sit on. 'I can't take you up to my room. It's not allowed. I can't make you a cuppa, either. The kitchen is locked till the others get back from their daytime jobs. I wouldn't normally be back this early . . .' She glanced away, fidgeting with the neck of her cheap black T-shirt.

Ellie asked the right question. 'So, where's Liddy?'

Dolores winced. 'She's poorly. Couldn't work this afternoon.' Her hands twisted. Was she about to cry?

A lie? Ellie said, 'Do you want to go up to her room to see if she's all right? She did come back here, didn't she?'

'No, she . . . We're not allowed in our rooms in the daytime.'

'But if she's ill . . .?'

Dolores broke into a laugh, which degenerated into a coughing fit. 'If you must know, I took her to the dentist. She's had awful toothache for over a week now, and she knows it's all in the mind and she ought to be able to rise above it, but it got so bad that I . . . I don't know how I'm going to tell him. We're not supposed to seek treatment . . . but she was in such pain. She wasn't putting it on, honest.'

'I'm sure she wasn't. Toothache's unbearable, isn't it? I've had some, and I know.'

'It's all very well for you. You can afford it.' Dolores bit her lip. She hadn't meant to say that, had she?

Ellie said, 'I think I understand. Liddy wasn't on a dentist's books hereabouts? She wasn't registered as a National Health patient?'

Dolores shook her head. 'I took her to the dentist in the Avenue. She was crying with pain. The dentist was kind. He said he'd fit her in somehow or other as a private patient, but it might be some time as he was fully booked this afternoon. We were dead worried because we have to clean the school at the end of the Avenue after half-past three, so I went along and said what had happened. They were pretty shirty about it, and I suppose I can't blame them. So I cleaned the rooms I usually do and one of hers, but then the caretaker came round to close up so I had to leave the rest.

'I went back to the dentist for her, and they said she'd been dealt with at last but was supposed to take some antibiotics and she had the prescription all ready, but Ambrose doesn't agree with our taking any medication, and we didn't know what to do because the dentist said she really must. Liddy was crying, in a terrible state. In the end she asked the receptionist if she could use their phone, and she arranged to go and stay with her sister in North London for a bit, just till she'd finished the antibiotics. I couldn't talk her out of it.'

'Why should you? It sounds a sensible solution.'

'Her sister's man is a dealer.'

Dolores meant the man was dealing in hard drugs? Oh.

Dolores twisted her hands. 'We've been working together for five months now, and I thought we were friends, but she's all take, take, take! Now I'm right in it, aren't I? She didn't care one bit that I was going to have to tell Ambrose what's happened, and he's going to be livid. And what about the school? I couldn't manage her work as well as mine, and they aren't going to be pleased about that, are they? And when *he* hears about it . . . I would go in over the weekend and do it then, only I don't know how I can as I haven't got the keys and the caretaker doesn't live on site, and we've got all our usual work to do and the services to attend. I'm at my wits' end.'

Ellie tried to work it out. 'Liddy had to go as an emergency; she wasn't registered as a National Health patient. The dentist took her in and treated her privately, but he must have wanted to be paid. You're not supposed to handle money. So, what did you do?'

A deep breath. 'I went and cashed the cheque you gave us the other day. We'd meant to hand it in, honest, but there's been this and that, and . . . we'd held on to it. I didn't know what else to do. It seemed as if it were meant, that we had that money to hand. We paid the dentist fifty pounds, and then we took the prescription to the chemist and he gave her the tablets, but we had to pay for those, too.'

She was on the verge of tears. 'I couldn't ask Ambrose what to do because he's never here on Friday afternoons. When he finds out, he'll go spare! The only thing I have left to sell is . . . But I swore I wouldn't, not again, and if he found out he'd half kill me.'

Ellie interpreted that without any trouble. Dolores would go back on the streets if necessary, but if Ambrose caught her at it she'd be in for a beating. All right, you could say she'd stolen the money they'd earned, but she'd done it for Liddy, who'd then run out on her.

Ellie had some money in her handbag. She could give Dolores enough to cover the cheque that had been cashed. But, ought she to do so? If Ambrose took the girls' earnings all the time, surely he was the one who was responsible for seeing they were signed up with a doctor and a dentist, and sent for eye tests if appropriate? Ambrose had, it seemed, fallen down on his duty to his employees . . . if that was what they were. Wouldn't it be right for him to cover the cost himself? Yes. But.

Dolores had let Ellie in and talked to her because she knew Ellie had money and was known to be a soft touch. Perhaps Dolores had hoped all along that Ellie would replace the money she'd given the dentist? Dolores was not as straightforward as she had seemed.

Neither was Ellie. She patted Dolores' arm. 'We'll sort it, between us. Now tell me; how did you get into this pickle?'

The old, old story. Absent father, drunken mother. Poor grades at school. Fabulous boyfriend who left her when her little boy was one year old and she had another on the way. New boyfriend, who introduced her to drugs. Social housing. Children taken into care. Thrown out of her flat by new boyfriend, who sent her on to a third man. Kept primed with drugs, on the streets for her pimp, until she was worn out. Up in court for the umpteenth time, rescued by Ambrose who had saved her. Wonderful Ambrose. He'd given her new life and hope, and she'd let him down by stealing that cheque, which he was going to take very hard, because there were rules; they had to have rules, didn't they? If he threw her out, she didn't know what she would do, and she'd be back behind bars in no time.

'How many times have you been in prison?'

'Well, none, really. My man bailed me out every time, so I've never been inside, not properly, only overnight once or twice.'

'What happened to your pimp?'

'Ambrose dealt with him.' In reverent tones.

Ellie could well believe that someone Ambrose had dealt with would stay dealt.

Dolores was thirty-one years old and looked sixty.

Ellie said, 'How do you see the future?'

Dolores' eyes lit up. 'It's a hard road, but I have the light of the Vision in my eyes, and if I keep on relying not on my own strength, but in the Word of our leader, I shall one day be free of my sinful past, and the angels will welcome me into the Land of the Forever Living.'

'You mean heaven?'

Dolores nodded. 'The Land of the Everlasting. The land of those who live for ever.'

'Right,' said Ellie, not willing to challenge Dolores' somewhat unusual theology. 'Now, I'll talk to Ambrose about Liddy when he gets back. When do you think he'll surface?'

'Supper time. He's always here to say grace and hear our reports.'

Ellie checked her watch. She had promised to be back for supper herself. 'I may have to come back tomorrow to speak to him. Meantime, could you tell me something about the project here? There are ordinary tenants, and then there are the people Ambrose has rescued. Is that right?'

'That's right. Some are, and some aren't.'

'Who lives in the old part of the building?'

Dolores gestured back to the hall. 'That's his flat, there. He has to have space and peace and quiet in which to meditate and to pray for the good work.'

'Does he live alone, or is there a Mrs Ambrose?'

Dolores looked shocked. 'He's celibate. He has to be, to become the channel for the Vision.'

Hmph. Well, anyway, if he's got a girlfriend, he's not keeping her here.

'That's all on the ground floor,' said Dolores, 'except for this meeting room and the kitchen, of course.'

So Ambrose's rooms must occupy the major part of the ground floor in the old building. 'Upstairs?'

'They're mostly people who were here before us. They've been put here by the Social, and they're all much of a muchness, if you know what I mean. The people on the first floor at the front, he was made redundant, got into debt and lost their house. They don't speak to us even if we meet in the hall. Ambrose goes up to talk to them now and again, but they're steeped in sin and obstinacy and refuse to repent. One of these days they'll drop dead and find themselves in the flames of hell, and then they'll be sorry, won't they?'

'Er, yes. On the other side?'

'They're actors, or so they say. More like they sweep the studio floors. It's a nice flat. That's the one Claire used to have, before . . . before.'

'The actors don't listen to Ambrose, either?'

'You've said it. Up top, there's the one we call the Fat Lady. Husband disappeared long ago, and then she lost all her hair and ballooned out till she looks like one of those Russian dolls. As Ambrose says, she's a perfect example of being poisoned by the doctors. She was quite a slim little thing once. At least, that's what she says.'

'You said Gail's mother left some time ago. She did live here once, though?'

'At the top on the other side. I dunno where she went. Shocking thing, that; finding the daughter in the canal. Who'd have thought? Mind you, she was bound to come to a bad end. Ambrose tried to talk to her . . .' She shook her head. 'She was asking for it; skirts up to here and neckline down to there. If she'd listened to us she'd still be with us today, wouldn't she?'

'You knew Gail?'

'Not to say *know* her. I saw her about now and then. Hanging around in the Broadway, flirting with men; you could see where she was going to end up, all right. If she'd really had a feeling for the game, I could have taught her a thing or two, but she never paid me no mind. Stuck up little bitch. As if her sort of looks would last! I reckon someone picked her up and taught her the trade. She wasn't much good for anything else. And –' warming to her theme – 'the ones who've come in instead? They're scum, too.'

'You mean the people now living in the flat which Gail and her mother had?'

'Another single parent family, wouldn't you know? The mother's got a part-time job somewhere, two children by different fathers: one of them's a tart, and the other's got special needs, or that's what they say. Ambrose says it's an opportunity to spread the word. We must pray until eventually we get through to them. He wrestles in prayer for us every day. Great drops of sweat start out all over him, and he roars like a wounded animal. He feels everything so deeply; the sin, the grimy sludge from the bottom of the human chain—'

'Yes, yes. Most disconcerting. I suppose he gets an income from the people of the Vision, though?'

Dolores sniffed. 'Yes and no. Our rents used to be paid direct to him, but now we have them paid to us and make them over to him. Some of us have a spot of difficulty with that. It's a temptation we needn't have, that's what Ambrose says, and he's right, isn't he? Many's the time I've looked at my cheque and thought about getting drugs with it, just to ease me along for a bit, but I haven't, so far. Ambrose wants to take over more of the building as the others leave because they're standing in the way of our purpose in life. Trailer trash, they call them in the States. And that's what they are. Fit for nothing but the bin.'

Ellie reflected that Dolores herself would be considered trailer trash by some people. 'Surely they have jobs?'

'Some do. Some do nothing but watch the telly, drink straight out of cans and smoke. As for their morals . . . Ambrose says that those who aren't past it are a hotbed of sin and lust. The only one of them has got work every day is Hector, the decorator, but he lives over the garage at the back. He's not really one of us, but he joins us for services sometimes. He takes one or other of our lads out with him, tries to keep them out of mischief. He's not a junkie or an alkie, but he's weird in a different way.'

So that blue van outside would belong to him, and he'd be the man who tried to paint Ellie's rooms green. 'What sort of "weird"?'

'Oh, I dunno.' A wriggle. 'Ambrose says we shouldn't fall into conversation with him because we might be tempted to have impure thoughts. Chance would be a fine thing.' Almost a blush. 'No, I didn't mean that I would want to, even if . . . and believe me, there's nothing like that goes on here.'

'What about Claire?'

'Oh. Her. Well.' Dolores shot a sideways glance at Ellie and grimaced. 'Claire is, well, Claire. One of those who has to work to make recompense for their sins. She has to be watched.'

'Do you watch her?'

A shrug. 'We all watch one another.'

'How many of you are there in the annex? You and Liddy. Claire. That lad the decorator brought with him when he tried to paint my house green. Any more?'

'Big Ruby and her friend that's both alkies, but they're following the trail of the Light and, Hallelujah, they'll see the Vision when they leave this mortal coil behind. They've got voices now that raise the hairs on your back when they sing. Then there's poor old Lenny that's working in the dry cleaners now, but I'm thinking he's back on the meths, and we'll have to have him up in the next meeting and wash his blood clean.

Oh, and there were two more lads, junkies, that were with us, but they got picked up by the filth last weekend and are back inside.'

The filth? The police. Those two had probably been on remand or probation and infringed the terms of their licence. Ambrose was trying to help those at the bottom of the pile, and he couldn't win all of the time.

Ellie sighed and got to her feet. Time was marching, etcetera. 'I don't think I can wait any longer. Will you tell Pastor Ambrose that I'd like to call round to see him tomorrow morning sometime?'

Dolores scrambled to her feet, her eyes widening. 'The money . . .!'

'Tell him I want to speak to him about the money. And Liddy.'

Dolores grabbed Ellie's arm. 'When I tell him about Liddy, he'll go mental! She's not supposed to have anything more to do with her family; she had to swear to put all her past behind her—'

'That's his problem and hers. Not yours.'

'He'll take it out on me, and if I haven't got the money to hand over—'

'Why, what can he do? Shout at you? Surely you can stand up to that? You did what you thought was best. He knows where to find Liddy, doesn't he? He can ring her and check for himself that she's all right.'

Dolores gave a little sob. 'So you won't help me? If you'd only give me the money, I could hand that over and say Liddy walked off and left me.'

'It's better not to lie. Tell him I'd like to talk to him about it. All right?'

Ellie almost ran out of the house, pulling the front door to behind her. She was breathing hard. She was sorry for Dolores, but the woman had got herself in such a mess that Ellie could see no quick and easy way out – except by giving her the money – and that wouldn't be the right thing to do. It would let Dolores off the hook temporarily, but the truth was bound to come out, and . . .

Ellie told herself to breathe in and out. Slowly.

The van had gone. Well, it would have, wouldn't it? No self-respecting workmen would work after six o'clock, unless they were getting treble time. She wondered if she ought to walk round and have a look at the garages and the flat above it . . . but what was the point?

Ellie looked at her watch. She'd have to step on it, if she was to be home in time for supper.

ELEVEN

Friday evening

Supper was over. It had been tasty and digestible, and Rose was glowing with pleasure.

Mikey had popped in while Ellie was out and had left Rose a multicoloured lollipop, which she alternatively admired and sucked. Second childhood, thought Ellie, and then had a sneaky thought that perhaps she would have liked to have one, too. The lollipop was all the colours of the rainbow, and Rose said it tasted as good as it looked.

Susan had settled in, and all was right with the world.

Except, someone was pounding on the door AND leaning on the doorbell. Not Diana, who rang but didn't pound. So . . . Ambrose?

Oh dear.

Ellie let him in. He was in a towering rage, claws ready to strike. Well, not actually, of course, but that's the impression he was giving.

'What,' he thundered, 'have you done with Liddy? How dare you encourage her to run away!'

'Oh, for heaven's sake. Come in and calm down.'

'You cannot deceive me! Dolores has told me ALL!'

'Dolores,' said Ellie, 'is so afraid of you that she'd accuse her own mother of murder rather than risk your wrath.'

'What do you know about Dolores' mother?'

'Nothing. Only—'

'You're lying!'

Ellie contemplated the uselessness of saying, 'No, I'm not!' to be followed by him saying, 'Yes, you are!' That puerile exchange could go on for hours.

Meantime, Susan and Rose had come out from the kitchen to see what all the noise was about. Rose, bright-eyed, was still sucking her lollipop.

Ellie said, 'Ambrose, we have an audience.'

Susan, being the niece of a serving police officer, knew what to do. 'Shall I call the police?'

'No, no. He'll calm down in a minute. Ambrose, shall we go into the sitting room and discuss this matter? Would you like some tea or coffee?'

'I don't allow caffeine into my body.'

'Silly of me. It pollutes the kidneys or something, doesn't it? Susan, do you think you could bring us both a cup of peppermint tea?' Ellie led the way into the sitting room without waiting to see if he would follow. Which he did.

The phone rang in the hall. Susan answered it and called out, 'Mrs Quicke, it's my aunt for you. She says it's urgent.'

'Tell her I'll ring her back in ten minutes. Now, Mr Ambrose, I don't know what Dolores has said to you, but—'

'Don't you dare deny it! You have encouraged one of my flock to abscond, to return to the den of iniquity from which I rescued her! More, you have stolen monies due to me.'

'Dolores has a vivid imagination.'

'Dolores would not lie to me!'

'Of course she would. She's terrified of you, and so, apparently, is Liddy. Dolores told me that Liddy needed treatment for toothache—'

'All in the mind!'

'Pardon me, but for most people toothache is not "all in the mind". I observe you have perfect teeth. Perhaps you have never even needed a filling? Dolores told me that Liddy is not so blessed. She was in so much pain that, in fear and trembling, she risked your displeasure in order to visit a dentist. For some reason she was not on a National Health dentist's list, but she found one which would treat her if she went privately. No—' She held up her hand. 'Don't interrupt. I'm sure you would have seen to it that she was registered with a dentist if you had thought of it, but you didn't. If you had, it would have saved you a considerable sum of money.'

He was astounded. 'You are saying that she used my money to pay a dentist to treat her? That she actually went to him privately?'

'That's what happens if you aren't registered and need emergency care. The dentist said she must have antibiotics—'

'Poisoning her system!'

'Do you know,' said Ellie, in a conversational tone, 'I thought at first that what Liddy had done was wrong, but I'm beginning to think otherwise. She took the money she'd earned and spent it on emergency dental treatment. What's wrong with that?'

'She stole, and she lied! She is expressly forbidden to harm her body by using noxious substances of any kind! Now she has fled to the very people who used and abused her. Ah, you didn't know that, did you, Mrs Clever Clever? Her sister is a drug addict who is beyond saving. She encouraged her pimp to lure Liddy into his clutches, too. He works the two of them for his friends, keeping them docile with cocaine. I was unable to save her sister, but I managed to rescue Liddy and set her on the road to recovery. Who else would have tried to save her? The doctors? Don't make me laugh. Now she has gone back to that evil man, and in a few days' time she'll be back, grovelling in the gutter, beyond salvation, beyond redemption, bound for the pit of hell. And you are responsible!'

Ellie blinked. Did this angle on the story make a difference? Well, no. 'It's a sad story, but I am in no way responsible. From what you say, Liddy is an adult who has made some wrong decisions in her life. In this case she was torn between obeying you and her need for treatment. The pain won, and she didn't dare face you. If you had been more approachable and allowed her to go to a dentist in the normal way then she might still be under your roof. She was too scared of you to risk it. I think you must shoulder part of the blame for what has happened.'

'I offer my followers salvation!'

'You offer them shelter, under certain conditions. You provide them with work, you house and feed them, and in return you take their earnings—'

'That is to prevent their buying the poisons that were killing them.'

'I can see you believe you are doing the right thing by these people, but your regime is too harsh. It does not surprise me that some rebel. Whether the decisions they then make are wise or not, I cannot say.'

'You refuse to recognize your part in Liddy's descent into hell?'

Ellie almost giggled at that, but managed to stop herself just in time. Ambrose in a rage was alarming. 'You must know where her sister lives. Why don't you go and see if you can get Liddy to return to you, allowing her to take the antibiotics and saying nothing about the missing money?'

'So you think it is right to overlook—'

'If what you say is true about her sister and her boyfriend, then you probably don't have much time to rescue Liddy. Your choice.'

He opened and shut his mouth several times, then strode out of the room, across the hall, and left.

Susan was on the phone in the hall. Again? Or on a fresh call? She held out the phone to Ellie. 'Aunt Lesley, in a panic.'

Ellie took the phone, thinking that she was tired and could do with an early night. 'What's up now?'

'Did you visit the Vision place today?'

'Yes, and Ambrose came round to see me afterwards.'

'Did he, now! I'll be round in ten minutes, right?'

'No, you won't. I'm tired, and I want to go to bed. Yes, I know it's early yet, but that's not what my body is telling me. Come round tomorrow morning.'

'Very well. Answer me this. What time did you visit the Vision?'

'I don't know. It was after Susan came. She said she'd cook us some supper, so I had a spot of free time and walked on up the hill . . . About five? Maybe a bit later.'

'Tell me exactly what you did and what you saw.'

'What is this?'

'Just tell me. You got there about five? Susan may be able to tell me exactly when you left. Oh, Ellie. How do you manage it? You walk through battlefields and don't even notice the shells falling around you.'

'What should I have noticed?'

'A girl called Karen on her way back home from school. She lives on the top floor of the big house with her mother and a very much younger brother, who is handicapped. The mother works on a till at the supermarket in the Broadway Centre. She collects the boy from a special school on her way home. Karen should have been home about five. She sometimes stays on after school for some club or other. She hasn't turned up, and her mother's going frantic. Are you sure you didn't see her?'

'Definitely not.' Ellie found the news disturbing. She hadn't seen anyone but Dolores, had she? She looked at her watch. 'I didn't think the police took notice of missing girls until they'd been absent for more than four or five hours. Don't they usually assume she's gone to a friend's house to watch a film or something?'

'I agree. Nobody would be panicking if this girl hadn't disappeared from the same house as Gail. As it is, they've logged the mother's complaint, but are watching the clock, hoping against hope the girl will turn up. I don't think she will, do you?'

Ellie shook her head. 'I really don't know. Depends on the girl. On balance, I think you're right to worry. It's too much of a coincidence, isn't it?'

'If she doesn't turn up by tomorrow morning, there'll be all hell to pay.'

'You'll keep me informed?' Ellie put the phone down, thinking back. No, she really hadn't seen a schoolgirl. She'd seen Dolores and heard her story, had learned something about the other people who lived in the building, and that was it.

She would wait up till Thomas rang, and then she'd be off to bed.

Prompt on cue, the phone rang. Ellie nearly dissolved into tears at hearing Thomas's voice, as clear as if he were in the room next door.

'My dear one, I've been so worried about you.'

Ellie made an effort to keep calm. 'Oh, you know me, all sorts of things happen, and—'

'What? Tell me what's been happening.'

So she told him, trying not to cry because that would waste time and transatlantic phone calls cost money. She ended, 'I'm in such a muddle. I think Ambrose is something of a nut case. He thinks he's a prophet, talks wildly about receiving heavenly visions, but there's no love in his relationship with people. It's all hell fire and cursing.' She tried to laugh. 'He cursed Diana, and she was so upset, you can't believe! She went so far as to say that if you'd been here, you'd have protected her from him.'

Thomas was amused. 'There's a turn-up for the books. She really thinks I could be of use to her?' Then his natural kindliness took over. 'Poor creature. Yes, I will bear her in mind. What about you? I've only got a couple more days here. I could cut my stay short and—'

'No, don't do that. I'm all right, really I am. If I could only sort out what I think of Ambrose and his project—'

'The church side, or the care of his people? As to the visions and so on, it may be that he needs to test where they come from; his imagination, God or the devil? Perhaps he needs guidance to help him decide. Next, does he run this group by himself? He should have someone he can go to, someone he can ask for advice. And lastly, who is his doctor?'

Common sense speaks, and all is made clear. 'You think he ought to be on some kind of medication?'

'Without speaking to him personally, I can't tell, but from what you say of his behaviour and wild words he might be in need of help.'

'Suppose he's genuine? Suppose he really is receiving orders from God?'

'Do you think he is?'

Ellie sat down on the chair nearby and considered the matter. 'I think he believes in himself, believes he receives messages from on high, but his behaviour is not Christian. He doesn't love and care for people. He seeks to dominate. Also, he sometimes gets hysterical. He is charismatic, can dominate a meeting. He has no doubts. He thinks his followers should obey him implicitly. I'm reminded of the saying that the only people who should have power are those who don't want it. He relishes it. He's a despot, a tyrant. He thinks he's acting for the best, but his methods are questionable. I'm worried that his actions have driven Liddy back on to the streets.'

'Addicts can't be rescued unless they want to be, but you have a point. I will pray that he reaches her in time and has the sense to relax his regime.'

'They are adults,' said Ellie, trying to think this through. 'Surely by law they have the right to make their own decisions, provided only that they are not harming others. Submitting to his regime is keeping them off the streets and away from the temptations of their former lives. I don't know what his success rate may be, but I've heard that some have lapsed recently. Dolores said that two of their lads returned to their former ways and are now back in prison. At least, that's what I think she meant. I'm not sure she always tells the truth.'

'In a programme such as this, it's normal for a certain percentage to lapse.'

'I think his success rate is higher than the usual programmes which treat the client with substitute drugs while leaving them in the community, exposed to all the old temptations. He's backed by Social Services – or so he says. I shall have to check that.'

'The key must be how he treats his followers. I don't think Social Services would approve of a regimen which is not overseen by a doctor. His people should definitely have been registered with one, and with a dentist and an optician, too. There are some grounds for concern here.'

'Yes.' And there was the case of the missing girls, too. But that lay outside Thomas's remit, and she didn't want to bother him with it now. It really was none of her business, not like the Vision's application for funds. She said, 'You'll be glad to hear we have a new cook-cum-carer. Lesley's niece is moving in for a couple of weeks. She's a food technology student and an enormous improvement upon Claire the Tearful . . . whom I hope we never see again. So we're fine, now you've sorted me out about Ambrose.'

'Are you sure you don't want me back straight away?' He sounded as if he were torn.

'I'm sure.' Smiling. 'Enjoy yourself. Take care. Let me know if your plane is delayed, or early, or something.'

Saturday morning

Vera and Mikey arrived as breakfast was being cleared away. As usual after a meal, Rose had dropped off to sleep. Vera wanted to know if there was anything Mikey could do for Ellie that morning as, she said with a meaningful glint in her eye, she'd be glad to get him gainfully employed under the eye of an adult. Which meant she really wanted Ellie to have him that morning. Vera added that Dan was supervising a football match and she was due at work in ten, no, five minutes' time. But not, said Vera, frowning at Mikey, if he were going to cause any trouble.

Susan said she intended to try out a variation on a recipe that morning, which meant she didn't want Mikey around, either.

Ellie wondered what Mikey had been doing to cause Vera to want him supervised that morning, but refrained from asking. Sometimes it was better *not* to know. She said, 'I'd be happy for Mikey to help me out with this and that.' Without specifying what.

Vera departed with a sharp word to Mikey to behave himself.

Mikey grinned at Ellie, and Ellie grinned back. She beckoned him to follow her into her study. Ellie remarked to the air that she wondered if anyone could find out where Claire Bonner used to live. Somewhere in Perivale, she thought. Did Mikey think he might be able to find out?

Would Mikey bite? He was so much better at finding things on the computer than she was. And, he was at a loose end, so he might deign to help her.

He said, 'Have you tried the BT phone book? It has addresses and phone numbers. And, all that stuff you can find online.'

She blenched. She hadn't tried online. She didn't know how to and didn't want to know how to, either. 'Couldn't you do it for me?'

'Leave it to me,' he said, easing into Ellie's seat at her computer. 'A tenner?'

Ellie found her handbag and put the money on her desk beside him.

What next? Rose wanted to make another will, which meant Ellie needed to contact her solicitor, Gunnar, who was also an old friend. She withdrew to the hall and, because it was a Saturday and he wouldn't be at work, phoned him at home. After the usual exchange of courtesies, she explained the situation. He tutted. She sighed and agreed that leaving Rose in the clutches of someone from the Vision had not been wise, that Rose regretted making a will in their favour and wanted to put the matter right. 'Do you think you could manage to fit her in as soon as possible?'

'Tell me more about these people of the Vision.'

Ellie obliged, trying to be concise.

'The police are involved?'

'Yes, but I really don't know what's happening. Another girl may have disappeared . . . and they're still after me for money. But, I'll cope.'

'I'm sure you will.'

A vote for Ellie. She hoped his confidence in her was not misplaced.

And then what? Time out in the Quiet Room?

Chance would be a fine thing. The doorbell rang. Lesley arrived in a rush.

'Ellie, the girl Karen is still missing. Let me get this straight. You went up to the Vision house yesterday evening and saw . . . who? Yes, I know I asked you yesterday, but indulge me. Talk me through it.'

Ellie sighed. Was she never to have any peace and quiet? 'I didn't see any young girl. Would you like some coffee? I'm having some.' She served them both coffee and retreated to the sitting room. Lesley got out her notebook, and Ellie concentrated.

'I went up there to see if I could have a word with Ambrose and to take a look at the place. The people of the Vision occupy part of a big Edwardian house which has a modern extension at one side. Ambrose didn't answer his bell, and I didn't have his telephone number. Someone was in one of the upstairs flats. I could hear the television faintly, but as I understand it the tenants in that part of the building don't have anything to do with the people of the Vision, and they didn't come down to speak to me. I was on the point of leaving a note for Ambrose when Dolores arrived – she was one of the cleaners foisted on me by Claire – and she let me in.'

'What about Karen?'

Ellie shook her head. 'I didn't see anyone but Dolores.'

'Dolores . . . What's her second name?'

'Haven't a clue. She told me something about herself and the other people who live in the house. The ground floor is occupied by Ambrose and communal rooms for the Vision. Upstairs in the big house are flats of varying sizes, occupied by council tenants. The extension is occupied by Ambrose's waifs and strays, but Dolores wasn't allowed to show me them. She couldn't even give me a cup of tea. The kitchen is locked up till they prepare the evening meal. Dolores was in a state over Liddy, the girl that she usually works with, who'd been taken poorly and gone back to stay with her sister, which apparently was not a good thing. And then I left.'

'You didn't see anyone else, coming or going?'

'No, I didn't.'

'Or hear anyone? No one came to the door? What about someone coming down the stairs?'

'No one. We were in the communal dining room. I was facing the open door into the hall. I'd have seen if anyone else had crossed the hall.'

'Bear with me for a minute. You left at what time?'

A shrug. 'Half-past five? I was back here before six. We had supper together, and then Ambrose hurtled in, accusing me of doing away with Liddy.'

'What!'

'The cleaner I told you about, who works with Dolores. He was furious because she's not supposed to go back to her sister's, which is what she has done . . . and, to be frank, I don't blame her. At least, I blame him for creating a climate of fear which meant Liddy couldn't go to him when she needed the attention of a dentist. This has nothing to do with the latest girl, Karen, disappearing, has it?'

'Ambrose wanted to know what you'd done with Liddy? He didn't mention anyone else?'

'No. I suggested he went off to rescue Liddy if he could, and he did so. At least, I assume that is what he did. He left, and then you rang.'

'Did he visit you to establish some sort of alibi, do you think?'

Ellie thought about that. 'No. He was concentrating on Liddy's disappearance. I honestly don't think he knew about Karen going AWOL, and as far as I know, she was not a member of his group. I wonder . . . Dolores said the people at the top of the house were trailer trash. Does that description fit Karen?'

'Sixteen, looking twenty-five? Badly bleached blonde hair, boobs out to here . . .?' Lesley produced a photo. 'Take a look.'

Ellie looked. Pouting lips and slumberous eyes. A mass of hair which was a tousled mess, dark brown at the roots, brassy blonde at the tips. 'No, I haven't seen her. What's the betting she's gone the same way as Jenna and Gail? If so, she's still alive. The man kept both girls for some months, didn't he?'

'If she doesn't turn up by tomorrow, Forensics will pull the Vision place apart, and the Murder Squad will want to know you were there about the time the girl went missing.'

'Do I need my solicitor?'

'I wouldn't think so.'

Ellie sighed. 'What I have to say is not going to help you much, is it?'

Lesley left. Ellie checked that Mikey was still happily working away on her computer and made her way into Thomas's Quiet Room, which was a refuge for them all when the world became too demanding.

She sank into her chair and closed her eyes. She wouldn't go to sleep. No. She was far too wound up for that. But, if she could manage it, she might just drift away from all her troubles, placing them firmly in the hands of someone who knew the answers to everything.

If you please, Lord. This is a tangle too far for me to cope with. Oh, and please will you look after Diana, who pretends she doesn't believe in you, but does, and is very distressed about being cursed by Ambrose . . . which is a bit of a laugh, really.

Now, these missing girls . . . Oh dear. And now another one? Somehow, I can't feel involved. It honestly doesn't seem to have anything to do with me.

Ambrose, now. Thomas was right. How he operates his

*project is Social Services' concern. Not mine. Ought I perhaps
to point them in that direction? Well, they won't be open on
a Saturday, will they?*

*I can't see a happy ending there. The trust should not – will
not – give him the money he wants, for two reasons; one,
because he is clearly off his rocker, and two, because we can't
fund a regime which neglects its clients' health. If 'client' is
the right word. Yes, I worry about what will happen to the
likes of Liddy and Dolores if the project has to end, but . . .
No, that is not my problem.*

*Claire. She's my problem. I don't know why. I don't like
her. I think she's one of those seemingly harmless people of
limited intelligence who can actually do a great deal of harm.
Just look at the way she worked on Rose. Ugh! And the way
she crawls to people . . . Ugh! And, ugh again!*

*She pleaded with me to help her. So I suppose . . . What do
you think, Lord? Do you think I should?*

*Her descent from self-sufficiency to dependency and menial
jobs is intriguing. There must be a flaw in the woman's character to account for it. Perhaps it's her uncertain temper?
Something must have happened to trigger her descent from
riches to rags.*

*Well, it's no use sitting here, wishing that things were
different. Up and at 'em!*

She made her way to the study and found Mikey working on
the computer. She said, 'How are you getting on with your
search for Claire?'

He passed her a note. 'There's only one Bonner listed in
Perivale. That's his address and telephone number. Malcolm
by name. Would that be Claire's father or her brother? I
went on to the Google map place and found a picture of the
house. Here it is. Ordinary three or four bed, two reception,
semi-d, with a loft extension, built on a steep slope. By the
look of it the earth has been scooped out of the hill at
the side of the house, allowing for a garage to be built there
with an extension on top. The house next door is the same.
Steps up the garden to the front door, and a drive down a
slope into the garage. Well-maintained, but the present

occupant doesn't seem to have any interest in the garden. Rockery which is mostly rocks.'

Ellie looked at the picture he'd given her. A very ordinary-looking house. Velux windows on the sloping roof, indicating a loft extension.

Mikey said, 'I looked up similar houses for sale in the area. Some have a loft conversion like this one. Surprisingly pricey. Nice area. Quiet. Near a good school. Five minutes from the nearest bus stop.'

'I got the impression that the house was supposed to have been sold after the mother died. Claire said . . . Now, what exactly did she say? Or Rose said . . . Yes, that's it. Something about Claire having been badly treated by her family. Can we discover the terms of Mrs Bonner's will? That's all in the public domain, isn't it?'

'I suppose I could, but it would take time. Why are you so interested in Claire's past?'

Yes, why? Ellie struggled to work it out. 'A steep rise to riches from rags is always interesting. You want to know how they did it. Likewise, a drop from riches to rags. If they had so much, why did they lose it? Claire had a good job, a car, lived with her family in this desirable residence. The mother dies and this Malcolm keeps the house. If he was the father then it makes sense that she'd want to leave . . . I suppose. But if he was her brother, why wasn't it shared between them? Perhaps he bought her out? At that point Claire departs from her job and her home. I sense something rotten in the state of Denmark – to misquote Hamlet.'

'"Fee-fi-fo-fum!"' quoted Mikey. 'I smell the blood of rotten old Claire. She tried to get Rose to leave all her worldly goods to her, you know. That wasn't fair. Also, she smells.'

'A rose scents, a person smells. I mean, smelling is a verb. I think. Or does no one care nowadays? Oh, now you've got me muddled.'

Mikey grinned, turning up his nose and pretending he could sense a bad odour. 'She smells of boiled cabbage.'

Ellie sighed. It was true; Claire did. Infrequently washed underwear? Ellie shuddered. Yuk.

Mikey said, 'Do you want to talk to Malcolm about Claire?

I wouldn't mind coming with you. I've got nothing better to do today.'

'Are you sure?'

'This is more interesting than homework, which, in case you're asking, I have already finished, right? So let's go and have a look at Claire's old stamping ground. Shall I order a cab to take us there?'

Ellie's long-deceased first husband had told her she'd never be able to drive a car, and for many years she had accepted that. When he died, she did try, once. Only to realize that he had been right. If she'd started younger . . .? But she hadn't. So, she hired a cab from a local firm when she needed one. 'Yes,' she said. 'We'll go after we've had a spot of lunch.'

Mikey said, 'Your computer ought to be updated. I'll do it for you sometime, shall I?'

Ellie shuddered. 'I can't face learning a new system.'

Mikey almost, but not quite, patted her on the head. 'You can do it. I'll help you.'

TWELVE

Saturday afternoon

Mikey watched their cab driver turn smoothly out of a side road into the busy stream of traffic on the A40. 'How soon do you think I could learn to drive? It's legal off road, isn't it?'

Ellie gave him a Look. He was, after all, only thirteen years old. Nearly fourteen, but nowhere near the legal age for learning to drive on British roads.

He grinned. 'All right. Probably not yet.'

Their cab turned off the A40 into Perivale, which was a quieter suburb than the one in which Ellie lived. Wide, tree-lined roads, buses, a school and a tube station . . . acres of housing built to the same pattern, three bed, two reception, semi-detached. And on to an area of slightly larger, better-built semis climbing a hillside.

The driver drew up to the kerb and let them out. 'Shall I wait for you?'

Ellie shook her head. 'I don't know how long we're going to be. We'll ring for you to fetch us when we're done.'

Most of the gardens hereabouts were well tended. Residents' cars were parked on the driveways and in the road. The houses on the left were on steeply rising ground, which meant there'd be a good view from their top windows. Those on the right dropped down the hill.

Mikey said, 'This is the house.' Just as it had looked on Google. Well-maintained, semi-detached. Bay windows to ground and first floors, Velux windows in the roof. Broad steps climbed the slope to the front door, while to the left the driveway descended to a garage, the electrically-operated door of which was closed.

'Shall I ring the bell?' He climbed the steps to the front door without waiting for her and rang the bell. Ding dong. Ellie toiled up the steps after him.

There were some of these newfangled blinds at the window; slats which theoretically could be adjusted to let the light in or keep it out. Ellie's mother had always told her that Venetian blinds – which is what they were called in her day – were more trouble than they were worth, collecting dust and with a tendency to stick at an angle. These were already showing signs of age. Ah well, each generation seemed to need to reinvent the wheel.

They stood in the porch and tried to see through the slats into the bay window. To no avail. Mikey pressed the bell again. No reply.

Ellie stepped back on to the path and looked up. It was a fine, bright blue day, but there were no windows open anywhere.

'He's out. What do we do now?'

Ellie descended the steps to the road with care. A fall here might have nasty consequences. 'It's a Saturday. He may be out shopping.'

'Or at a football match. You want to wait?'

'We've sent the cab away, so let's think about it.' She seated herself on the low wall which kept the garden from tumbling on to the pavement. Not that it was much of a garden. A rockery with nothing but rocks in it . . . and a few weeds. Not like next door, which was a riot of colourful shrubs, some of which Ellie was hard put to it to name.

Ellie looked up and down the road. 'I may not be much good at computers, but I'm quite good at getting information from neighbours who like to chat.'

The street was deserted. Mikey shifted from one foot to the other. He liked action. 'Shall I try the house next door?' A similar house, bay windows, loft conversion. Their garage doors, however, were wooden with panes of glass to give light to the interior.

Without waiting for a reply, Mikey climbed the steps to the next house and rang the doorbell.

Ellie spotted a nasty bit of milkweed just about to send its fluffy seeds all over the neighbouring gardens. That would not please the householders. Not one bit. She pulled it out. Saw another a little further on and got to her feet to attend to that, too.

'Has he actually employed a gardener?' A scarecrow of a man, bent over a walker from which dangled various plastic bags. One of them clinked. Saturday morning shopping spree? An interested neighbour?

Ellie blushed. 'Oh, no. Not really. I mean, I was wanting a word with Mr Bonner, and then I was thinking of my own garden and how easily weeds can spread if you let them seed, and I didn't think. It was silly of me. I don't know what I was going to do with them, once I'd pulled them out. I can't just leave them in the gutter.'

'You were wanting a word with Malcolm?' Bright eyes that missed nothing. Clothes which had once been good and which were still well cared for. A retired professional, bent over with arthritis, not as old as Methuselah, but getting on that way. His voice was still strong. 'Now why would that be?'

A door slammed above them, and Mikey half tumbled and half slid down the slope to the road. 'She slammed the door in my face!'

The elderly man looked from Mikey to Ellie. 'Your grandson?'

'Not exactly,' said Ellie. 'Well, sort of. My name's Ellie Quicke, and this is Mikey.'

'So, why were you after a word with young Malcolm?'

'Well,' said Ellie, 'it's a long story, but someone called Claire Bonner who used to live here came to me for a job. It didn't work out, and I had to let her go. But I feel sorry for her, in a way, and—'

'What's she done now, then?'

'Done?' Ellie wasn't sure what he meant. 'I don't know that she's done anything wrong, exactly—'

Mikey interrupted. 'Except feed Rose that stuff which made her go all doolally. Rose is an elderly lady who used to be Mrs Quicke's housekeeper, but is part of the family now. Claire was supposed to be looking after Rose while Mrs Quicke was away, but I saw her putting cough mixture into Rose's food, and it seemed to make her lose the plot.'

'Ah,' said the old man. 'A bottle of linctus, was it?'

Ellie stared at him. 'How did you know?'

Mikey clicked his fingers. 'She's done it before, right?'

The elderly man squinched his eyes shut, rocking his walker to and fro. Thinking. Then he made up his mind. He pointed his chin at Mikey. 'You go back up there. Tell that old ratbag to put the kettle on, as I'm coming up for a cuppa and bringing some friends with me. She usually comes to my house because my path isn't so steep, but I can still get up to her place if I take a breather halfway up.'

'She threw me out just now,' said Mikey.

'She won't throw me out. Tell her Emmanuel Cook's on his way.'

Mikey raced up the slope while Mr Cook, disdaining Ellie's proffered hand, set off along the pavement and up the steps to the next house door.

Ding dong. This time when the door was opened, the house-holder said, 'Oh, it's you, is it?'

'Bringing tidings. Let us in why don't you, Agnes?'

Agnes ushered them inside. Spotlessly clean, the house had probably been furnished when the woman had got married. Nothing much seemed to have been changed since then except the size of the television and the introduction of a modern phone.

Agnes was probably only in her early fifties, much younger than Mr Cook. She was a wisp of a woman with a ramrod straight back and large, flashing spectacles. Her hair was tightly permed, she had slashed a bright-red lipstick on, and she was wearing what used to be called a sundress, which allowed for unintentional glimpses of bra and vest straps. Her ankles were neat, and her high-heeled sandals matched the red of her dress, as did her painted toenails. Agnes was informing the world that she might be past the age of childbearing, but she was Not Giving Up.

The elderly man charged into the sitting room and seated himself with a sigh, saying, 'Agnes, this is Mrs Quicke and her sort-of-grandson Mikey, and they have a story to tell about our neighbour-that-was, Claire. Before they start, a cup of tea wouldn't come amiss.'

A pot of tea was duly produced, and an array of biscuits on a doily on a china plate. The tea was served in matching china cups and saucers, and very welcome it was, too.

Mr Cook placed his cup on the coffee table and nodded to Ellie. 'Now, you tell Agnes what you told me.'

Ellie told. She concluded, 'Claire has asked me for help, but to tell the truth, I'm not sure I trust her. On the other hand, I do feel sorry for her. A bit.'

'You needn't,' said the elderly man. 'We've known her since she was ten.'

Agnes nodded agreement. 'Claire was always difficult.'

Ellie said, 'Could you bear to tell us what you know about her?'

Agnes looked at Emmanuel, who sighed and said, 'Tell them.'

Agnes took a deep breath. 'We moved into this neighbourhood, Emmanuel and his wife, me and my hubby, about the same time. Beryl and her man were already there, next door, with the one girl, that's Claire, who was . . . How would you describe her, Emmanuel?'

Emmanuel grunted, pulling a face.

Agnes shook her head. 'At that time the garden here was a mess and next door's not much better. The fence between had blown down and not been replaced. Soon after we moved in, I was upstairs making the beds when I spotted Claire in our garden, poking at something in our water butt. Something that was splashing, trying to get out. I was pregnant and it made me slow, getting down. It was a little white cat that had been a birthday present to Claire, though apparently she'd never liked it. I got the cat out, but it was too late. Claire said she'd been trying to teach it a lesson because it had scratched her, but there was never a sign on her that she'd been hurt. We were new to the neighbourhood, we didn't want to make a big fuss, but we had to tell Beryl what had happened. I know Claire's dad walloped her for it, but . . .'

Ellie wondered whether this incident was behind Claire's fear of her own cat, Midge. Had Claire's father smacked her too hard, or was she allergic to cats? It was a puzzle.

'. . . and then Beryl was having trouble, miscarriage after miscarriage. I was sorry for her because I'd had my first easily enough, and the second came along soon after. Beryl was desperate for a son. She got him a couple of years later, and that was Malcolm. A nice enough lad, if not the brightest coin in the treasury.'

Emmanuel interrupted. 'Malcolm's all right.'

Ellie heard a note of warning in the old man's voice. Was he telling Agnes not to gossip?

Yes, Agnes had heard the warning and coloured up. 'Well, we made allowances for Claire, as one does. We thought she might have felt pushed out of the limelight because her mother wanted a boy so much, but she wasn't easy to like. She was a whiny little thing, never satisfied. Her dad used to say the girl took after one of his aunts, who'd never been known to smile unless someone fell over and hurt themselves. After Malcolm was born she got worse. I caught her pinching her brother one day and told her off for it, but . . . If Claire broke something she'd cry buckets and blame it on Malcolm, when he'd been nowhere near.'

'That was just for starters,' said Emmanuel. 'When the boys were all in their teens she said that Malcolm, and our boys as well, had been interfering with her.' His hand shook as he replaced his cup in its saucer. 'At first we wondered if it might be true, seeing as they were all of an age to experiment, though it seemed odd as Claire was so much older and . . . I'm sorry to say this, but it's true . . . she was no raving beauty. The boys all swore that they'd been out together on the evening Claire said they'd been doing things to her. So we knew she'd been lying. It caused us all a lot of grief.'

Ellie could well imagine. Mikey was wide-eyed. Did he understand what they were talking about? Probably. Oh dear.

Agnes said, 'You can imagine how miserable it made us all feel. It was hard to see her about the place, knowing what she'd said. Our boys avoided her. Malcolm was so upset; I reckon it was that which put him off girls for a long time. He installed a lock on his bedroom door and spent more time with us than in his own home, which was nice for us but hard for Beryl, especially since shortly after her husband had a series of strokes and died.'

'Malcolm was pretty cut up about his dad's death. He blamed it on all the trouble Claire had caused, and maybe he was right. Beryl kept excusing Claire, saying she was having a

difficult time at work, but we were all going through a difficult
time. One by one we lost our partners; first Beryl's man, then
my husband, and finally Emmanuel's wife. The boys went off
to college and university and got themselves jobs. One of
mine's working in Scotland on the oil rigs, and the other's in
local government and lives locally. Both married, both with
sprogs.'

Emmanuel chipped in: 'One of my boys is in Leeds, he's
something high up in IT and is in a long-term relationship,
while the other is working in Australia and has just got engaged.
Only Malcolm stayed at home and stayed single. Well, and
Claire, of course. She never had a man interested in her. She
took a secretarial course after school and got an office job at
the local supermarket. She even got promotion eventually.
Things settled down, after a fashion.'

'But it wasn't the same,' said Agnes, with a sigh. 'It couldn't
be the same. Malcolm and Claire were hardly on speaking
terms. As soon as you opened their front door, you could tell
that it was an unhappy house. Malcolm was always good with
his hands, and he went for an apprenticeship with a builder
and, if he was a bit on the slow side, he was also conscien-
tious. He built up a nice little connection, getting jobs all over
the place, not only local. He couldn't afford a place of his
own, and why should he have to? It was his mother's house,
and of course she'd leave it to him and Claire eventually.'

'No girlfriends,' said Emmanuel. 'He used to take a girl out
now and then, but nothing ever came of it. In any case, he
was out late and early, working. And, to give her her due, so
was Claire. Beryl; well, she went a bit funny. Someone she
met at a jumble sale told her about a wonderful preacher she'd
heard and invited Beryl along to one of his meetings. No
church that I've ever heard of carries on like that, but Beryl
loved it. Soon she was going twice a day on Sundays and
several times in the week, too. Then she started on at us to
go with her. She went on and on about it. Agnes went once,
didn't you, Agnes?'

Agnes shook her head. 'You've never seen the like. They
were all weeping and wailing and chanting. I think it's called
a Love Fest, or is it Love Bombing? Would that be right?

They were almost tearing the trousers off this big black man, who was screaming at them about repentance and I don't know what else. As I said to Beryl, "I've always been a Methodist, and a Methodist I shall die." Not that I go to church every week, but I never miss Easter and Christmas.'

Ellie said, 'Where did these people meet, and what did they call themselves?'

'They used to meet in a big house about a mile from here, though they moved away later. The room was heaving with people, I'll give them that. They called themselves the people of the Vision. There wasn't much about God or loving your neighbours, but a lot about worshipping this man they called their leader. Beryl was captivated. She said that following him made sense of her life, though I couldn't see it, myself.'

The old man chuckled. 'Malcolm went once and came in afterwards to tell us all about it. He was laughing, but angry, too. He said the leader had worked the congregation up till a woman had a seizure or a fit and the pastor "healed" her. Malcolm reckoned it was all faked. He wouldn't go again, no matter how much his mother asked. Claire started to go and was there morning, noon and night; well, apart from work hours, that is. What I think is that those two women needed someone to boss them around once they'd lost their husband and father. Malcolm distanced himself from them. He wouldn't even sit down at the table and eat with his mother if Claire was there. I told him, families ought to eat together, but he couldn't bring himself to do it.'

Agnes said, 'Our boys have all kept in touch, mind you, and when one comes home we all try to get together again.'

Emmanuel blew his nose. 'Anyone could see what these Vision people were after. First they cut you off from your friends, and then, when they have you where they want you, they raid your purse. After a while Beryl came round to say she couldn't "consort" with us any more if we didn't repent, mend our ways and start going to this Vision thing with her. "Consort", indeed! By that she meant she'd put a chain on the door and she and Claire refused to let us in if we called on them. That was when Malcolm had that electronic door put on the garage, which has a door into the cellar, the same as all the houses have on this side of the road. So he could come and go without running into them. We didn't think . . . We never suspected . . . But what could we have done more than we did?'

Agnes shook her head. 'We'd been friends for so long. We tried, you know. To keep in touch. Even if I met her out shopping, Beryl'd start on at me to repent and give my life to some Vision of heaven that this "leader" had had. One day I made her sit down and have a cuppa with me, and she took a dose of something out of a bottle with her glass of water. No more tea or coffee for her. I said I hadn't known she was poorly and asked her what the doctor had said, but she said doctors were all rubbish and the stuff in the bottle was harmless, you could buy it over the counter, and it was to keep her mind focused on what was important. She told me a rambling tale about how Claire was being persecuted at work by some woman or other, but had got the better of her by feeding her some of this same syrupy stuff and asking the pastor to put a curse on her. The woman had then gone off sick permanently, and what did I think of that!'

Ellie tried to put the pieces of the puzzle together. 'A woman at the supermarket had crossed Claire, who fed her some medication until she went off sick?'

Agnes nodded. 'I said to her, "Wasn't that very wrong?" Beryl got really angry with me and said I was an agent of Satan, which as far as I know, I never have been. So I told Emmanuel here, and he didn't know what to do either, because it might all have been something Beryl had imagined, but he said I should tell my son that's in local government and see what he thought. And *he* said he'd have a quiet word with someone he knew in the supermarket chain to see if they'd like to look into it. He did have a word, as we found out later. But what happened next was . . .' A sigh. 'You tell it, Emmanuel.'

Emmanuel shook his head. 'It was bad, very bad. Agnes had her son and his wife over one evening with the baby, and they asked me and Malcolm round for a bite. Malcolm was working late, but said he'd try to pop in later. Anyway, we were having a good time catching up when Beryl hammered on the door and demanded to be let in. She was in a right state, her hair loose and in her nightie, if you please. She said she'd made a will which Malcolm had torn up before she could sign it. So she'd got another will form from the stationer's and written it all out again, and she wanted us, there and then, to act as witnesses to her signature. She said she knew what she was doing and the house was going half to some people who were doing some good in society and the other half to Claire. She said that Malcolm was bound for hell and would get nothing.'

Agnes picked up the tale. 'She was acting so strangely, unsteady on her feet, slurring her words. I thought she must be drunk, though as far as I know she never used to touch the stuff. My son's wife is a practice nurse, and she said Beryl ought to see a doctor. Beryl started screaming that we were all out to get her, and the baby started crying, and . . . we didn't know what to do. Then Beryl sort of slumped down into a chair and started snoring. My daughter-in-law felt for her pulse which was a mite fast but steady enough. She woke her up long enough to make sure Beryl hadn't had a stroke or anything, and she hadn't. My son popped round next door to see if Malcolm or Claire were in. Claire was out – at the Vision, I suppose – but Malcolm had come back by that time.

'Between us we carried Beryl back home and put her to bed. Then Malcolm broke down completely. He said he'd been covering up for her for ages, that she was getting worse, that he didn't know what to do about it. She twisted everything he said, making out he wanted her dead. She'd hallucinated a couple of times, thinking he was her own father taking her to task for some childish offence. Malcolm had tried and tried to get her to go and see a doctor, but she wouldn't. He'd asked Claire to help him persuade Beryl to see someone, but Claire said the doctors didn't understand their mother's condition and she was perfectly all right as she was – though she obviously wasn't. All right, I mean. He didn't know what to do for the best. None of us did. Except we all thought she must see a doctor. Malcolm said he had an early start to work next morning, but he'd try to talk to her about it when he got home in the evening. We showed Malcolm this will form that she'd brought over for us to witness her signature and, well, we gave it to him to do what he thought best with.'

Ellie said, 'You think he destroyed it?'

Emmanuel shrugged. 'We don't know what he did with it. She didn't sign it when she was over at our house, and we didn't witness her signature, so it couldn't be valid. We thought we shouldn't interfere. There was nothing to stop her writing a will again. But, we were dead worried about her.'

Agnes said, 'I made up my mind that the very next day I'd tackle her about her health and going to the doctor, but that morning she got up early and went down to the supermarket, before I was up. She walked straight into a stand of cut flowers and dropped dead. Heart attack. Apparently, she'd had a heart condition that she hadn't known about. There was a post-mortem because she hadn't been near a doctor for a long time, but the coroner said it was heart failure, and she was cremated. The family's solicitor produced a will that Beryl had made years before, shortly after her husband died, when there'd been all that fuss about Claire saying she'd been interfered with when she hadn't. That will left Claire ten thousand pounds with the house and contents going to Malcolm.'

Ellie said, 'You didn't say anything about Beryl wanting to make a later will?'

Emmanuel shook his head. 'It seemed to us that Beryl wasn't in her right mind when she brought the will form over for us to sign. We thought we should let sleeping dogs lie. Then we heard Claire had got the sack from her job, and we felt a bit bad about that, but not much, because if she'd been giving the same medi-cation to some woman at the supermarket and arranging for her to be cursed . . . well, that wasn't right, either. So Malcolm borrowed the money to pay Claire what she was owed and told her to get out. He said he'd adapt the house to take in a couple of lodgers to make ends meet, and that's what he's done.' He stopped, looking as if he'd said too much. Or too little?

Ellie said, 'The lodgers are living there now? We tried the bell, but there was no answer.'

'No, no,' said Agnes. 'That didn't work out. He didn't really like people staying in the house when he was out, so . . . He did a beautiful job on it, too.'

Ellie tried to work it out. 'Claire took her ten thousand and moved away. The Vision had by that time moved down to Ealing, so she followed them. Ambrose arranged for her to rent one of the larger flats in the same house, and she started looking for work, but with her employment record, she couldn't find much.'

Mikey spoke up. 'What I think is, they should have done her for murder!'

THIRTEEN

Ellie said, 'What do you mean, Mikey? Claire didn't kill her mother. Granted, she ought to have queried Beryl's use of her medication, but you can't stop an adult if they want to dose themselves with something they've bought over the counter. It's up to them to decide whether to take it or not. I suppose, if the family had intervened and got her doctor to look at her . . . But unless Beryl were sectioned they couldn't stop her taking the stuff, could they?'

Mikey said, 'If Claire had been questioned about her mother's doping herself silly with medication and the supermarket had publicized the fact that she'd also harmed someone at work, she wouldn't have dared to go on and try it again, would she?'

'We don't know that the medication was the same,' said Ellie, acting the part of the devil's advocate. 'It might have been something different. Granted, Rose admitted that she hadn't known what she was doing while I was away, but that could just have been old age catching up with her.'

Emmanuel and Agnes's heads turned from one to the other, trying to make sense of what was being said.

Mikey shrugged. 'Well, all I can say is that I was pretty glad to see you back early. Rose was not sure how to get her food from her plate to her mouth. If you'd left it any longer, like, she'd have been a goner.'

Ellie winced. Had Rose really been that bad?

'And,' said Mikey, 'Claire got her to make that stupid will, remember?'

Emmanuel frowned. 'Another will? For the Vision people?'

Mikey said, 'That's right. For the same people. Rose wants to change it now she's back in her right mind. Claire tried dosing you, too, didn't she, Mrs Quicke?'

Ellie thought back. 'You mean, the day I returned, she made us some soup for supper. Rose didn't drink it, but I did, and

I ate the meal she'd prepared for Rose, too. I didn't think it was very nice, but I did sleep well that night.'

'Which was a bit odd if you'd got jet lag,' said Mikey. 'I looked it up, and you ought to have been wide awake till the next day.'

'And then,' said Ellie, remembering, 'she did give me something to drink the next day when I felt a bit odd, but I put it down to jet lag.'

'She doctored your food?' Agnes had her fingers to her mouth.

Emmanuel's face seemed to sag. 'We thought we were doing the right thing by not dragging it all out into the open—'

'And not telling anyone that Beryl had wanted to make another will while she was off her trolley?' Ellie sighed. 'Well, if she had, it would have had to be challenged in the courts, and what a fuss that would have made. If I'd been in your shoes, I expect I'd have kept quiet, too.'

Mikey bounced on his seat. 'So what happens now? Is Claire going to find another old person and poison them, too?'

Ellie shot out of her seat. 'Oh, dear lord above! Why didn't I see it? Diana told me, in words of one syllable . . . Oh, my goodness gracious me!'

Emmanuel said, 'You mean, you know of another case?'

'What do I do now? Tell Lesley, I suppose. Although it's probably far too late if the woman was cremated, though I don't know that she was. If she was buried, could they tell after so much time has passed? Wait a minute, didn't Diana say the whole thing's going to court, or is it just at the stage where the solicitors are arguing about it?'

Mikey filled Emmanuel and Agnes in. 'This "Lesley" she's talking about is a police woman, who's not bad-looking either. But she's all tied up at the moment with the case of the missing girls.'

'Missing girls?' Agnes frowned and glanced at Emmanuel. For information?

Emmanuel frowned, too. 'You mean the girl they found in the canal? What's she got to do with this?'

'Nothing, I suppose,' said Ellie distractedly, looking in her bag for her mobile phone and coming across a bunch of weeds. She stared at them. 'Now where did those come from?' Ah, milkweed. Plucked from next door's garden. She felt rather foolish. Whatever had made her put them in her handbag? 'Oh, I remember. Where's my phone? I ought to tell Lesley, oughtn't I? Or no, perhaps I'd better speak to Diana first, get some details, because if the woman was cremated, there's no point making a fuss. And, it's no good saying anything now, is it? It's all hearsay.' She held up the milkweed. 'Where can I put . . .? Do you have a bin?'

Agnes took the weeds off her and dumped them in the waste paper basket. 'They weren't from my garden, I assume.'

'No, of course not,' said Ellie. 'From next door. I really don't know why I picked them up, except that I couldn't bear to let them seed all over your beautiful garden. Who do you have to help you? I have a gardener once a week, but he's not much good.'

'A local lad. Mind, I have to stand over him. They don't teach them anything practical nowadays, do they?'

Ellie wasn't really listening. She told herself that there was no point panicking about something that was all over and done with months ago. She said, 'I should explain that some time ago Claire went to work for an elderly lady who died, leaving something to the Vision, and now there's a fuss about her will and selling her house. I'm wondering if Claire hastened her end, too.'

Mikey was on his smartphone. 'Shouldn't she be had up for manslaughter, like, if not for murder?'

Agnes leaned forward. 'Beryl said it was something for her cough. She'd got it over the counter and not from the doctor, so it can't have done her that much harm, can it?'

Mikey was frowning. 'Cough linctus can make you sleepy, can't it?'

Ellie tried to think straight. 'I can't be sure that Claire did spike my food, but Rose did say she was given a linctus for her cough, and she certainly was confused.'

Agnes nodded. 'Dizzy. Beryl was that dizzy she was staggering about all over the place.'

Mr Cook said, 'Nobody realized Beryl had a heart condition

until it was too late. They did do a post-mortem so it must be right that she had a heart condition but, as we all know, Beryl wouldn't hear of going to the doctor. So it was natural causes and not murder.'

Agnes was having nothing of that. 'If she hadn't been feeling so dizzy, she wouldn't have fallen into the flowers and had a heart attack, and she might have lived to make another will. It was the syrup that did for her.'

Mikey mouthed, 'Manslaughter,' but only Ellie noticed.

Emmanuel guffawed. 'Well, whatever it was, the medicine did for Claire's hope of inheriting.'

Agnes tapped him on the back of his hand. 'Now, then; you can't prove anything. So it's best we don't chatter about it.'

They'd discussed this many times before?

Ellie looked at her watch. Was it running fast or slow? It was a bit erratic. 'We must go. Look at the time. What I think is that we ought to ask a doctor what medication might make someone so confused that they'd walk under a car or whatever. Or, rather, the police ought to. I'll phone Diana and get all the details for Lesley when I get back.'

Mikey looked up from his iPad. 'Whose is the Wi-Fi I'm using?'

'Next door,' said Emmanuel, heaving himself to his feet. 'Malcolm uses it for his business, getting work in and invoices out, getting the bills paid. He's properly clued up, banking online, all that. Me, I like a piece of paper in my hands.'

Agnes agreed. 'My sons tried to show me, wanted to set me up with Slype or something, but I said if I hadn't got my lipstick on, I didn't want people looking at me.'

'I'm with you there,' said Ellie, 'but it's the coming thing. I suppose.'

Mikey lifted his forefinger. 'Taxi ordered. Here in half an hour.'

'Time for another cuppa?' said Agnes. 'Or would you like a turn round the garden?'

'There's nothing I'd like better than taking a turn round your garden,' said Ellie, with truth. 'There's a hydrangea you've got in the front that I'm not familiar with. Is it a lace-cap?

And your Japanese anemones . . . Where did you get the purple one?'

Mikey and Emmanuel cast their eyes to heaven. 'She'll be for ever,' said Mikey.

'My gardening days are over,' said Emmanuel. 'Now, lad; help me down the steps to the pavement, will you? I can manage it all right if I take my time, but today I've got a couple of bottles in my shopping that I don't want to drop . . .'

Going home in the cab, Ellie was quiet. Counting on her fingers.

Mikey sighed. 'What is it?' He shucked off his jacket and settled into a corner of the cab.

'I think the Vision is in trouble financially. The operation they run must eat money, and Ambrose has an expensive life-style judging by his clothes and his car. I'm trying to work out what happened and when. For instance, how long ago did Beryl start going to the Vision and when did she start taking Claire? Who was it who suggested Beryl take the medication that affected her so badly? Did Claire think of it, or was Beryl introduced to it by someone at the Vision?'

Mikey yawned widely. Had he been up all night, watching television? Well, that was no business of hers.

Ellie worried away at the problem. Claire didn't take the medication herself. No, she wasn't exhibiting any of the symptoms. If anything, she was on the nervous side of the spectrum. But, Claire had seen what the linctus had done to her mother, had fed it to Rose and probably also to Ellie.

Had she also fed it to the elderly lady she'd been working for, before she took the job of looking after Diana's lively toddler?

The Vision had occupied a large house in North London before they moved to Ealing. At that time they were already taking in waifs and strays, presumably recommended by . . . who? Local doctors? Hospitals? Social Services? Ambrose must be paid a whack for looking after them. Or, if they were unable to work and were on benefits, they must be getting some kind of living allowance. Dolores had said they were supposed to pass their benefit cheques on to Ambrose, but in the same breath admitted that some might have difficulty in doing so.

Ellie had heard that Ambrose attracted a good crowd to his services. This must bring him in some sort of income, but would it be enough to cover the rent of a big house, feed all those dependants and subsidize his lifestyle? Um, probably not. The rent of even half of such a big house in that part of London would be astronomical.

Ellie decided she really didn't know enough about how such places were run.

Back to when Beryl started to attend the Vision services. Ambrose was living in another rented house nearby, working his magic on a group of addicts and milking his fans for funds. Along comes the widowed Beryl and her unappetizing daughter Claire. Beryl falls under his spell and so does Claire, the ugly duckling who will never become a swan. Claire is earning good money, and presumably much of that finds its way into Ambrose's hands.

Ambrose notes that the two women are living in a pricey semi-detached house. Pound signs ring up in his eyes. Ambrose counts his chickens before they're hatched and looks forward to getting his hands on Beryl and Claire's house.

He moves his operation to another, even bigger house in Ealing. Why? Perhaps the previous house was on a short lease? In this new place he finds himself with lots of room for his dependent addicts and a spacious flat all to himself.

Query: 'all to himself', as there might be a Mrs around? Dolores had said Ambrose was celibate, but Ellie wasn't sure about that. For instance, where did he go on Friday afternoons, that he couldn't be contacted?

Back to the present. He's ensconced in his nice new house. What are the drawbacks? Well, for one thing, a big old house like that would need a lot of maintenance, and there were all those mouths to feed. It must be like running a hotel; food and cleaning and linen and general wear and tear. Also, the new house came with some sitting tenants who would be paying rent to the council, and not to him.

On the other hand, some of the original tenants were elderly and not likely to cause any trouble. Others seemed to be there for a while and then move on, like Gail and her mother. Ambrose must have regarded them as an opportunity, rather than a problem, as Dolores had said he did try to convert them to his cause.

On the plus side, with plenty of rooms to spare, Social Services – or whoever – could be invited to send him more clients.

Ellie wondered who she might know in Social Services who could give her the low-down on Ambrose's occupation of this new house. Perhaps she should ask Lesley?

Back to the present; if Ambrose was being backed by Social Security, he should by now be coining it with a bit over for his personal kitty, but it was possible that his eyes had been bigger than his stomach, that he hadn't done his sums and was only just making ends meet.

He'd have been thinking that when he got Beryl and Claire's house, he'd be in clover. Only, when Beryl pops her clogs the house doesn't fall into Ambrose's hands. What's more, Claire loses her job at the supermarket, so can't contribute any more to his coffers. What a setback!

So, what next? Claire was still under his spell. With the money she'd got out of Malcolm she bought a car, rented a decent flat in the Vision's new house and took a job at the school while waiting for something better to come along.

Then, oh dear! Claire lost her temper and her job in quick succession.

Ellie sighed. Why hadn't Ambrose realized that keeping Claire around was like handling a double-edged sword?

Yes, she could earn money to give him, but her methods of earning her living were not exactly squeaky clean.

Still, even after the court case, Ambrose persevered with Claire. He paid her fine, which got her off the hook in one way but was an entry on the wrong side of the red line in his accounts. How did he plan to recoup this loss? Well, he forced her to sell her car, and he moved her into spartan accommodation in the annexe. He told her to find another job. She did just that, looking after an old lady who, under the influence of some linctus or other – that's not proven, but it seemed likely – departed this life leaving a will in Ambrose's favour which this time had been properly signed and witnessed.

Only, according to Diana, the family intervened, and the sale of the house was stopped.

Then came the threat of the new house being sold over Ambrose's head. A house could be sold if there were existing tenants, but the price would be low . . . Unless it depended on what sort of lease the tenants might have? The people put into the house by Social Services might be on monthly contracts and could easily be shifted elsewhere, but what about the old couple who'd been there for ever? It would cost something to get them to move, but it could be done. Likewise, Ambrose and his lot could be given notice to quit.

The site would then be clear for redevelopment.

Ellie wondered if Ambrose had ever tried to get a mortgage. Given his clientele, would anybody give him one? Probably not.

Could he get Social Services to buy another property for him? No, they wouldn't have several million to spare, and it was probably in their best interests to sell to a developer and pocket the cash.

A clinging chorus of sycophants at his services might be good for Ambrose's ego and bring in enough to pay the bills if he lived modestly, but would not be enough to purchase a large house in a good part of Ealing, where prices had gone through the roof.

Back to Claire, out of a job when the old woman died. Claire then went to work for Diana, who must have seemed at first sight to be an easy touch . . . until she got to know her employer and realized that prizing Diana off her money bags was next to impossible. Anyway, little Evan was far too much for Claire to cope with.

So, on to Rose. Ah, dear sweet Rose, who thought the best of everyone, and who had a pleasant little nest egg that would do nicely . . . until it was apparent that Rose's estate was peanuts compared to the money in Ellie's trust fund. And, just look! Ellie lived in such a nice, big house. Why, the Vision could almost fit into it . . . Or would it do for a second project?

Ellie sighed. She thought she'd worked out what had happened, more or less, but there were a lot of things she needed to check.

She poked Mikey, who had fallen asleep. 'What have you been up to? Were you up late, watching the telly?'

He stirred, but did not wake.

Oh, the delights of being able to drop off to sleep, just like that. In the middle of the afternoon, too.

Mikey was still asleep when they drew up outside his home, another big old house – though not as big as Ellie's, or as that which the Vision currently occupied. Dan was rescuing it from years of neglect, and there was still some scaffolding up. Ellie asked the driver to toot his horn. Fortunately, Dan was at home and came out to see what the matter was.

Ellie indicated the sleeping boy. 'Too big for me to carry, and too deeply asleep for me to rouse.'

Dan shook his head, smiling. 'I'm so proud of the lad. He plays chess at night with some grandmaster in the States over the Internet. We allow him to do it at the weekends, provided he's done his homework and some household chores. Thanks for bringing him back. Is his bike at your place? If so, I'll get him to come round for it tomorrow. Are you coming in? Vera should be back in a minute.' He lifted Mikey out of the cab and carried him inside the house.

'No, I can't stay.' Ellie told the cab driver to wait while she collected Mikey's satchel and jacket and followed Dan into the house. He laid Mikey out on the settee in the comfortable, not-too-tidy living room, while Ellie dumped his things in the hall.

She said, 'Will you tell Vera I've found someone to live in for a bit? Nice girl. Trainee chef.'

'Tell me what?' said Vera, who that very minute came through the front door. 'Hi, Ellie. I've finished for the weekend. Want a cuppa? By the way, it was on the news last night about another local girl going missing, and I asked Dan if he knew her. Guess what! He does.'

'Really? I'm all ears.'

Dan shook his head. 'She left us a year ago, so I really don't . . .'

Vera put her arm around him and kissed his ear. 'It may be important. Tell her.'

'Oh well . . . At the end of the summer term last year this girl was found after hours in the gym, with a queue of boys waiting their turn. She'd set it up. She wasn't being pressured into giving sex. Far from it. She boasted that she'd had every member of the football team, and that checked out, too. She was just turned sixteen, which is the age of consent for sex, and she certainly had consented! So we informed Social Services and suggested the girl transferred to an all-girls school. Which I believe she did.'

Oh. So the girl really was trailer trash. Ellie hesitated. 'Would the police have been informed about this? She might have cleaned up her act since then. I wouldn't want to blacken her name unnecessarily.'

'I doubt if the police would have been told unless they checked with Social Services, who have a limited number of options in cases like this. They might have taken her into care, but they don't like to do that unless the home circumstances are pretty dire, which in this case I don't think they were. If she had been victimized . . .? But she wasn't. Rather the reverse. It sounds as if they left her at home, put her into a different school and kept an eye on her. How much time she spent in her new school and how often she truanted, I can't say. At seventeen she could legally leave school. She must be nearly that now.'

Ellie sighed. 'These young ones think sex is the answer to everything. I'll pass the tip on. I'm sorry, Vera, I can't stop today. Thomas is due back tomorrow, but we'll catch up soon, all right?'

Ellie got back into the cab and directed him to Diana's house, trying to switch her mind back to Claire and away from a girl who might be no better than she should be, but who didn't deserve to be kidnapped and held captive. How terrifying that must be. Oh, the poor thing . . .

Another big, imposing house. Well, it suited Diana, who'd married a much older man. It was his fourth and her second marriage. It might last. With luck. Anyway, her grandson, little Evan, was a total delight when he wasn't wrecking everything in sight.

Ellie told the driver not to wait and rang the doorbell. Ellie could see the top of Diana's husband's head through the window in the snug. He was watching the sports channel. He might or might not have heard the bell, but he wouldn't answer the door. In fact, he was probably having a nap.

Diana came to the door with Evan on her hip. Evan adored his mother, and the feeling, much to everyone's surprise, was reciprocated. Diana did not normally 'do' lovey-dovey. With the exception of Evan, Diana did not believe in wasting energy on anyone who couldn't do something for her in return.

In Diana's world, Ellie was judged to be useful. Ellie had babysat when Evan had been tiny, and she controlled all that lovely money through her trust, so must be accorded the minimum of respect. Most of the time, anyway.

Typically, Diana's opening words were not an invitation to come in and have a cup of tea but, 'What do you want?'

Ellie held back a sigh and stepped inside. 'Yes, I'm very well, thank you. Expecting Thomas back tomorrow. I won't take up much of your time, but your ex-nanny, Claire, has asked me for help, which I am not at all sure I want to give. I've been trying to trace her career. You told me you'd been asked to sell the house of an elderly lady who'd been looked after by Claire, and to whom she left an inheritance. Could you remember the woman's name, by any chance?'

'I'm all at sixes and sevens today.' Diana shut the front door with some force, put Evan on the floor and set off down the passage, saying, 'Hold on a minute. I've just put something on the stove. Give me one good reason why I should help Claire. After what that dreadful man said . . .'

She went on talking as she disappeared, but Evan clamped his arms around Ellie's leg and grinned up at her. She melted into a smile and said, 'Let go, there's a love.'

'No!'

Ellie knew that the first word most babies master is: 'No!' Perhaps Evan had been no earlier than others to say it, but he certainly knew what it meant. And used it. She tried to pry his fingers away. Result: another 'No!' Louder than the first.

'Evan, darling, let Granny go.' As if! It was never any good trying reason. She knew that. She tried to move, and he clung on. He was too heavy for her to carry.

Diana called out something.

Ellie lifted her voice in reply. 'I can't hear you. Evan's holding me prisoner.'

'What?' Diana appeared in the doorway to the kitchen.

'Evan.' Ellie gestured downwards. 'Where's his nanny?'

Diana disappeared again. 'Nanny's got a headache. My darling husband won't lift a finger, and . . .'

With some difficulty Ellie heaved Evan off the floor and into her arms.

'NO!' He beat at her arms with his fists. She stumbled to the stairs and managed to sit down before he had her tumbling to the floor. Diana was still talking, but Ellie couldn't make out what she was saying.

Evan, however, was now all smiles, sitting on her lap and tugging at the handbag she wore over one shoulder. 'Ganny, Ganny, Ganny . . .' Looking for sweets. The little love couldn't say his 'r's properly yet. She made sure the clasp on her bag was firmly closed. He started chewing on the strap. Poor boy; another tooth coming? Teeth were a bother, coming and going, weren't they?

Diana reappeared with a piece of paper in her hands. '. . . so I have to see to everything. I had to take Evan into work with me this morning, can you believe? He loved the swinging door, the darling boy! Until he got his fingers trapped in it. I'm going to sack that girl, next week. She ought never to have let him play with the filing cabinet. Papers, everywhere! I told her she must stay on to get things straight, and she had the nerve to say—'

Ellie held out her hand for the paper. 'Is that the name of the woman Claire was working for? You did say the will's being contested?'

'And it looks as if we've lost the sale. Yes, that's her name and address.' Diana thrust the piece of paper at her mother and scooped Evan up into her arms, separating him from the strap of Ellie's bag with some difficulty. 'Don't do that, darling. You don't know where it's been.'

Evan roared his disapproval, but she kept a firm hold of

him and he didn't try beating her up. Perhaps he knew she was stronger than him. So far, anyway.

Once freed, Ellie hoisted herself to her feet and said she must be going. She didn't think it likely that Diana would offer her a cuppa, and she didn't. Only, Diana wasn't finished yet.

'That man, the one who was so rude to me. Mad as a hatter, but he's no right to go round upsetting people like that. I'm thinking of complaining to the police.'

Ellie was interested. 'On what grounds?'

A shrug. 'Assault? Harassment? I mean –' teeth were bared in what was meant to be a smile – 'no one could take that rubbish about a curse seriously.'

Ellie knew it was naughty of her, but she couldn't resist. 'I've heard tell of a woman he cursed a while back, who's off sick. Permanently.'

Diana forced a laugh, but her eyes were wide. 'How absurd! As if one could be affected by a few words!'

'Indeed,' said Ellie, 'but I suppose if you have a bad conscience, it might get to you.'

Another laugh, a trifle on the wild side. 'As if!'

Ellie repented her mischievous words. 'Don't you let it worry you. I'm on the case.'

Diana didn't seem reassured.

On the way home, Ellie called in at the chemist in the Avenue. It was getting to the end of the day and there weren't many people out and about. Luckily, the pharmacist was able to drop what he was doing and have a quiet word with her in the consulting room at the back. He was a fine-looking youngish man of Asian origin, always courteous.

As soon as they were seated, she told herself she was over-reacting and shouldn't be wasting his time. But there he was and there she was, so she might as well go through with it.

'I'm really sorry to bother you, and it's probably nothing. The police haven't been involved, and the coroner said it was a heart attack, but . . .'

Not a good start. He was polite and waited for her to sort herself out. She tried again. 'Someone I know is suspected of

having given her employer some medicine which may have
hastened her death. It seems a bit far-fetched to me that an
over-the-counter medicine could produce disorientation,
sleepiness and even death . . . Do you know of any such?'

FOURTEEN

'Yes, of course,' said the pharmacist. 'If too many doses of certain types of cough linctus are taken, there will be the side effects you have described.'

Ellie rocked back in her chair. 'You mean ordinary, over-the-counter cough medicines? Really?'

'If misused, yes. Sleepiness, some disorientation, even hallucinations have been recorded. And, if there is a history of heart problems . . .?'

'Oh, yes. There was.' There goes Beryl, glugging down the linctus, with a heart problem rumbling away in the background. Exit Beryl. 'You said there might even be hallucinations?' Hadn't Beryl thought Malcolm was his father at one point?

'It's on record, yes. You really must read the accompanying leaflet when you buy an over-the-counter medicine.'

'Oh, it's not for me. At least, I might have been given a couple of doses, but . . . How much would you have to take for it to affect you?'

'The normal dose would be one spoonful, up to four times a day.'

'So, if you took twice that . . .?'

'You'd probably drop off to sleep. Some addicts misuse it.'

'It shortens their lives?'

He nodded. 'I'll write the name of the top-selling brand of linctus down for you.' Which he did.

She blinked. 'I've taken that myself when I had a cough some years ago. It wasn't expensive, was it? I can't remember how much it was.'

A shrug. 'A couple of pounds for a small bottle. A large bottle would be under three.'

Her mouth fell open. 'You can kill with something bought over the counter for as little as three pounds?'

'Not in one go, no. Everybody's different, but if you overdo it every day, you will become increasingly addicted and there will be side effects of greater or lesser severity.'

'If you stop, you're all right?'

He smiled and nodded. 'Provided you haven't got a heart condition. If you had, then a lesser amount might kill you.'

'Is there anything else that could produce the same symptoms?'

'Not really. There's sleeping tablets and paracetamol, of course, but people know about the risks there. The thing is, if you want to kill yourself, there's plenty of quicker ways of doing it.'

'Agreed,' said Ellie, getting to her feet, 'but if you want to disorientate someone and you don't want them to know you're doing it, then this linctus fits the bill?'

'Correct. Er, you suspect someone may be misusing the product?'

'Someone who died. Heart disease. I'm wondering if the linctus might have hastened her end.'

A shrug. 'If she read the instructions and continued to take the linctus, there's nothing to be done.'

'I realize that. But I might mention it to the police, to be on the safe side.'

He nodded and went back to measuring out his pills and potions.

Home at last. It had been a long day.

She shed her coat and bag, noting the strap was discoloured where little Evan had chewed on it, bless his heart.

The house felt warm, and the door to the kitchen quarters had been propped open, in case Rose needed to summon help. The grandfather clock ticked away, the conservatory at the back of the house was full of colour and there was a fresh vase of flowers on the chest in the hall.

All was right with the world. Tomorrow Thomas would be back and they could all relax. Well, except for telling Ambrose and Claire to go and take a jump . . . and for telling Lesley what she'd learned about this and that. Ellie decided to phone the police after she'd checked on Rose and Susan.

In the kitchen, the radio was playing softly. Susan, solid

and comfortable, was putting the finishing touches to a pie. She smiled at Ellie and indicated with her elbow that Rose was asleep in her big chair.

Dear Rose. She looked smaller every day. Ellie cleared a lump in her throat and nodded when Susan indicated the kettle. Yes, she'd love a cup. Thanks.

'I'll bring it in to you in the sitting room,' said Susan.

Ellie relaxed in her big chair, and soon enough Susan came in, placing a cup of tea on a little mat on the table at Ellie's side.

Ellie dried her eyes. 'You see, Rose doesn't want a fuss. She doesn't want me to call the doctor, and indeed there's not much they can do for her now. She'd like to stay here until . . . until. I realize you might not want to—'

'She's a darling. She reminds me of my gran. I'll stay.'

'Thank you.' Ellie realized that Susan had brought the tea in to her because she had something to say.

Susan said, 'Your solicitor came while you were out. He had a clerk with him, carrying a laptop and a printer and I don't know what. Rose wanted me to give him some special cake or other, but he said it didn't matter.'

'He likes Rose's Victoria sponge, but he'll have realized that she can't . . .' Ellie blew her nose. 'It's a Saturday. Gunnar doesn't usually work at weekends, so that was good of him.'

'He left this envelope for you.' Susan handed it over and continued, 'He said he was glad he'd come, as Rose told him she doesn't think she's got much time left.'

'No, I don't suppose she has. Was she able to sign her will there and then?'

'Yes. His clerk and I witnessed her signature. Then she dropped off to sleep again.'

'Thank you, Susan. I'm so pleased you could be here. I shouldn't have gone out, really, but—'

'She said you were out doing good, that that was what you were supposed to be doing, and I was not under any circumstances to call you back. She said what an interesting life she'd led, and that everything good had come to her through you or your aunt before you. She said I was to look after you when . . .'

Ellie reached a hand out. Susan took it and held it fast. It was most comforting.

Ellie said, 'Thank you, Susan. I'll be all right, you know. I'm crying for myself and not for her.'

Susan said, 'Rose fancied an apple pie for supper. She says you always like her apple pies, and that Thomas will like it, too. I hope you like flaky pastry. I'm doing a big lamb stew with veg for starters.'

'That sounds good, but Thomas is not due back till tomorrow.'

'Oh? Rose said . . . Well, it's no wonder if she got the dates wrong.'

Ellie nodded. 'I must make some phone calls. You'll call me if she wants anything? Or if she rings her little bell?'

Susan withdrew, and Ellie opened the envelope which Gunnar had left for her. The note inside read:

> *My dear Ellie,*
> *I am angry when I think how that woman bamboozled Rose into signing a will in her favour. I hope you track her down and deal with her. Let me know if you need any help.*
> *Gunnar*

Ellie nodded to herself. Gunnar would indeed be a powerful ally if she needed help in this matter. Which, she reflected, she might well do.

She sat down to make some notes.

Claire's background, her mother's death and the disappointment over the house.

Her subsequent career. Short temper. Death of elderly lady to be queried?

Then on to the vexed question of Ambrose and the Vision.

How much do the police know about him?

Has he ever been in trouble?

What is his tie-in with Social Services?

Is bullying a crime?

No, bullying was probably not a crime. She didn't think he'd actually broken any of the laws of the land, unless there was some law – probably an archaic one – which said he was responsible for the health and well-being of his 'clients'? Lesley could check on the actual wording. Or would it come under 'human rights'? Almost everything seemed to come under that heading nowadays.

Next: the affair of Karen. Or, if you preferred it, Karen's affairs.

Did Social Services know of Karen's spotty past?

Were they still keeping an eye on her?

Possibly not if she was now about to turn seventeen.

Did this new information about the girl make any difference to the hunt for her?

The phone rang, and it was Lesley.

'Sorry about that. All systems go. Karen's mother phoned to say the girl had rung her, saying she was safe and well and having the time of her life with a new boyfriend. Apparently, they're off to Ireland for a holiday. Karen says she was bored with school, and she'll be seventeen next week, so that's that.'

'Really? I suppose I shouldn't be surprised, but I am.'

'The mother told Karen we'd all been going bananas looking for her, and that Karen must ring the police and apologize. Between you and me, I think the mother's relieved to have got rid of such a troublesome daughter, what with being a single parent and having a disabled son to look after as well.'

'Did Karen ring the police too?'

'She did. We checked where she was phoning from. She used a pay as you go phone, and it was moving around. In her boyfriend's car, we think. On the M25, some distance away. She thought it hilarious that we'd been looking for her. She says she's not going home to Mum, but promised to keep in touch with her now and then. That was it. End of.'

Ellie said, 'Oh well. I had heard she was a right little raver, into sex at the drop of a hat. She was brought to the attention of Social Services a while ago, but I suppose they decided not to take her into care because, well, the damage was done, and it wasn't the home environment that was exposing her to trouble. Did you know about it?'

'Only after she disappeared. It seems clear that the cases

of the other two girls are not connected with Karen. The police will carry on working on the others, but Karen cocks a snook and walks.'

'It definitely was her on the phone? She wasn't under duress?'

'Believe me, we'd know the difference. She wasn't hysterical, or frightened, or even pretending to be sorry she'd caused us all so much bother. As and when she turns up, we might give her a dressing-down for wasting police time, but I don't count on it.'

'Understood. I suppose it's a relief to know she's safe and well.'

A pause. 'Is Susan working out all right?'

'She's wonderful. Thank you. By the way, if you're still interested, I've learned a bit more about Claire.'

'Nothing that needs attention urgently?'

'No. It's all rather sad, really. A difficult personality, doing a lot of damage through spite and through being in thrall to Pastor Ambrose. Now he really could do with a cold eye being cast over the way he works, though I don't suppose you'll find anything criminal. What they both need is a good talking to.'

'I'll drop in on Monday, maybe. I'm exhausted.'

'Pamper yourself for a change.'

Lesley killed the call. At which point Ellie became aware of a commotion in the hall, of a deep man's voice greeting Rose, and a well-known laugh.

She flew out into the hall, half-laughing, half-crying . . .

. . . and was caught up in a bear hug and lifted off her feet.

'Thomas! You weren't due back till—'

'I thought you might be needing me.'

'Oh, Thomas! Always!'

'I missed you!'

'I missed you, too!'

Rose was there, clapping her hands. 'There. I told you he'd be back today.'

'So you did,' said Ellie, mopping tears again. 'Oh, Thomas, am I glad to see you!'

Sunday morning

Ellie woke, smiling to herself.

She was beautifully warm, with Thomas lying at her back. He might have come to bed late – well, jet lag had afflicted him, too – but her world had righted itself now that he had returned. A mountain of work would await him when he got into his study, but now she could always trot along to have a word with him about whatever it was that was bothering her, instead of having to wait till the evening for a phone call, and then worry about what she could say to him that wouldn't cause him to abandon his conference and get him on the next plane home.

He said he was pleased with the way things had worked out at the conference. He'd had opportunities to rub up against other bright minds. He was a modest man, but Ellie could tell from this and that, and things left unsaid, that his attendance had been appreciated, and that yet more opportunities were opening up for him to influence official thinking in future. Altogether, it had been a good thing that he'd gone.

She eased herself out of bed and made for the bathroom. Thomas didn't stir. He said he'd slept for a while in the plane, but had spent most of the time praying. He'd decided to take an earlier plane because he'd been worried about her. It was a good feeling to know that he'd been worried about her and had done something about it.

He hadn't moved by the time she went down for breakfast. Rose wasn't up yet, but Susan was standing in the garden, looking around her. There'd been a shower in the night, and everything looked and smelled fresh.

Susan lifted her arms wide. 'This is so beautiful. I grew up in a flat. No garden. I had a window-box once, but the cat from across the road used it as a dirt tray.'

Prompt on cue, Midge scrambled down from a nearby laburnum tree. Ellie and Susan both laughed. Midge ignored Ellie to make a beeline for Susan's legs and wound around them. *I like you. I'm going to love-bomb you so that you will admire and appreciate me. Feed me. Now!*

Ellie said, 'He's supposed to be a good judge of character.'

Susan picked Midge up and rubbed his head. 'We couldn't have a cat, either, in our block of flats.'

Ellie saw that Midge was, incredibly, tolerating Susan's advances, and that the girl was on the verge of tears. 'You have no home of your own?'

A sniff. 'Dad's dead, and Mum's going through the menopause. She's into yoga and health supplements. She hates it that I'm into catering. Aunt Lesley's been good to me, putting me up recently, but I can see it's not convenient. I've been getting by, sharing with friends during term time, but I like my own space. One day, when I'm through with college, I'll earn enough to get a place of my own.'

'My dear, you can stay here as long as you like. That is, if you'd like to?'

Susan looked back and up at the big house. 'The space . . . The peace and quiet . . . A bathroom to myself! I'd love to stay.' She put Midge down and made for the house. 'Would Thomas like a full English breakfast?'

Ellie pulled up a couple of weeds from a patch of cosmos and followed her in. Thomas had insisted on hearing all about Claire and Ambrose the previous night, and in telling him, her mind had cleared and she'd realized what needed to be done.

Firstly, Ambrose was keeping his clients in conditions that amounted to slavery, so something must be done about that. Cue the entry of Social Services?

Secondly, Claire had contributed to the death of the elderly woman she'd been working for. If she hadn't actually been guilty of murder, she had certainly committed manslaughter. If the victim had been cremated it might not be possible to prove this, but a stern warning ought to be given to Claire so that she didn't try it again. Cue the police.

As for the murdered girls; there was nothing to link Claire with the first one. Nothing at all. Yes, Claire had had a spat with the second victim, whose mobile phone had been found in Claire's car, but the girl might well have dropped it when given a lift home. There'd been no forensic, nothing else to indicate that Claire had any connection with the girl. What's more, when Claire had said she had not killed Gail, Ellie had believed her.

So there was no need for Ellie to do anything about either of the murdered girls, was there?

Sundays were usually a busy time for Thomas who, though he no longer had a parish, was frequently asked to fill in for a neighbouring clergyman who might be ill or on holiday. So today, it was a treat to have him home for a leisurely breakfast and then to give him a cup of real coffee to enjoy while he read the newspapers. Ellie smiled to herself as he discarded different sections of *The Times*, dropping them on the floor around his chair. Yes, it was good to have him back. And, it was predictable that as soon as he had got through the papers, he went off to spend time in his Quiet Room.

Ellie unpacked his cases, rescued the presents she'd bought and placed in his luggage for him to bring back, and started the washing machine. Susan began to prepare a roast dinner, while Rose sat in her big chair, humming along to a programme on the radio. Midge took up a position on the top of the fridge so that he could monitor everything that happened.

The phone rang. It was Vera. 'Hi there. I think Mikey left his bicycle with you yesterday, didn't he? Did he leave his phone as well? He can't find it anywhere.'

Ellie thought back. 'He used it to call a cab when we were ready to come back from Perivale. I'm not sure I saw it after that. I'll try the cab company, see if he left it on his seat, but I'm pretty sure he didn't. I'll ring you back, shall I?'

She tried the cab company. No, they hadn't had a smartphone handed in. In any case, Ellie was pretty sure she'd collected everything of Mikey's from the cab when they'd got to his place. She looked up Emmanuel's phone number, because she knew his surname, Cook, while Agnes's hadn't been mentioned. Mr Cook gave her Agnes's number, and yes, Agnes had found the smartphone when she'd been plumping up the cushions that morning.

Should Mikey ride his bike over there to collect it? Um. No. There was some very heavy traffic on those roads, and it was quite a way. Ellie phoned Vera and said the phone had been found, and where. Vera agreed Mikey shouldn't try to ride over there. She said she would have gone to fetch it herself, but Dan had arranged for them to visit some friends in the country that afternoon. Mikey would have to do without it until someone could get over to retrieve it. It served him right, said Vera, for having been so careless.

Ellie hesitated. 'I might be going back there myself some time to have a word with Claire's brother. If I do, I'll let you know, shall I?'

Vera welcomed the suggestion with enthusiasm, but as soon as Ellie had put the phone down, she wondered what on earth had made her offer. Young Mikey ought to be told to go over there by tube and bus. It would take him half a day and might reinforce the idea that he should take more care of his belongings.

What did she want with Malcolm, anyway? She knew already what sort of linctus his mother had been throwing down her throat, and he couldn't confirm or deny what Claire had been up to since he threw her out. No, let sleeping dogs lie.

The doorbell rang again. Tentatively. So, it wasn't Diana, it wasn't Mikey and it wasn't Ambrose. Ellie looked down the passage, but Thomas had not yet emerged from his Quiet Room. He might even have dozed off there. Jet lag must be allowed to run its course.

It was Claire, with a painful smile on her face. Fidgeting. 'May I come in for a moment? I won't be long. Promise.'

Ellie's first reaction was to slam the door in Claire's face. She even started to do so, and then stopped. If what she suspected was true, then Claire had been going around dosing those nearest to her with linctus without anyone daring to say, 'Stop, thief!' Well, not *thief*, but *murderer* wasn't the right word, either. Or was it? If there were any evidence . . . but there wasn't, unless Claire's elderly victim had been buried and not cremated? Was this a chance for Ellie to find out what had happened?

Ellie dithered for a moment, then ushered Claire in. 'Come in and sit down.' Ellie led the way to the sitting room.

'Oh,' said Claire, looking around her. 'You've put the furniture back where it used to be, and you really shouldn't allow flowers in the house. They're all God's creatures, you know, and it's not right to cut their lives short.'

Ellie sighed. Claire did have the most unfortunate habit of

rubbing people up the wrong way, didn't she? 'Each to his own. What you do in your own place is up to you, and what I do is mine. You wanted to see me?'

Claire leaned forward in her chair, clasping her hands between her knees. 'You promised to help me, and I want to tell you how grateful I am that you, who have so much, should take the time and trouble to do so. I realize you are struggling against the bonds of Mammon to reach up to the Vision of heaven, but—'

'Yes, let's take that bit for granted,' said Ellie. 'What did you really come for?'

'Why, I . . .' Again, she produced a grimace which was intended to be a smile. 'I wanted to invite you to join us for our service this evening. How can you judge of our sincerity, our striving for perfection, unless—'

'My husband has returned from America and is at this moment spending time with God. Would you like to join him in his Quiet Room?'

The woman reared back. 'What? No! Never! How could you suggest such a thing? I could not possibly, not ever, allow myself to be contaminated by—'

'That's enough,' said Ellie. 'More than enough. Let's change the subject. You worked for an elderly lady before you went to my daughter, right? I have her name and address here.' She held up the details she'd got from Diana.

Eyelids flickered. 'Yes, a woman with a beautiful soul, reaching towards the light . . .'

Oh, yeah!

'. . . now resting in the arms of the Vision!'

'Was she cremated or buried?'

Claire sat back in her chair. Another painful smile. 'She was cremated at her own wish.'

Ellie sighed. Oh well, that answered the question, didn't it? Next: someone had to frighten Claire into behaving herself in future, and it looked as if Ellie had been elected to do the dirty work. 'You killed her, didn't you?'

FIFTEEN

'What! How dare you!' Claire didn't appear surprised by Ellie's question. It certainly didn't distress her. She was very confident that she had nothing to worry about, wasn't she? Perhaps she was right to be confident. If her employer had been cremated, there was no evidence that Claire had ever done anything wrong.

Ellie said, 'You tried it on Rose, too; didn't you?'

A toss of the head. Another self-conscious smile. 'Tried what?'

'Linctus. Overdoses mean disorientation, sleepiness, even hallucinations.'

'What rubbish.' An even broader smile. 'You are not well. Have you yourself been taking some medication? It sounds as if you have. I am sure that you will feel better once you have admitted that you are partaking of the poisons in a modern diet. You drank coffee and tea this morning, I assume?'

'I think you should know that my solicitor called on Rose yesterday. She has made a new will. It was signed and witnessed there and then.'

Claire didn't like that. She passed her tongue over her lips. 'There was undue influence, no doubt. You stood over her while she signed.'

'I was out for the day. I didn't hear about it until later. You can tear up the earlier will you asked her to sign. It is no longer valid.'

'You have persuaded her—'

'Not so. What's more, you should know that I myself made a will some time ago which leaves everything to my husband and to a charitable trust. Even if you sedated me until I didn't know what I was doing and got me to sign another will, the trustees would fight whatever you produced, and I don't think Ambrose has enough money to take it through the courts, has he?'

That had been a shot in the dark, but it appeared to strike home. Claire's eyes lost intensity, wavered and sank.

'Claire, I believe you are more foolish than evil. You are your own worst enemy. Your temper lets you down, and you take short cuts. We won't call it murder, but I believe you contributed to the death of the elderly woman you once worked for, and I'm going to make sure that the police start a file on you. Yes, it's all suspicion. I realize that. But if for instance it ever crossed your mind to misuse linctus in that way again, then you should remember that in such circumstances the police would look very hard in your direction. Next time you might not be lucky enough to get your victim cremated.'

'How could you say such a thing!' Tears flowed. 'I've never been so insulted—'

'Yes, yes. Now, you'd better go.'

'Hello?' Thomas opened the door and stood there, clearly unsure whether their visitor was going or staying.

Ellie said, 'This is Claire. She's just leaving.'

Claire used her handkerchief to good effect, appealing to Thomas. 'I'm so upset! Your wife has—'

Thomas said gently, 'She's told me about you, yes. I'll see you out, shall I?'

A moment later Ellie heard the front door open and close. Thomas came back into the room and put his arm round Ellie.

Ellie said, 'You saw what she was like?'

A nod. 'A weak brew, with a dash of bitters. She's dangerous and not as helpless as she would like to seem. Watch your back, my love.'

The phone rang. It was Mikey. Well, it would be, wouldn't it? 'Mum said you might be going back to Agnes's to fetch my phone?'

Ellie tried to be severe. 'It serves you right if I don't. You are careless, Mikey.'

'But you will?' Wheedling.

She tried not to laugh. He had got her where he wanted her, the young rapscallion.

'I might, but I don't promise to get it back today, understand?'

'Cross my heart, I'll never let it out of my hands again.'

'Promises, promises. Mikey, did you notice anything in particular about our conversation with Agnes and Emmanuel?' She wondered why she was asking this of a young boy . . . but Mikey wasn't your usual teenager, was he?

'I don't think so.'

She reflected that there had been something, but . . . Ah, she had it. Agnes and Emmanuel had talked a blue streak about Claire and Beryl, but hadn't seemed bothered about the missing girls. Now, why was that? Oh, it probably meant nothing. It was only natural that the old people were more interested in their own family problems than in the lives of some girls they'd never met.

'Mrs Quicke, if you're going over there this afternoon, like, may I come, too?'

'No, you can't. You're going out with your parents.'

'Dan's not my father.' A sulky voice.

'Say that to his face and you'll get an earful. He's a better father than your birth parent.'

A sigh. 'Yes. I know.' He put the phone down.

Thomas said, 'Are you going out again, my love? Do you want me for anything?'

Which meant that Sunday or not, Thomas was itching to see what had landed up on his computer while he'd been away. So she might as well track down Mikey's smartphone.

Sunday afternoon

A grey afternoon. Ellie phoned Agnes again to ask if it would be convenient for her to come over to fetch Mikey's smartphone.

'Why not? Emmanuel said he might pop round, too.'

Ellie put the phone down, wondering how often Mr Cook 'popped' round to see Agnes. Was there a hint of a romantic involvement there? Possibly. But there had been a certain sharpness in Agnes's tone when Ellie had suggested making a second visit in two days, which reinforced her feeling that those two nice people hadn't been entirely open with her before. Did they really know something about the vanished girls? Or was she imagining things?

Once Ellie would have dashed out of the house without leaving a note as to where she might be going, but Thomas had taught her the wisdom of taking safety precautions. As if she needed safety precautions when dealing with the likes of Agnes and Emmanuel!

Nevertheless, she went down the passage to Thomas's study, where . . . Yes, he was on his computer . . . She managed to catch his attention long enough to indicate that she was writing a note to tell him where she was going to be.

As she got out of the minicab, the driver asked if he should wait for her.

Ellie dithered. If this interview were only about collecting Mikey's smartphone she'd have said 'yes'. But it was more than that . . . or was she misreading the signs? Agnes would offer another cup of tea. Ellie thought she might well accept, and that in turn might lead on to further confidences.

'No, don't wait. I'll ring when I'm ready to be collected.'

The front door opened as Ellie climbed the steep path, and there was Agnes, brightly lipsticked, wearing high heeled sandals, a formal blouse and skirt. Smiling.

What big teeth you have, grandma.

'Lucky you rang. I found his smartphone this morning.' Agnes ushered Ellie into the big room at the front, where the tea things had been set out on a small table. Emmanuel was already there. He made as if to rise, but gave up the effort and subsided back into his chair. All was as before, with one big difference.

Two large young men were also in the room, one on the settee and the other on an upright chair.

Two. Large. Young. Men.

Ellie felt as if she'd walked into a trap. These two men were very large, and the room seemed to have shrunk. On the other hand, they were both drinking beer, which meant they regarded this as a social occasion. She hoped.

'This is Malcolm,' said Agnes, indicating a heavily built young man with thinning dark hair who looked as if he did physical work for a living. Capable hands, and feet in heavy boots. Worried grey eyes, ancient jeans and a clean T-shirt.

A nice boy. Not all that intelligent.

'And this is my son Edward, who is never called Teddy . . .'

'Except by my wife.' Edward brayed a laugh. No one else even smiled. Edward was taller than Malcolm, with a flop of fair hair and a rounded chin. He had a big nose, and his eyes were bold and brown. Good, casual clothes.

Malcolm earned his living with his hands, but Edward had 'office worker' written all over him. Upper management?

A predator. Beware!

'Do take a seat,' said Agnes. 'Cuppa? Milk, no sugar, I seem to remember?'

Ellie sat. 'Milk, no sugar. Thank you. So you are all involved, are you? I did wonder.'

'Yes and no,' said Edward. 'I had nothing whatever to do with the girls being murdered.' Here he directed a look marked 'poison' at Malcolm.

Malcolm shuffled his feet, his colour rising. 'Nor me. Honest. Let God strike me dead.'

Agnes patted his arm. 'No one ever thought you had, dear.' She sent a look to Edward which Ellie interpreted as a warning. *Don't upset the apple cart!*

Ellie wondered what sort of trap this was going to be. 'You guessed I'd be back?'

Agnes nodded. 'We hoped you'd come without the boy. We might have filled in the gaps a bit last time if he hadn't been around. A nice lad. Clever at his schooling, I expect.'

Emmanuel grimaced. 'He's not as clever as he thinks he is. There was a pair of Karen's shoes under the table there, and he never even noticed.'

What!

Ellie had to peer round her chair to look where he'd pointed, and there they were: a pair of black ballerina shoes, the kind the teenagers wear when they aren't in high heels. Agnes would never have been seen dead in shoes without heels. And neither Ellie nor Mikey had noticed them!

'You mean that she's living here, with you?' said Ellie, her brain zigzagging through so many possibilities that she felt she might faint. She lifted her cup to her mouth and sipped. Good, strong tea. Not doctored in any way. So far, so good.

Malcolm cracked his knuckles. 'She came for the weekend. Says she's bored with school and doesn't want to go back.'

'She's living next door, really,' said Agnes. 'Same as the others.'

The others? Ellie wondered if she'd gone deaf or something. Why hadn't she seen that Malcolm's place offered a perfect refuge for runaway teenagers? Now she came to think of it, Ellie had noticed, when she was being shown the back garden, that there was an unobtrusive door out of Agnes's scullery which could connect with Malcolm's, and the fence around his garden had been built up so that no one could see inside. And she hadn't put two and two together! She was losing her touch.

Edward sneered. 'Malcolm's got cold feet and wants to get rid of her. He says she's too expensive, when what he really means is that—'

'Shut up!' Malcolm reddened. 'It's just too risky.'

Ellie blinked. What was going on here? 'You mean the police might—'

'Nah,' said the old man, rubbing his arthritic knees. 'The police can't find their own notebooks, never mind girls as want to go missing.'

Malcolm cracked his knuckles again. He edged forward on his chair. 'It wasn't me, but it's happened twice now. I can't risk it happening to her as well. We've got to get Karen away before . . .' He swallowed hard.

Agnes sighed. 'What he means is, Mrs Quicke, can you take the girl off our hands? We know you've got a trust fund. Perhaps you could get her set up somewhere to learn the beauty business?'

'Yes, but—' said Malcolm. An uncomfortable silence ensued, which Ellie couldn't interpret.

Ellie's brain went into overdrive. *I'm gobsmacked! Do they really think I'd remove the girl and . . . what! Set her up in business? They must be joking! But at least they don't mean me any harm . . . or do they? They're after my money and not my death. Well, I suppose that's a relief.*

Agnes recollected her duties as hostess. 'More tea, anyone? Another beer, boys? Well, Mrs Quicke, I see that we've taken you by surprise with our little plan.'

Our little plan? Was Emmanuel in on this, too? His eyelids were drooping. He was falling into an afternoon doze in his armchair.

Ellie put her empty cup down. 'Will someone please start from the beginning?'

Silence.

No one was prepared to meet Ellie's eye. Eventually, she said, 'Suppose you tell me about Jenna?'

They all looked at Malcolm. He threw up his hands. 'She shot out into the road in front of the van. In the dark. Late at night. I nearly ran her over. She was in a bad way. Blood all over, clothes torn. I wanted to take her to the hospital. She wouldn't let me. She'd found her uncle waiting for her when she got back from school. He raped her, but her family wouldn't help. Her mother had been pushing her into his arms for weeks, telling her to "be nice to him", because they all depend on him for a living. Her father and brother both work for him, you see. So she fled, nearly committed suicide under my wheels. I brought her home to—'

'To me,' said Agnes. 'I cleaned her up. It was rape, all right. She was exhausted. I wanted to get the police, and she became hysterical, said she'd kill herself. I let her sleep it off in the back bedroom here, thinking that in the morning I'd be able to talk some sense into her, but it was no good. Any mention of the police or the doctor and she became hysterical, saying he'd find and kill her. She swore she'd top herself if we didn't hide her. I believed her. Malcolm was the only one she'd talk to. She trusted him.'

'I liked her,' said Malcolm, tears in his eyes, 'but I swear I never touched her.'

Ellie believed him. A nasty thought wormed its way up out of the back of her mind. She didn't want to believe it. How many months had Jenna been pregnant when she died? Four months? If the rapist hadn't been responsible, then who had been?

Her eyes switched to Edward, who was smiling at her. Not nicely. 'It was you!'

'Mum asked me to think of some way to help the girl, and she came on to me.'

Ellie could feel Agnes wanting to say, *Oh, Edward!* And restraining herself. After all, Edward was her son.

Ellie looked at Malcolm, who turned his head away, big hands clenching as they hung between his knees. He wasn't going to accuse Edward, but it was clear to Ellie what had happened. She switched her eyes back to Edward. 'Jenna was helpless, and you . . . comforted her?'

Those bold eyes of his! He poured on the charm, half smiling, expecting Ellie to be overwhelmed by his good looks and fake sincerity. 'I married far too young. My fiancé was pregnant, and I wanted to do the right thing. But as soon as she'd got my ring on her finger, she said she'd lost the baby. Between you and me, I don't think it ever existed. She trapped me into marriage, which wouldn't be so bad if she'd only be a decent wife, but she's got such a temper you wouldn't believe, and she only lets me into her bed when she feels like it, although God knows that, as a man, I have my needs. She's miscarried several times – she says. All but the once. She never thinks how that makes me feel. Jenna was, well, different. She came on to me.' He repeated the words in a loud tone. 'I said, she came on to me. And if I responded . . . well, I'm only human.'

Agnes stared into the past, not disagreeing out loud, but obviously not liking her thoughts much. So she thought as Ellie did, that Edward had probably taken out his frustrations on a vulnerable girl?

Malcolm had tears in his eyes. 'She was such a pretty little thing. I swear I never touched her. Only, after Edward did that to her, she said she'd like to move over into my house, and I made her a lovely bed-sitting-room in what had been the utility room in the basement, next to the garage, and I put up screens to make an outdoor room in the garden so she could get some sun. After a while she calmed down and began to smile again.'

The difficult bit of the story skated over, Agnes was prepared to tell more. 'Jenna came over to visit with me whenever she wanted – there's a communicating door between our two utility rooms. I got her some clothes and women's things from the market, and we talked it over, and we planned that when she was old enough, eighteen or thereabouts, Malcolm would marry her, and they'd look after the baby between them.'

'I never touched her.' Malcolm, sending another arrow glance at Edward.

Ellie did the sums in her head. Jenna had been made pregnant by Edward. Jenna trusted Malcolm, moved over to live with him in secret. Four months after she became pregnant something happened.

Ellie said, 'Until the snake entered the Garden of Eden. Was it Claire . . .?'

Malcolm lifted his hands in a gesture of defeat. 'Claire came back one day to fetch an old desk which had been Dad's. I hadn't known she'd wanted it. If she'd only said, I'd have taken it over to her flat for her, but I suppose she thought I'd stop her taking it, although honestly, if that was all she wanted, I'd have let her have it. I'd asked her to leave her keys when she left, and she had. I never imagined she'd be sneaky enough to have them copied. I blame myself. I ought to have had the locks changed. But I never thought! When I got back that evening Jenna said that someone who'd said she was my sister had walked in and surprised her, and had got the whole story out of her. Claire promised Jenna – she promised! – that she wouldn't tell the police. I was dead worried, but nothing happened for a fortnight, and then . . . oh God! I got back one evening and found Jenna dead. On the bed. Naked.'

'Malcolm thought it was me!' Edward, through clenched teeth. 'But it wasn't. I'd been nowhere near the house that day, and I could prove it.'

'I know, I know.' Yet Malcolm's sideways look showed that he still feared it might have been Edward.

Agnes gestured helplessly. 'The boys each thought the other had done it. We didn't dare go to the police. They'd have thought Malcolm had done it, or at the very least have charged him with kidnapping, which it wasn't, but it couldn't be proved. Then we thought of burying her in the garden, but Malcolm said her family had the right to bury her, even if they hadn't treated her well in life. So I bought a niqab from a stall in Southall, thinking this was the nearest we could get to a proper shroud. I told the girl in the shop that it was for a fancy-dress party, and Malcolm took her to the canal and laid her out under the bridge.'

Oh dear, oh dear. It all made a horrible kind of sense.

Malcolm said, in a thick voice, 'I loved her. We could have been happy together.'

It came to Ellie that, if it wasn't Edward, she knew who had killed Jenna. Well, she didn't *know*. But she had a strong suspicion, which was such a revolting idea that she gasped. Could it possibly be that . . . Ambrose? No, no! She'd dismissed him from her mind when she'd had a look at the house in which he lived. And, surely, he wasn't a killer? She couldn't quite fit her mind around that thought. She would put it at the back of her mind and deal with it later.

On the heels of that thought came another one. Once Claire realized she'd got the two young men over a barrel, wouldn't she have moved on to blackmailing them? Malcolm, the builder, who could easily be fitted up as a murderer. Edward, with the bold eyes and the frustrations that came from marrying a woman who didn't understand his needs . . . Well, that was the way he'd put it, but maybe his wife had a different point of view . . .?

Ellie realized she'd been given another clue to Claire's behaviour. Edward was a sexual predator. How early had he started? Was it possible that Claire's story about having been interfered with at an early age was true? Hm. Yes. Malcolm, too? And the other boys, now safely living far away? They'd all alibied one another, hadn't they?

Well, they would, wouldn't they?

As a child Claire had been the odd one out, the one who was so easy to dislike . . . If her allegation had been true . . .? The adults wouldn't have wanted to believe it, of course. But, if it was true . . . well, that didn't explain Claire's present behaviour altogether, but it did cast a sidelight upon her hang-ups.

'Claire said . . .' Malcolm shivered and licked his lips. 'She said that I had to be punished for breaking God's laws and the laws of the country, and of course she was right. I had hidden Jenna and put her body where I knew it would be found. Yes, I realized I'd sinned. I said I'd go to the police and explain, and risk them accusing me of murder. Claire said that was too easy. That I had to show I had repented by working for the Vision people at their new place, for free. I said I couldn't do it for free, or I couldn't make ends meet. But eventually, I agreed. I had to set aside one whole day a week to do the repairs at their new place.'

'And that's when you met Gail?'

He nodded. 'I was working late. She shot into the yard when I was packing up for the night. She was in a right royal rage. The pastor had had her in and given her a dressing-down, and as she said, he had no right. She wasn't even a member of his so-called church. She was fizzing with temper at him and at Claire, who'd betrayed her in some way, I couldn't exactly make out what.

'I tried to get Gail to calm down, because she said she was going to set the Vision place on fire as a goodbye present, and she might have done, she was in such a temper. She said her mother didn't give tuppence about her, and she was going to run away to meet up with some man, only he'd just told her he was married and couldn't see her any more. She asked me to give her a lift to the tube station and to lend her some money to get over to her friend's place and have it out with his wife. I said she mustn't do that or the police would be after her, and she said they wouldn't because she was old enough to leave school and take care of herself. She said she was going to be eighteen next week, which was a lie, but I didn't discover that till later.

'So I told her about Jenna, how she'd taken refuge with us for a while, and how that had turned out so badly, thinking that she'd see the dangers of running away, but she said she'd make it up to me if I took her home. She climbed into the van and said I should get going, so I did, thinking she didn't really mean it and would ask to be let out any minute, thinking she'd want to go back home after a few hours, or the next day. Agnes was furious with me, but agreed we could keep her overnight. Only . . . only Edward came by that evening and . . .' He clapped both hands over his ears and closed his eyes.

Edward folded his arms and laughed, uneasy but still

showing off about his 'needs'. 'She was aching for it. Full strength.'

Agnes cast her son a look which said that she loved him, but that he'd got a bit above himself. 'I was furious with him. And her. And Malcolm. It placed us all in such a difficult situation.'

Edward was belligerent. 'Being with Gail saved my marriage, and you wanted that, didn't you? You were always saying it would make you happy if I could only settle down and give you a grandchild or two. Gail didn't care about anything except sex, watching the telly and having enough cigarettes to smoke and junk food to eat. Oh, and not having to go to school, and not having to work for a living. I kept her happy, didn't I? Almost every day I managed to pop in and satisfy her. It satisfied me, too, so that my dear wife didn't annoy me so much. Gail and I had our little disagreements, of course. She wanted me to divorce my wife and marry her, but that was never on the cards. You know my wife; she'd have skinned me alive, taken the house and half my income. I really believe it was being with Gail, being more relaxed at home, that meant I didn't mind so much when my wife had a tantrum . . . and I was right, because in the end she did carry a baby to term, and he's a fine little boy now.'

Ellie switched her eyes to Malcolm, who had his head in his hands. Poor man; taking girls home for Edward to have fun with. That couldn't have been a happy time for him. And who had paid to provide Gail with junk food, cigarettes and clothes? Answer: Malcolm.

Ellie said, 'Malcolm, why didn't you go to the police and tell them you'd got Gail?'

'I wanted to. She said that if I did, she'd tell them about how I'd hidden Jenna and then killed her. I couldn't prove I hadn't. I didn't like it. I tried to get her to ring her mother and tell her she was all right, but she said . . .'

Edward laughed. 'She said, "Let the cow suffer for a bit."'

Malcolm's big hands wrung one another. 'It wasn't right. Well, she did ring in the end. She had me over a barrel. I hated it, actually. But I was stuck.'

Ellie saw how it was. Once started down the slippery

slope . . . 'How soon did Claire suspect that it was you who'd taken Gail?'

'Almost straight away. She caught up with me when I was working on the plumbing at the Vision and taxed me with it. I told her what had happened and that Gail was refusing to go home. Claire said she could see how it was and that she'd try to cover for me because I was her brother, but that the police did suspect her of doing away with Gail, so if they charged her with murder, she'd have to give me away. I was on tenterhooks.'

'What! What?!' Emmanuel roused himself from his forty winks.

Edward said, 'Gail understood that telling the police would have ruined me.'

Wait a minute! How did Claire cotton on to the fact that Gail had run off with Malcolm so quickly? Had she remembered his van had been in the drive the evening Gail disappeared and put two and two together? I'm amazed she didn't give him away to the police . . . but then the Vision would have lost their handyman and . . . How much did Edward have to pay for her silence? I wonder how long she'd have kept his secret if the police had charged her with murder?

Ellie turned back to Malcolm. 'Then one day you returned from work to find Gail dead, in the same way as Jenna? And you still had no idea who'd done it?'

He snorted, nodded, wiped his nose with the back of his hand. Agnes said, 'Tck,' and handed him a box of tissues. He blew his nose.

Let's think about Ambrose being the killer. Claire would have told Ambrose everything, wouldn't she? I did wonder who was keeping his bed warm at night. He might be celibate, but on balance I think it unlikely. Perhaps he tried to be celibate, fought against temptation, until he learned about poor little Jenna, who'd already been raped by her uncle and by Edward. Perhaps he went to visit her in a spirit of kindness . . . No, he is not kind. He went to denounce and rape. The same with Gail. In his mind he probably thought that any woman was fair game, but he hadn't any in his congregation of misfits and addicts who appealed to him. He borrowed the

keys from Claire and killed both girls. Do the boys realize
that? No, I don't think they do. But Claire must suspect . . .
    I must talk to Lesley about this.
    She tried to tie up some loose ends. 'Malcolm, was it you
who dropped Gail's body into the canal, near where you'd left
Jenna?'
    'Edward did that,' said Malcolm. 'I said that she was his
girl, and I wouldn't have anything to do with getting rid of
her body.'
    He hadn't liked Edward taking Gail over, had he? Ellie
wondered at the tangled relationships between the two families,
growing up together, experimenting together and sharing the
same girls. Not a healthy situation.
    What about Agnes and Emmanuel? What share had they
had in all this? Had they been innocent bystanders, driven to
helping out because their boys had got into something too
difficult for them to deal with? Probably. Neither of them
seemed to enjoy knowing about what had happened.
    'What about Karen?' said Ellie. 'Malcolm, was that you as
well? A third time? You were over at the Vision house at least
once a week. You saw the girls coming and going. You could
see Karen was ripe for conquest, going the same way as Gail.
Surely, Malcolm, you must have guessed that if you took
another girl in, Edward would only move in on her?'
    Malcolm groaned, rubbing his forehead. 'I . . . I always lagged
behind the others, and they made fun of me; always late, they
used to say. And I was. I didn't even think about girls much
until . . . but Jenna was so sweet, and I had thought we might
make a go of it in spite of the baby, and we'd talked about it,
and she'd liked the idea of settling down with me, and I'd been
looking at engagement rings when . . . I wouldn't have harmed
a hair of her head.'
    'Yes, but Gail was different. When she crawled into your
van, it must have crossed your mind that this time she might
be the one to break your duck. She wasn't one to hold back,
was she? You must have felt jealous when Edward moved in
on her.'
    He flared up. 'I didn't kill her. I didn't even like her, much.
She was . . .' He threw his arms up. 'She wasn't my sort.'

'Granted. Is Karen any different?'

He turned a dull red. 'No, she's not. She's a real cracker. Gail used to laugh at me, and I never, ever . . . No, I didn't. I never touched her that way. But Karen, well, she came back from school while I was sitting at the back of the van, having a cuppa from my flask of tea, and she stopped to talk to me, winding her hair round her finger, pushing her hip out at me and licking her lips. All the signs of . . . Well, I didn't know what to think. I told her that they'd found Gail, because I thought Karen might know her, and she did, of course, and she said that Gail had had it coming to her, but that she, Karen, knew a thing or two, and couldn't she have a sip from my cup and . . . well, I could feel myself getting all hot and bothered, you know . . . and she climbed up into the van and shut the door, and . . . I hadn't realized how much I'd been wanting it, until then. She kept saying what a big boy I was, and she stroked me and . . . until . . . and then . . . Afterwards I felt great, but of course I knew it was foolish, more than foolish. But she bounced up and sat in the front seat and asked where we could go so that we could do it again, and it was like all my dreams come true.'

Ellie tried to think straight. Had all this been happening outside in Malcolm's van while she'd been inside the house talking to Dolores? It sounded like it. And she'd missed it completely!

Malcolm said, 'Only, then she said she needed a drink and promised I could have some more of what she had to offer if I took her to a pub, but she said it couldn't be local or someone might see her and tell her mother, who was strictly off the booze, so I came back to these parts where she's not known, and then she said it would be more comfortable if I had a bed to offer, and . . . well, it was quite something. But, later that evening, when I suggested I took her home, she . . . Karen is not . . . I mean, she's got a mind of her own, and once she'd seen the set-up here, she started bossing me around and . . . Don't get me wrong, sex is wonderful, but it's not love, or anything. It's like . . . having flu. And I'm over it. I'm not worried about her doing it with Edward, because of course he wanted to have his turn, and she . . . she loves it! She's always

thinking up new . . . Don't get me wrong. We still do it, now
and then, but I don't think we should get married or anything.
I know I brought her here and didn't tell her mother, and yes,
it was my responsibility to see that she got back home, but
. . . you don't know what she's like. Every time I suggested
she ought to ring her mother she threw a wobbly, and I realized, too late, that it was a mistake to give in to her. She's not
. . . well, she's not my sort.'

He sent a look of uneasy triumph in Edward's direction.
'She does say I'm better value.'

'Hah!' said Edward. 'She tells me that, too.'

Ellie wanted to laugh, even though it was a dreadful situation. The two young bucks each trying to out-sex one another.
She said, 'Was it you, Malcolm, or was it Edward, who finally
got Karen to ring the police while you were driving around?'

Edward laughed. 'It was Malcolm's idea, but we did it in
my car. It worked, didn't it?'

'And now . . .?'

The words dragged out of Malcolm. 'I want rid of her.
Safely. I don't want her around any longer, but I don't want
her to get killed like the others. Aunt Agnes said she thought
you might help.'

Ellie took a deep breath. 'She's here in this house, at this
very minute, isn't she? Listening to everything we've said?'

Agnes twitched her eyes towards the hall. 'Oh, no. I don't
think so.'

The others looked that way, too.

It was the cue for Karen to enter.

SIXTEEN

Ellie got up and wrenched the door open. 'Do join us, Karen.' And then she gaped, because the girl in the doorway had no hair.

None.

Bald as the proverbial coot.

Malcolm cried, 'It wasn't me, honest. I didn't, I wouldn't . . .'

Edward gave a high-pitched laugh, which descended into a giggle. 'Oh, Malcolm, you bit off more than you could chew with this one.'

Karen minced into the room on some of the highest heels Ellie had ever seen. She was smoking and wearing a glittery, sleeveless top, the tightest of jeans and a mountain of make-up. Eyebrows, false eyelashes, eyeliner, foundation, blusher, the lot. Her skull shone white against the tan on her arms and shoulders.

She was stunningly, shockingly beautiful. Her hair had been a tousled mess; unkempt, dry, half brown and half yellow. Now everyone could see what a pretty shape her head was. She no longer looked like a schoolgirl from St Trinian's. She looked like one of the amazing women from outer space to be seen in Hollywood films.

'So . . .?' She threw herself, legs sprawling, on to the settee beside Edward.

Agnes said, in a dull voice, 'She did it to herself. She got into a tantrum, wanting Malcolm to spring to bleach and some more new clothes. When he said he couldn't afford to spend any more money on her, she took his razor and shaved her head.'

Karen blew smoke. 'So what? I said, it'll save him a bleach job at the hairdressers. I thought he might spring to a tattoo. I rather fancy a tattoo.' She addressed Ellie. 'So you're the rich woman who's going to set me up in business, are you? I really did fancy running a tattoo parlour at one time. I used to think how it would be, all those beautiful, hunky men coming in to have themselves decorated, but this . . . this is much better.' She ran sharp, scarlet fingernails down Edward's arm.

He laughed again. Was he sexually aroused because Karen had done it to him, and not to Malcolm? He was certainly looking at Malcolm and not at Karen.

Malcolm muttered, 'It's not funny.'

Karen lay back with her bald head on Edward's shoulder. 'I like Edward. He's so full of good ideas. I like Malcolm, too. He gets so hot and bothered, he makes me laugh.' She handed her cigarette butt to Edward. 'Put this out for me. If I drop it on the floor, dear auntie will have another fit. I'm in her bad books, you see. I can't cook, and I don't see any reason why I should do the housework for her. Or for Malcolm. He brought me here, and as far as I'm concerned, it's up to him to look after me.' She pointed one scarlet-tipped finger at Ellie. 'Auntie here seems to think I can be bought off. I warn you, you'll have to come up with something good. I like it here, and if I had something regular coming in, I wouldn't mind staying.'

'Out of the question,' said Ellie, dazed by this turn of events.

Karen smiled. Not nicely. 'Then I'll just have to toddle along to the police station and have these dear people arrested. Malcolm told me all about Jenna and Gail. I knew Gail from school. The police will be so thrilled to hear what happened to her and to Jenna. Twenty years apiece for the boys, I should think. I don't suppose Auntie Agnes or the old man will last that long, but you never know. They'll only be fit for an old people's home when they come out . . . if they ever do.'

'What! What?' the old man started up again. He looked around, seemingly not sure where he was or what he was doing there. He struggled to his feet and reached for his walker. 'I've got to visit the little boy's room.' He tottered off to the hall and beyond.

'Same here,' said Ellie, following him.

Agnes twittered to her feet. 'Mrs Quicke, there's one through the kitchen and another upstairs. Let me put out a clean towel for you.'

'Upstairs? I'll find it.' Ellie needed time to think.

Up the stairs she went. There were four doors on the first-floor landing. Overlooking the road was the master bedroom, all flowered wallpaper and curtains. There was built-in furniture, painted white with gilt trims, and a flounced dressing-table. Clearly, this was the marital bedroom, and Agnes still occupied it.

Next to it was a small bedroom over the porch. It had the unused look of a spare room, occupied occasionally. An old-fashioned wooden cot stood under the window, waiting for the grand-babies to make an appearance.

At the back, overlooking the garden, was the bedroom in which Edward had had his wicked way with the girls from next door. A double bed, rumpled. A man's dressing-gown hung behind the door, a woman's underwear was strewn around. Ellie picked up a shopping bag from Zara's, tissue paper and cashmere. Karen knew what she wanted, didn't she? Ellie could see her poring over fashion magazines, thinking she'd have this garment or that when she was rich . . . or had struck lucky with a wealthy suitor.

The bathroom. Oh. Ellie almost backed out again. A powerful scent. Clumps of dirty particoloured hair on every surface. This was where Karen had shaved her head?

There was a rim around the bath. Towels had been used and thrown on the floor in a puddle of water. Make-up items were everywhere; opened, used and left without their lids. A magazine had been propped up against the window, showing how a film star applied her make-up. Ellie recognized the look and had to admit that Karen was a quick learner. But the cosmetics she'd chosen . . . Whew! No wonder Malcolm was pleading poverty.

A timid knock on the half-open door. Agnes, with a clean hand-towel. 'I'm sorry about the mess. When I saw it . . .!' She says the mirror is better in here than in Malcolm's bath-room, and of course last night she was out at the disco with Edward and slept late . . . I did say she should clear it up, but . . . you can see what she's like.'

Ellie nodded. Yes, she could see.

There were tears in Agnes' eyes. 'You're not going to go

to the police, are you? Malcolm doesn't deserve . . . And poor old Emmanuel, he's said all along that we ought not to have let things get out of hand, but now they have and . . .' She clasped her hands in a prayerful position.

'I don't know what to think,' said Ellie, with truth. 'Thank you for the towel.'

She pushed Agnes gently out of the bathroom, locked the door, cleaned round the toilet and washbasin, and replaced the caps and lids on the make-up. Then she sat on the toilet, wondering if she could possibly make her escape out of the bathroom window . . . and realized that at her age and with her, er, not exactly supple limbs, she couldn't.

Dear Lord, I didn't see this coming. What am I to do? Help, please!

In fact, Edward's the only one of the lot of them whom I think ought to be locked up. His conduct is disgraceful. But that's not how the law of the land works, is it?

Poor Malcolm. Foolish, soft-hearted. Yes, he's behaved in idiotic fashion, but he doesn't deserve to be hanged, drawn and quartered . . . Not that they do that nowadays . . . although I suppose he'd think going to prison would be just as painful.

Agnes. Covering for that nasty son of hers. Understandable, if unwise. But that's parents for you.

Emmanuel. Probably thinks he's well out of it. Neither of his sons is involved in this situation. Or are they? That's a nasty thought.

Karen. I have absolutely no idea what to do about her. Help, please!

Ellie began to laugh at the thought of Karen turning the tables on those two silly young men. Oh, their faces when they realized what she was like. Worse, far worse than Gail . . .

Not, of course, that one could condone kidnapping. But then, it wasn't exactly kidnapping, either, because if you believed Malcolm – and Ellie did – then all three girls had taken the initiative. No, it wasn't kidnapping, but it was . . . There would be a law covering it. Detention of a minor? Something like that. Except that, according to them, they were only guilty of taking in girls who had run away from home.

What about the two deaths? Ah, that was a different matter

altogether. Ellie did not feel at all inclined to laugh about them.

She unlocked the door and went downstairs and into the kitchen, from which she could hear shuffling noises. Emmanuel, at the sink, washing his hands over and over. He said, 'You will help us, won't you?'

Ellie said truthfully, 'I really don't know. Mr Cook, when Claire said the boys had been interfering with her, she spoke the truth, didn't she?'

He went on washing his hands. 'They said not.'

'They gave one another an alibi. I get that.'

'My boys said she made it up.'

'They're well out of it, aren't they?'

His chin went down. And up. Perhaps he'd nodded. Perhaps it was the onset of Parkinson's. He transferred his attention to drying his hands, finger by finger, on a towel.

'They don't listen to me. Think I'm past it. You see, I was well into middle age when we had the boys, and I suppose I've been more like a grandfather than a father to them. Now, don't you get the wrong idea: they're good lads, and they come back to see me when they can. I've always been fond of Agnes, and I don't like seeing her in trouble. There's too much of an age gap for her to think of marrying me. I'd have her like a shot if she would, but there . . . It wouldn't be fair to her . . . even if she agreed, which she hasn't. I have a little money saved. Could you use it to help her? Can't you fix it so that she doesn't have to go to prison?'

He was being realistic, wasn't he?

She said, 'Can you "fix" Edward?'

His neck swelled, and he began to laugh. She patted him on his back when he began to choke. He took long, slow breaths. 'Thanks.'

Ellie said, 'What about Agnes's other son? Would he be any help to her in this? Get her a good lawyer, for instance.'

He shook his head. 'He's another like Edward. Two peas in a pod. Take after their father, God rest him.' He gave her a shrewd look. 'So you've decided not to throw good money after bad?'

'That's one way of putting it. I haven't exactly decided what to do, but it's in my mind that it's no good doing something wrong, hoping that good will come of it. I don't think Malcolm meant any harm, but he treated those girls as if they were adults and had the right to take control of their lives, whereas by law they were still school children and not capable of deciding things for themselves. Malcolm has wasted a lot of police time, and something else: he didn't intend to put the girls in danger, but that's what he did.'

'He didn't kill those girls, and neither did Edward.'

'Proving who did might be tricky because the police were not brought on to the scene of the crime when the girls were killed. There might well have been forensic evidence in Malcolm's house which could have led the police to the murderer. Instead, he decided to cover up the deaths. I think there's a law about not reporting a death as well.'

He didn't want to think about that. 'But if it wasn't the boys – and it wasn't – then who else could it be?'

'Let's go and ask them, shall we?'

Agnes had set about clearing the tea things away. Noisily. Casting baleful glances at her uninvited guest.

Malcolm was locked into his own thoughts. Edward was stroking Karen's head. Karen lay back, eyes half closed, enjoying the attention. She had another cigarette between her fingers. Agnes plonked an ashtray on to the arm of the settee. Karen, typically, ignored it.

Agnes looked up when Ellie and Emmanuel returned. 'You've decided to help us?'

'Not so fast. First things first. Malcolm, you are concerned for Karen's safety. I think you're right to be afraid for her.'

'You believe me?'

'I do. If she stays here, she'll go the way the others did.'

Karen lifted heavy eyelids. 'You don't frighten me. Go on, Edward: don't stop.'

Ellie wanted to slap the girl, but refrained. With difficulty. 'Karen, both the girls Malcolm brought home in the past ended up dead. What makes you think you won't meet the same fate?'

'Well, neither of the boys want to kill me, do they?'

'No. But someone else knew about the other girls, didn't

they? Come on, think about it. Surely you must have suspected . . .' Ellie could hardly believe that they hadn't worked it out.

Both young men shook their heads. So did Agnes and Emmanuel.

Ellie realized that if they'd never seen Ambrose in action, or understood how the Vision worked, they probably wouldn't ever have had cause to suspect him.

'Malcolm, who is the only other person who knows about the girls being here?'

'Claire, you mean? But she wouldn't have killed them.'

Ellie said, 'I don't think for a minute that she did, but I would like you all to consider what sort of person Claire has become and why. I believe that in your teens you boys did interfere with her.'

'Certainly not!' said Agnes, colouring up.

'Oh, come on!' said Edward, rolling his eyes. 'Why would we want to play around with that whiny little monster?'

Ellie sighed. 'Of course, you denied it. Yes, you covered for one another. But it did happen, didn't it, Malcolm?'

Malcolm, eyes on the carpet, nodded.

Ellie said, 'I suspect Edward started it.'

Edward laughed, neither denying nor admitting it.

'And then,' said Ellie, 'it was Edward, wasn't it, who lost Claire her job at the supermarket?'

Edward explained it to Karen. 'I asked one of her bosses to look into the matter, yes. They'd dismissed someone who'd quarrelled with Claire at work and had fallen sick. I said, "When Claire takes a dislike to someone, they'd better watch out, especially if she's always making the tea or coffee!" It turned out she'd been putting something in her colleague's drink which made her dizzy and unable to operate her computer. Also, Claire told the woman she'd got someone to lay a curse on her. Talk about the Dark Ages! You won't believe this, but the poor creature got the local dog-collar round to exorcize her. Yes, I did ask someone to look into it; the woman was reinstated, and Claire got the sack.'

Ellie frowned. 'Claire knew it was you who'd got her the sack?'

'Of course. But she couldn't do anything to harm me.' A flashing smile.

'I wouldn't count on it,' said Ellie. 'As for you, Malcolm. You knew that your mother wanted to leave her estate divided between the Vision and Claire. You destroyed the unsigned will she'd written to that effect, which meant that when your mother died, you could produce an earlier will which left ten thousand to Claire and the rest to you.'

'I did,' said Malcolm. 'Mum was not herself at that time. She'd been taking some linctus or other which was turning her into a zombie. She was getting dizzy and sleepy, and sometimes she didn't seem to know who I was. I wanted her to go to the doctor, but she wouldn't. I was afraid she'd walk under a bus one day, or burn the house down. Every time I said something about it, Claire would urge my mother to take a double dose.' A gesture of frustration. 'I didn't know what to do. She was getting worse every day, and . . . when she had that heart attack and died, well, I know you're not supposed to feel that way, but I was relieved.'

'Why did Claire encourage your mother to keep taking the linctus?'

'I really don't know, unless it was to spite me. We never got on, you know.'

'Did you realize your mother planned to cut you out of her will?'

'Not until the day before she died, when she showed me a will form and said what she wanted to do, and I . . . I was so upset. I hadn't had any idea. You see, when Dad died things weren't too easy. Mum had her little pension, but it didn't go far. I took over paying the mortgage, and Claire helped at first, but after she and Mum started going to the Vision, they hadn't a penny between them and I had to come up with money for everything: rates, electricity, telephone, food . . . everything. I managed, but it was a struggle.'

'So when your mother said she was planning to leave the house to the Vision and to Claire, you felt it was unjust?'

A grimace. 'Mum was raving about hellfire and damnation. I thought she'd gone out of her mind. I'd been carrying the burden of the household all that time and . . . Yes, I guess I lost my temper. It was all too much! I stormed out of the house and walked around the streets for a while. When I got back Edward was knocking on my door. Claire had gone out to an evening prayer meeting, so she wasn't around to help. Edward said Mum had fallen asleep in here. We carried her back to her own bed and tucked her in. Edward gave me the will form which she'd been wanting them to witness, and yes, I tore that up. The next morning Mum said she was going down to the shops early for something she needed, so I said I was going to have a serious talk with her when I got back from work, and I went off as usual. They called me back later that morning to say she'd had a heart attack and died.'

'Do you think you were right to tear up the will she'd tried to make and not mention it?'

'At first, yes. I was so angry. Angry with her, and angry with Claire, and angry with myself for not having made her go to the doctor. We hadn't known about the heart complaint, and if I'd made her go, she might have lived. The doctor could have made her see sense about that linctus.'

'So you were right to tear it up?'

He looked away. 'No, probably not. If that was what she wanted . . .'

'It would have made you homeless.'

Another grimace. 'I know. But if I'd told them about it, I'm sure they would have made some readjustment so that I could have gone on living here. As it was, I was so skint when she died that I had to borrow the money to pay Claire off. Since then, I reckon I've repaid Claire by spending so much on the Vision.'

'Do you still feel you were right to throw Claire out when your mother died?'

A shrug. 'Rightly or wrongly, I felt she'd helped Mum to an early grave. If she'd only backed me up when I wanted Mum to see the doctor . . . but she never did. We never got on. Even when I was small, Claire would pinch herself and say I'd done it. She used to pour ink on my school homework, hide and destroy my gym kit. Little things, I know. I used to look at her and wonder why she hated me. That sounds ridiculous; that a child should hate her younger brother. I didn't want to believe it. You don't, do you? Not in your own family. But yes, I did think she contributed to our mother's death, and I was glad to see the back of her.'

Ellie repeated, 'Do you still think you were right to throw her out?'

He met Ellie's eyes squarely. 'Perhaps not. When I stopped being angry with her, I thought maybe I ought to have been more generous, given her more money to start over – but I hadn't a penny to spare, then, and . . . well, since then she's done pretty well out of me.'

'You planned to take in lodgers?'

'At first, yes. I did the work, and then Jenna came to stay, so I couldn't risk having anyone else in the house.'

'You said Claire came back for your father's old desk. How did she get in? Didn't you ask her to leave her house keys behind when she left?'

'Yes. She must have had copies made because she walked in on Jenna without ringing the bell. But I don't believe that Claire could have killed Jenna. Not even to spite me.'

'I don't think she did kill her. She gets her kicks another way. She's got you working for the Vision for no pay. That must make her feel wonderful. And it's quite a punishment for you, isn't it?'

He nodded. 'It's a serious problem. This new big house of theirs has not been well looked after. I thought it was owned by Ealing Council at first, but the Vision have got it on a repairing lease, which means they have to maintain it. I've been patching the roof, replacing lead flashing, repainting the outside, hanging new doors, mending cupboards . . . It's never-ending.'

'Right. Now, Edward. How has Claire been using you?'

Edward's eyes narrowed. 'Don't be ridiculous! She can't do anything to me.'

'Be your age,' advised Ellie. 'Of course she could. She knew about you and Jenna, and she knew about you and Gail. So what did she do about it?'

'Nothing, I tell you!'

He protested too much. What was he hiding? She said, 'Well, I'm sure she's worked it out by now that Karen went off with Malcolm. If I'm right, she'll be calling round here any day now to check.'

Karen languidly tapped the ash from her cigarette on the carpet. 'Oh, yes. She came around when dear auntie was out, on Saturday. Didn't I tell you, Edward? I suppose we had other things to think about.' Giggle. 'I was so surprised to see her. I hadn't realized she was Malcolm's sister. She asked if Malcolm were looking after me properly, and I said he was. She wanted to know if I'd met Edward yet, and I said I had, and we had a little laugh about it.'

Everyone looked at her with rounded eyes. In shock.

'Why didn't you say?' That was Edward, alarmed.

'Why, what could she do about it?' said Karen.

Ellie worked it out. 'She didn't tell the police where you were, but she knew you were already having fun with Edward . . . as he did with Jenna and Gail. But she hasn't told Edward's wife about his involvement with any of the girls, which means . . .'

'Why would she?' But Edward removed his arm from around Karen.

Ellie felt sick. 'What borough do you work for, Edward? This one, or another? And which department of the Council offices? Social Services, or Housing?'

'Neither.' It was almost a shout.

Agnes was wide-eyed. 'But Edward, you told me that—'

'Social Services,' said Malcolm. 'I don't understand.'

'I think I do,' said Ellie. 'Claire is adept at blackmail, isn't she? She was a repressed personality, always the odd one out, until she discovered the joys of dedicating her life to a man whom she could do something for. She put that man on a pedestal. Whatever he said or did, she was his devoted servant. That man was Pastor Ambrose, the leader of the Vision cult. He is charismatic, powerful physically and mentally. He attracts a good congregation and, with the backing of Social Services, he takes addicts off the streets and makes them live a rigid routine which has a decent record of success. That's where Edward comes in, isn't it? Edward; you were responsible for Ambrose's project getting the backing of your department, right?'

A shrug. 'Why not? He does an outstandingly good job in a field most people can't even begin to understand.'

'I suppose you gave him your backing for the right reasons at the beginning.'

'I kept an eye on him.'

'Of course you did. Claire saw to that. There was no need for her to spell things out to you. If she'd told the police or your wife what she knew, you'd have been in deep trouble. There was no percentage in that for Claire. No, there was a better way to get her own back on you. She got you to help Ambrose instead.'

'Absolute rubbish,' said Edward. 'I've always gone by the book. My hands are clean.'

'Are they? I think you got your colleagues to help find new quarters for Ambrose, and you made sure Social Services continued to send him clients. But, he let you down. That great white elephant of a house eats money. Living expenses mount up, while the two inheritances, on which he'd depended, fell through. Ambrose began not to care about what other, inferior mortals thought. He cut corners, and you turned a blind eye to whatever he did or did not do.'

Red stained Edward's cheeks. 'That's libellous.'

Ellie said, 'There must be some legislation, something legally binding to cover his taking care of the addicts. They must surely be registered with a doctor and a dentist locally. An optician, as well. You must know, as well as I do, that addicts need their physical health monitored at regular intervals. It is possible that Ambrose has convinced himself he doesn't need to bother with all that, but I don't think Social Services would agree.'

Edward had begun to sweat. 'You don't know what you're talking about.'

'Ambrose's flock are supposed to give him everything they earn. Is that all right by Social Services? I don't think so, do you? One of his "clients" recently suffered an abscess under a tooth but was told it was all in her mind. She was driven mad by the pain. She used money she was supposed to have handed over to Ambrose, in order to get treatment from a dentist and antibiotics from the chemist. Then, unable to face

Ambrose's wrath, she fled back to her family, who are the ones who got her into drugs in the first place. Is this how Social Services would have wished him to handle the situation?'

Edward was now as pale as he had been red. 'This is the first I've heard of it. I suppose it will have to be looked into.'

Karen said, 'Enough of this. Mrs Quicke, I want you to buy me a nice little flat somewhere, so that I can see Edward whenever I wish . . . or whenever he wishes.' Another giggle.

Edward tried to respond with a smile. She lifted herself up to kiss him, open-mouthed. His arms closed around her.

Ellie said, 'Yes, that is enough! This has got to stop. All of it.'

SEVENTEEN

Ellie looked around the room to see how her words had been received. Mr Cook was nodding.

Malcolm was twisting his hands together, but also, if with reluctance, nodding. Malcolm had a conscience. Malcolm had been driven into a corner and wanted out. He knew what 'ending it' might mean and was prepared to face the consequences.

Agnes had her hand to her mouth, eyes flickering from her son Edward to Ellie and back. Agnes was weighing up the possible result of 'ending it' and not liking what she saw.

Edward unstuck himself from Karen. 'No.' He produced a travesty of a smile. 'I see no reason to "end things", exactly. If what you say about the way Ambrose has been carrying on is true, I agree it will have to be looked into. His heart is in the right place, and if he has overstepped the mark, well . . . A quiet word should do the trick.'

'No,' said Malcolm, washing his face with his hands. 'It's got to stop. I can't carry on any longer. I'll go to the police and—'

'You can't do that,' said Edward, fighting down panic. 'They'll charge you with murder. And really, there's no need. The search for Karen has been called off, and no one's looking this way for Jenna or Gail. Everything will be perfectly all right if you only keep your head.'

Mr Cook said, 'Malcolm's right. It's gone on far too long. I've been saying so all along. You should never pay a blackmailer.'

If that was what he thought, it explained why he'd invited Ellie in to visit Agnes in the first place. Taking a hand in the game? Bringing in an outsider to lance the boil?

'It's all right for you,' said Edward. 'Your boys are well out of it. But you know as well as I do that—'

'What?' Mr Cook picked up on that. 'What do I know? You

think my boys were involved with your mucky games with Claire? Yes, they watched, but—'

'They did more than watch,' said Edward. 'Right, Malcolm?'

Malcolm washed his face again. 'Leave me out of this. I watched, and so did they. Yes, we ought to have come clean and admitted it, but we didn't. We covered for you then, Edward, and we've gone on covering for you all these years, no matter how many girls you've brought home to "play with" under your mother's roof, but now . . . I can't take any more. It's got to stop.'

Silence while they all thought about this.

Karen twined herself around Edward. 'Who's been a naughty boy, then? But Karen loves naughty boys, like, if they are kind to her. You're not throwing me overboard, are you, lover boy?'

'I . . . no.' Edward took her chin in his hand and kissed her long and deep.

'What a pair!' said old man Cook, thumping the floor with his cane. 'If you ask me, they deserve one another.'

'Yes,' said Agnes, 'but if this all comes out, and I do see where Malcolm's at, and of course I haven't liked Edward bringing his girls here whenever he liked, and neither Gail nor Karen are exactly who I'd choose to have as house guests—'

'Thanks for nothing!' said Karen.

'But he's my son, and I have to think that he might lose his job, and his wife might divorce him . . . Which I'll agree I wouldn't lose any sleep over, because she's a cold fish if ever there was one . . . But then there's my little grandson that I love to bits. Of course, Ambrose should look after his people properly, but . . . Oh dear. I'm all of a tizz.'

'There, you see?' Edward was all smiles. 'No need to panic. I'll have a word with Ambrose, and we'll find somewhere else for Karen to stay. There's no need for us to do anything else, right?'

Mr Cook shook his head, but said no more.

Ellie looked at Malcolm, and he looked back at her.

Malcolm said, 'No. Mrs Quicke's right. It's gone on long enough. It's over. Finished, as far as I am concerned.'

Edward's mouth twisted. 'You're outvoted, mate. Karen and

I and Mother all agree that this can be smoothed over without
going to the police.'

'If it comes to a vote,' said Mr Cook, 'then I'm in it with
Malcolm. I'll even come with you to the station, lad, if you
wish.'

Ellie said, 'And I.'

'Two against three,' said Edward. 'As I said, you're outvoted.'

Agnes felt for a hanky in her bra and found one. She used
it. 'I'm so sorry, Edward. I'll stand by you, of course, but this
has gone beyond a joke. If it gets rid of that nasty wife of
yours then I'm all for it, and I'm sure the judge will let us
have access to my grandson if it comes to a divorce. Malcolm
is right. This has got to end.'

'There's no need for that.' Karen, back to stroking Edward's
cheek. 'Edward's my soulmate, like. Aren't you, my treasure?
No need for his wife to divorce him if I can be fixed up with
a little hidey-hole nearby.'

Ellie grasped at this. 'You're right. There's no need for
Edward's wife to divorce him, unless she wishes it. Financially,
she'll be better off if she doesn't. Divorcees don't usually have
a luxurious lifestyle, and though Edward may keep his job, I
doubt if his prospects will be enhanced by disclosure of his
blackmail and extramarital activities.'

Edward smiled, not nicely. 'Exactly. There's no need for it
all to come out, is there? Malcolm can own up to hiding Jenna
and Gail and take the consequences. I shall have a quiet word
with Ambrose, and all's well that ends well.'

Malcolm shook his head. 'No, you don't. They're going to
think I murdered them both unless I tell them about you and
Claire. I hope to God they don't think I killed them, but I'm
not keeping silent about your involvement if they do.'

Mr Cook twitched bushy eyebrows. 'You've forgotten something else, Edward. Claire knows what's been going on, and
Claire won't want to give up her hold on you lot in a hurry.'

Ellie said, 'We've all forgotten about Claire, haven't we?
Claire is the key to this whole sorry tale. She's known all
along about Jenna, Gail and Karen, but she hasn't seen fit to
pass this knowledge on to the police. Instead, she's indulged
in blackmail for the benefit of Ambrose, and it's got to stop.

Karen, may I suggest that you stand on your own two feet for a change? If you don't want to return to your mother, that's all well and good, but if you refuse that option, you may well have Social Services on your back until your next birthday. I don't think you'll like that, not at all. And, please get it into your head that I am *not* going to support you.'

Karen pouted. 'But what will I do? Edward . . .?'

Edward grimaced.

Ellie interpreted. 'Edward may choose to help you out, provided he keeps his job and comes to some kind of accommodation with his wife. I do advise you, Edward, to tell her everything straight away – and I mean, today!'

Karen wailed, 'I'll tell you something for nothing, like. I'm not going back to school!'

'You can go to college. How do you think you can support yourself without learning a trade?'

Karen flounced, muttering she didn't need no silly old trade.

Ellie thought, but did not say, that Karen would probably do well as a high-class tart. No, on consideration, not *high-class*, because she hadn't enough brains for that. But if she managed to hook up with a pimp who treated her well . . . Oh dear! What a terrible thought! But the good Lord only knew what else the lazy cow had got going for her. Perhaps it would be best if Edward managed to set her up somewhere . . . but that would cost a lot . . . and she'd have to take care she didn't lose her looks. The only other thing the girl might be good for was modelling. Mm. Would she have enough self-discipline for the job? Possibly not, but . . .

'Karen, you could sign up with an agency to do some modelling, couldn't you? And you might consider selling your story to the tabloids.'

Karen went all starry-eyed and even unstuck herself from Edward's side. 'Oh, yes! That's what I'll do. Thanks, Mrs Quicke. I thought you were, like, too ancient to come up with any good ideas, but this is ace. Don't you think so, Edward?'

Edward's face was a picture. Doubt fought with hope. Hope won. Edward would always expect things to be made easy for him, wouldn't he?

Ellie got out her phone. 'Now, before we summon the police

and, remembering it's a Sunday afternoon and the top people
may or may not be on duty, I'm going to ring my solicitor
and see if he's free to help us. That's where my having money
comes into this: I'll pay for him to represent Malcolm, Agnes
and Mr Cook. Also for Karen, provided she tells the truth and
clears Malcolm of rape and kidnapping. Is that all right by
everyone?'

'What about me?' said Edward, annoyed at being left out.

'You'll pay for yourself,' said Ellie.

Sunday, early evening

Home again. At last. The sun had lost its brilliance, but it
hadn't rained for a while and the air was dry and dusty. The
trees were still densely leaved and green, but every now and
then a brown leaf drifted down to the pavement. Soon autumn
would be upon them.

'Yoohoo, I'm back!'

Thomas appeared from his study, talking to someone on his
mobile, raising a hand to her and smiling. Thomas was all right.

Susan appeared from the kitchen, also smiling. Susan was
wearing an apron and carrying a mixing bowl. She also nodded
and smiled. So Susan and Rose were all right.

Susan said, 'Like a cuppa?'

'Bless you,' said Ellie and shucked off her jacket.

Only then did she see the black-clad figure sitting on the
hall chair.

Claire. Not smiling. Fidgeting. 'Oh, there you are at last.
I've been waiting for ages.'

Now what?

Ellie shrugged and led the way into the sitting room. Claire
followed. Ellie seated herself in her favourite chair and looked
around with pleasure. There were flowers on the table in the
window, and the furniture was just where she liked it.

Claire said, 'I'm so worried. I dropped over to see my
brother, and there were police cars all over the place so I didn't
dare go in. Has somebody died? You've got a friend in the
police, haven't you? I thought you could ring them and find
out what's happened.'

'What makes you think that someone's died?'

The woman was anxiety itself, leaning forward on the edge of her chair. She guessed that something had gone very wrong with her plans, but didn't know how much they'd been compromised. 'Was there an accident, maybe?'

'Why don't you ask your brother what has happened?'

Claire shook her head. 'I wouldn't like to intrude.'

Ellie sighed. What a mess these people had made of their lives! 'If you'd asked your brother, he'd have told you that they'd decided to tell the police what they know about Jenna, Gail and Karen.'

Knowledge flickered at the back of Claire's eyes. Ellie remembered seeing that flicker once before, when Claire had begged for help but had been less than free with the truth. All the time Claire had been asking for Ellie's help, she'd been withholding evidence. She was like a spider, trussing Malcolm and Edward into submission with the knowledge of what she knew. A deadly spider. One who could kill?

Thomas had told Ellie to be wary of the woman. But, surely, she was harmless? What damage could she inflict on Ellie? There was nothing she could use for blackmail . . . No, nothing that Ellie could think of.

Susan came in with a tea tray laden not only with teapot and cups and saucers, but also slices of a delicious Victoria sponge. For two.

Ellie took the tray from her. 'Nothing for Claire. She's not staying.'

Claire bridled. 'You would refuse me even a cup of tea?'

'Yes, I would.' Ellie poured herself a cup of tea, took a slice of cake and handed the tray with everything else on it back to Susan, saying, 'Claire is on her way to the police station, you see. To confess.'

'What?' Claire flushed beetroot red. 'Why, what have I done? You can't accuse me of wrongdoing! In front of a witness, too. I could have you for that.'

'Ah, yes. Perhaps you'd like to stay for a moment, Susan. You might like to hear what I've learned about Claire in the last few days.'

Susan put down the tray and took a seat.

Claire, predictably, began to weep. 'Oh, how could you! When I've tried so hard to help you. You were only too keen to employ me when you needed someone to look after Rose, weren't you? Didn't I do the best I could for her? Yes, I did. Then you threw me out, sacked me because you'd heard some ridiculous rumour. I could have you up before a tribunal for that, couldn't I?' Her gaze skittered around the room, and her hands tightened into fists.

Ellie sipped tea and ate a mouthful of cake. 'Three elderly ladies were given so much cough linctus by you that two of them died, and the third became so disorientated that she didn't know what she was doing.'

'I haven't heard it's a crime to treat a cough with linctus.'

'Overdosing brings about sleepiness, hallucinations, disorientation and, if there is a heart problem, death. Susan; Claire's mother died this way, and so did an elderly lady who Claire worked for recently. Rose was dosed with linctus too, though she has more or less recovered.'

'Which proves,' said Claire, 'that I was right to treat her cough with linctus. What else can you accuse me of?' Her eyes were wide with apprehension. If she'd seen the police cars at her old house, she must be aware her plans had gone awry. But by how much? That was the question that must be occupying her mind.

'Blackmail,' said Ellie. And left it at that.

Claire wriggled, eyes and mouth wide. 'Blackmail? Are you accusing me of blackmail?'

'I wouldn't dream of it,' said Ellie. 'But Malcolm, Edward and his mother, Mr Cook and Karen are all talking about it to the police as we speak. Oh, and just to make matters absolutely clear, I've got my solicitor on the case, looking after their interests.'

Now Claire didn't know what to think. She ran her tongue over her lips, her eyes searching the room again and again . . . worrying how much Ellie knew, and wondering how much she could deny. She chose to pretend ignorance. 'What for?' That was probably her best defence.

'Harbouring under-age girls who should have been at school.'

'Really? Malcolm, Mr Cook? Harbouring under-age girls? Oh, surely not!' She tried to produce a laugh. 'That is so ridiculous. I can't believe you'd really think that.'

'What about Edward? Do you think he's also innocent of the charge?'

'Edward?' Her tongue flickered in and out.

For a moment Ellie was reminded of a snake. Now that everything was going to come out, would Claire take the opportunity to revenge herself on Edward by agreeing he could have been responsible for harbouring an under-age girl?

Claire shook her head, smiling, dabbing at the tears on her cheeks. 'Oh, you'll have me in stitches. Whatever will you think of next?'

Almost, Ellie gave up. Better brains than hers would have the task of trying to work out how much Claire had known and what use she'd made of that knowledge. So she said, 'Do you think they'll get done for murder as well?'

The woman hissed, drawing back in her chair. 'What, what? Murder, you say? No, no. That's not . . . Oh, how could you tease me so? You're enjoying this, aren't you? Well, all I can say is that it takes a twisted, evil mind to torture me like this, after all I've tried to do to help you.'

Ellie suddenly felt very tired. 'Now don't go on about wanting to see me dead and in hell. I think hell is where you are right now, Claire. You may be able to talk yourself out of this, and you may not. That's not my problem. You may fool yourself into thinking that you have been doing wrong in order to benefit the Vision, but God is not fooled, and there will come a reckoning.'

'How dare you preach to me about—'

'Just stating facts. Here's another one. Malcolm may or may not go to prison for what he's done, but either way, he's stopped working for the Vision for free. Also, Edward has realized that his oversight of the addicts sent to Ambrose has been less than perfect. Even if he retains his job – which I think, myself, is doubtful – I don't think Ambrose will be getting any more referrals from Social Services.'

Claire's eyes went dull, and she seemed to shrink in her chair. A double blow.

Ellie turned her own eyes away and took another mouthful of cake. Got it down with a swallow of tea. Someone rang a bell. A double ring? Two people ringing the doorbell? Ellie got to her feet.

Susan's head turned to the hall. 'Was that Rose's bell?'

Claire struggled out of her seat, a smile on her face which looked painful. 'I'm not staying here to be insulted. You'll hear from my solicitors in the morning.'

'Splendid,' said Ellie, shepherding her out of the room.

Thomas, appearing from his study. 'Was that Rose's bell?'

Rose lay huddled in a heap on the hall floor.

Ellie cried out, 'No!'

Mikey, in the doorway, open-mouthed. 'I came for my bike. Did you find my phone . . .? Is that Rose? What . . .?'

Claire pushed past him and slid out of the house.

Ellie knelt down at Rose's side and reached for her hand. 'Rose? Rose, are you all right?'

Susan hovered. 'Shall I ring for an ambulance?'

Ellie couldn't think straight. 'Rose?'

Thomas was on his knees at Rose's other side, turning her towards him. 'Take it gently, now.'

'I tripped and fell,' said Rose. 'Silly me. Miss Quicke said to follow her, and I tripped over my own two feet. So sorry. I know you're busy.'

Ellie said, 'Are you all right?' thinking and not thinking, fearing the worst while hoping against hope.

Thomas helped Rose to sit up in his arms. 'Let's get you to bed.'

'No,' said Rose. 'I don't want to go to bed. Help me to my chair.'

Thomas picked Rose up and carried her back to her chair in the kitchen. The others followed. Midge arrived from nowhere and hunkered down on the ledge beside Rose's chair.

'That's good,' said Rose, smiling at them all. 'I like to see what's going on.'

Ellie propped Rose up with pillows and cushions.

Mikey rang his mother to say he'd be late and seated himself beside Rose, holding one of her hands, rubbing it gently, patting it.

'Supper?' said Susan. 'Or an ambulance?'

'Supper,' said Rose, smiling. She reached up a wavering hand to touch Ellie's cheek.

'We always feel better when we've eaten.' Her eyelids drooped.

Susan, while keeping an eye on Rose, foraged in the freezer and produced a lasagne which she'd made earlier. She put it in the microwave to cook and set about preparing a green salad to go with it.

Ellie held Rose's free hand.

Now and then Rose opened her eyes long enough to smile at them.

The minutes ticked on.

Rose dozed, and woke. Smiled at them, and dozed again.

Mikey found the box of tissues and blew his nose. 'I'm not going home, and you can't make me.'

Thomas brought a chair from the table and sat close to Rose, murmuring prayers.

Ellie continued to hold Rose's hand.

Each time Rose opened her eyes, Ellie smiled at her, and Rose smiled back.

The clock in the hall struck seven, and the microwave timer pinged.

Rose roused herself. 'Supper time? Keep some back for me, will you? Go on, eat; I can't bear food going to waste.'

Susan dished up. They ate at the big table, or tried to. In silence. Watching Rose gently breathing through the last hour of her life.

Thomas said, quietly, to Ellie. 'Shall I ring the doctor?'

Ellie shook her head. She left the table to sit beside Rose and hold her hand again.

Mikey stacked the plates in the dishwasher while Susan put some cling film over the uneaten portions of lasagne.

Rose opened her eyes, looking at someone the others couldn't see. 'Not long now,' Rose said. 'Miss Quicke says my clothes are a disgrace and we're going shopping for some more this afternoon . . . as if that matters where we're going. Tomorrow we're picking out some more roses at the garden centre. Peace, and that white one that I can't remember the name of . . .'

Her eyes closed again . . . for maybe two lightly-taken breaths.

Then she started upright in her chair. 'There's her bell. I must go to her . . .'

Thomas caught Rose as she fell back in her chair and closed her eyes.

Ellie held Mikey's hand in hers while Thomas said the prayers for the dying.

Midge stretched himself out, yawning. He jumped down from the ledge and made his exit through the cat flap.

Mikey rang his mother. Vera and Dan arrived. Vera wept with Mikey for Rose. Dan put his arms round both to comfort them and eventually took them both home with him.

Thomas laid Rose on her own bed and stayed beside her all night. He told Ellie to go to bed, but she couldn't rest. It was a long night.

Later

Thomas took Rose's funeral.

Ellie bought and planted two roses in the garden; one was called Peace, and the other was the white one which Rose couldn't remember the name of, but Ellie thought must be Iceberg.

Rose's will left half her estate to the daughter who'd ignored her for so many years – 'for old time's sake' – and the rest to be divided equally between Mikey and Ellie.

News drifted back to Ellie in dribs and drabs, mostly through Lesley's visits.

'I suppose you'll think it good news,' said Lesley, tackling a piece of Susan's chocolate cake. 'The Crown Prosecution service has decided not to press charges against Agnes and Mr Cook.'

'Yes, that is good news,' said Ellie, who was feeling very quiet since Rose's death.

'As for that Karen . . .' Lesley wet her finger and captured the last crumbs of cake from her plate. 'She's been driving everyone mad, taking selfies of herself with every member of the police force who interviews her and putting them on Facebook.'

'Still as bald as a coot?'

'She seems to think it will get her a modelling career. Quite the little businesswoman is our Karen, negotiating to sell her story to the tabloids. Maybe she'll make it on to television as a media personality. I wouldn't put it past her.'

Karen had exonerated Malcolm from charges of kidnapping and rape, which helped the powers that be to view his part in the disappearances of Jenna and Gail less severely than they might otherwise have done.

'Malcolm's the one I feel the most sorry for,' said Ellie, 'and he's the only one likely to go to prison.'

'Stupid lad. Led by his hormones. Cheer up, Ellie. He's been charged with manslaughter, but the case against him is circumstantial, and with a good barrister there's a chance he'll get off.' She put her empty cup down. 'My niece working out all right for you?'

'We've let her have the flat up at the top of the house. There's no separate entrance, unfortunately, but she says she loves it up there, though she's still using our big kitchen to try out this and that. Most days she cooks us something we can all eat together. It's suiting us just fine.'

'And young Mikey? Is he buying a racing bike with the money Rose left him?'

'Dan and Vera had a long talk with him about that. Mikey's real father is from a wealthy family, but their ideas for him may not chime with his, so he's starting a university fund of his own. The money will go into that. He misses Rose. And so does Midge . . .' Ellie said as that wily cat jumped up on to Lesley's lap to purr and beg for food.

'So do you. So, I know, do I.' Lesley heaved Midge off her lap. 'I must go.'

Ellie said, 'What about Claire?'

Lesley shrugged. 'What can we charge her with? Two elderly ladies died and were cremated. Claire might have hastened their ends, but there's no proof that she did so.'

'She blackmailed Malcolm and Edward into helping the Vision.'

'She says she never did. She says they offered to do it off their own bat. We can't make blackmail stick, Ellie. I know you don't like the woman – well, neither do I – but to bring charges we have to have some evidence of wrongdoing, and there is none.'

A few days later Ellie paid Agnes a visit and was not surprised to find Emmanuel Cook already there. Both were subdued, but cautiously hopeful for the future. Malcolm had been granted bail and was working all hours trying to make up for lost time.

Agnes said, 'He's feeling a bit depressed. He feels he's living under a cloud of suspicion and can't see any way out from under. All he can do is hope that some day, some how, the police will discover who really killed those two girls. But he's grateful that he no longer has to work for the Vision.'

'What about Edward?' said Ellie, touching a spot which she knew must be sore.

Agnes shook her head with a sigh. 'I told him all along that he was asking for trouble, but he wouldn't listen. I can only hope that this has been a lesson to him.'

'I doubt it,' said Mr Cook. 'Edward's never been able to keep it in his pants, has he?'

Ellie was intrigued. 'Is he still seeing Karen?'

'We wouldn't know about that,' said Agnes primly. 'All I said to him was that he shouldn't bring any more girls back here, and he promised me he wouldn't.'

Emmanuel chuckled. 'He got a right rollocking at the Town Hall, mind you. It was six of one and half a dozen of the other that he'd lose his job. He's survived after a fashion, but I don't think he'll be getting promotion in a hurry.'

'And his wife?' said Ellie.

Agnes arched her eyebrows. 'Refuses to believe her husband could ever have looked at anyone else. Says it's all lies. I suppose she can see only too clearly that life as a single parent is no fun. I wish he were rid of her in one way, but the maintenance money would cripple him.'

Emmanuel snorted. 'She's a tongue like an asp, that one. I don't envy him.'

No. Neither did Ellie.

Which left the question: who really had killed the two girls?

EIGHTEEN

Yes, who had actually killed Jenna and Gail?

Ellie did have an idea, but wasn't at all sure it was correct. This whole case had been confusing. First she'd thought it might be Malcolm, until she'd met him and heard his story. Then she'd thought it must have been Ambrose, even though she couldn't quite see him as Murderer One.

On and off she spent quite a bit of time thinking about it. It seemed to her that the murders had not been premeditated, but that someone had come across the girls and, driven by lust to rape, had then killed his victims to prevent them from talking.

Well, it was a theory.

She remembered bold eyes with heavy lids, which had dismissed her as being of no interest. Testosterone on legs.

Edward? It might have been him if he hadn't been getting what he wanted from the girls already. He wouldn't have killed them because it would have put a stop to his little games – unless, perhaps, they'd threatened to tell his wife? But no. That wouldn't work. He'd got round that problem without too much bother. Edward was Teflon man. Mud never stuck. Ellie could only hope, uncharitable though the thought might be, that some time soon the Council would look for an opportunity to dispense with his services. Except that this might mean the break-up of his marriage and Agnes' grandson moving away . . .

So, who . . .? There'd been someone else she'd met recently who fitted the part of Sex Starved Male. But, who?

A telephone call prompted her to take action.

She went down the corridor to tell Thomas she'd had a phone message asking her to meet Ambrose at the big house that afternoon, because he was about to leave the area. Thomas nodded, his eyes on the screen. She wasn't sure he'd really heard what she'd said. He was inclined to concentrate on one thing to the exclusion of everything else. So she kissed the top of his head, scribbled a note as to where she was going and left it on top of his printer.

Up the hill she went. A big sign had been erected at the entrance to the drive of the old house. *Sold. Twelve superb luxury flats to be erected on this site.* Followed by the name of the managing agents, who were not Diana's lot.

The blinds in the extension were all higgledy-piggledy. The drive was unswept, though the trees were shedding leaves like billy-o. One of the upstairs windows had been broken, and a curtain flapped forlornly half in and half outside the room. There was a Drive Yourself van by the front door.

Two removal men came out of the front door, carrying an old-fashioned settee with a floral-printed cover on it. They stowed it in the van, which already contained various household items. A third man emerged from the house to heave some black plastic bags on top of the settee. One of the tenants moving house?

Ellie stepped into the hall, unhindered. One of the notice boards hung askew; the other was on the floor, propped against the wall. The paintwork already looked scuffed. Down the stairs came a youngish couple carrying pot plants and more plastic bags. They glanced at Ellie and went on their way. Removal day. Please don't interrupt.

The door to the Vision's dining quarters stood ajar. Ellie looked in. The stacking tables and chairs had gone. The hatch to the kitchen beyond was open, disclosing empty shelves. Dust was everywhere.

It was sad, in a way.

The door to Ambrose's quarters was shut. Ellie knocked, and a voice told her to enter.

Ambrose was sitting on a stool, which was the only piece of furniture left in the room. Some suitcases and a couple of plastic bags huddled by the door. There were no curtains at the windows and no carpets on the floor. Darker shapes on the green-painted wallpaper showed where items of furniture had stood until recently.

Outside, the Drive Yourself van farted and was driven away.

Ambrose's hands were laid on his knees, palm upwards.

His eyes were closed. He was meditating? At least he was not in an aggressive mood.

He opened his eyes and brought his mind back from wherever it had been.

She said, 'You wanted to see me?'

He stirred and looked around. Did he even recognize her? She said, 'You're moving out. You have some place to go?'

'My car has been repossessed. I'm moving to a rented house south of the river. Hector took the last of the furniture over there this morning and will be back for me soon.'

Hector? Who was he? One of Ambrose's flock . . .? No, he was the decorator who'd tried to force his way into her house. She remembered bold, dark eyes. Like Edward's. Like those of the man she'd imagined might have killed the girls. Oh.

Ambrose got to his feet and stretched. He said, 'Pride blinded me to what was happening. I soared high on the wings of others, but they betrayed my trust and now I am fallen to the depths.'

'You trusted Claire, because you believed she was in love with you?'

He winced, and his eyes dropped from hers. 'I was totally absorbed by my mission. Everything else was sacrificed to that.'

'You know she was nearly charged with murder?'

He blinked. 'Why on earth should she be charged with murder?'

'You should ask her about that. Is she still with you?'

He blinked again. 'Why are you here? Have you come to gloat?'

'Didn't you leave a message on my answerphone, asking me to call?'

'No. Why would I do that?'

A chill ran down Ellie's back. 'Someone asked me to visit you this afternoon. If it wasn't you, then who . . .? Do you think Claire . . .? No, it was a man's voice. Was it Hector?'

'Why would he ask you to call on me?'

'Because I have obstructed his plans?'

He seemed genuinely bemused. 'What plans? Are you referring to the time when you refused him entry into your house? A misunderstanding.'

'Granted. He might have phoned me on your behalf, without your knowledge.'

'Why should he do that?'

'Claire acted on your behalf in various matters.'

Another shrug. 'She thought she was serving the Vision.'

'She wanted to please you in all things, but the methods she chose were not above reproach, were they?'

Heightened colour. 'She told me you had money for charitable purposes, and we duly applied for some. If you had given us what we asked for, we wouldn't be in this fix now.'

'You didn't meet our terms of reference. Did you know that Claire had blackmailed her brother into working for the Vision for free? And forced Edward to keep Social Services in your pocket?'

'They worked for us because they understood the Vision and wanted to be a part of it.'

'Don't fool yourself. Claire discovered something about them which put them in her power, and she used them to help you. Did you never suspect that her devotion to you was unhealthy? Or have you become so self-absorbed that you had not noticed?'

He stared at her, not willing to understand. 'Claire has devoted her life to the Vision. It is her calling, and she follows it to the best of her ability.'

Ellie thought Claire needed a psychiatrist, but didn't think it would do any good to say so.

Ambrose rolled his shoulders, easing tension. 'Now I have to start afresh, to cleanse myself from all that has gone wrong in the past. I trust in the Vision. It will guide me into pastures new.'

'I'm sorry things turned out so badly for you, but perhaps the regime you ran was a little too harsh for some people, those who are not as strong as you.'

He gave a tiny nod. 'Perhaps. I shall have to review my methods when troubled souls are sent to me in future.'

She rather hoped there would be no more, but you never knew. Where else would the likes of Liddy and Dolores find someone to help them back into the normal world? And what was going to happen to them now? Were they already back on the streets? Perhaps. Yet what else did the world have to offer them? Perhaps Social Services would allocate them to a doctor who would put them on a different course of treatment. Well, you could always hope.

She wondered if her trust could put some money into a programme for Dolores and Liddy, but realized it would require the sort of medical background which they did not have. Reluctantly, she abandoned the idea. As for Ambrose . . . what did the future look like for him?

Ambrose threw back his shoulders. 'I shall survive. Yes, I was cast down into the pit when they told me, when our support from Social Services came to an end, when we were given notice to quit. I couldn't believe it at first, but now I see it was all meant. One door has closed, but another will open for me to go through.'

Ellie said, 'You heard that the girl Karen has surfaced again? And that at one point the police were thinking of charging Claire's brother with the murders of two more girls? You'll laugh, but at one time I wondered if you yourself might have been responsible for their deaths.'

He was astounded. 'What!'

'Well . . .' She was conscious of her colour rising. 'It was that business of your being unavailable one afternoon a week and apparently living alone.'

'Oh, that.' A conscious smile. 'To serve the Vision, I must keep myself pure . . . and in good trim. I visit a masseur once a week.' His eyes darkened. 'He was expensive. I suppose that has to go now, as well.'

'There is something else I wanted to ask you. The man Hector, who does some decorating for you. You told Dolores and the other girls to be wary of him. Can you tell me why?'

A frown. 'Hector? The poor creature, driven mad by needs which are human, but if not controlled can lead to tragedy.'

'Such bold eyes,' Ellie ventured.

A nod. 'He sees the evil in the eyes of young girls, in the

way they flaunt their bodies, the sins they seduce men into committing.'

'He feels he has a duty to stop them?'

'What?' Another frown. 'What do you mean?'

'He did more than just look at the girls, didn't he?'

A long pause. 'We do not speak of his past here. It has no meaning, once you have been reborn in the spirit.'

'He molested young girls in the past? Before he came to you?'

A restless movement. 'He used to hang around the school gates where Claire worked. He told her he couldn't help himself. She was sorry for him and brought him to me for healing.'

'You took him in, assuming that you could help him to control his urges. You sheltered him, and you gave him work. But, you also told your girls to be wary of him, so you *did* worry that he might reoffend. Did you know that Claire herself had been interfered with as a child?'

He shook his head. 'What nonsense.'

So he didn't know that. It was quite possible that he'd never looked at Claire properly. He'd seen what he wanted to see; an acolyte, a slave, someone who tried to serve him to the best of her ability, but who would never be considered an equal.

He said, 'Hector has been a good friend to Claire. After she lost her job we had to sell her car to defray expenses, and he was always ready to help her out by giving her lifts.'

'That explains it. I'm talking about the time before she lost her job at the school and had to give up her car. She wanted to retrieve her father's desk from the house in which she'd grown up, but it was too big for her little car, so she asked Hector to give her a lift over there in his van. She planned to avoid Malcolm by going when he was working here, in case he objected to her taking the desk. When she got there, she used the keys she'd copied to get in . . . and found a strange girl living in the house. That was Jenna, a refugee from a rape in her family, who told the whole sorry tale to the woman who was Malcolm's sister. Did Hector go in with Claire? I assume he must have done. She couldn't have carried the desk out by herself.'

He frowned. 'What has that got to do with—'

'Claire had had a troubled relationship with her brother. Finding Jenna in his house, pregnant and happy, lit the fires of jealousy in her. Did Hector return at a later date to abuse and kill Jenna? Or did she watch while he did so?'

He stared at her, wide-eyed. 'No. No, it's not true!'

'Malcolm came home to find the girl dead and, because he'd given her shelter from the rapist in her family, he feared he might be accused of having killed her. So, instead of ringing the police, he left Jenna by the canal bridge . . . which meant that Claire had him in her toils. And not only Malcolm – whom she got working for you for nothing – but also Edward, who'd taken advantage of Jenna and got her pregnant. Coincidentally, Edward worked for Social Services, and so he could keep the Vision project afloat for you by referring suitable clients.

'It's ironic about Malcolm, isn't it? Because, if he hadn't had to report for duty here every week, he might never have come across another girl who was ripe for the plucking. But he saw Gail, and Gail saw him, and after a right dressing-down from you, Gail got Malcolm to take her out for the evening . . . and she ended up in the same place as Jenna.

'When Gail disappeared from this house, Claire was suspected of killing her. I wonder how long it took her to work out that Malcolm could have gone off with the girl? Not long. She knew he'd been working here. She taxed him with the knowledge, and he confirmed it. She could have passed the information on to the police, which would have got her out from under, but no; it was far more exciting, far more worthwhile for her to pretend she knew nothing, because it kept Malcolm and Edward tied to her side and working for the Vision. If the police had charged her with murder, I suppose she'd have told them what she knew. But they didn't, and she kept quiet. Now and then she'd see Malcolm about the place, working for you, and she'd get the latest news from him. She learned that Gail had moved in on Edward, and finally, she heard that Gail was pregnant. Every day she thought about Gail being pregnant and enjoying her new life, while Claire herself had no one interested in her.

'At last she could bear it no longer. She got Hector to take

her over to Malcolm's again. Did she tell Hector about Gail?
Hector had known Gail in the past. He'd seen her about the
place enough times. So she deliberately let him loose on
Gail, too. What satisfaction it must have given Claire to
destroy the happiness of her brother and Edward, not once
but twice!

'Claire herself was not bringing you in much money,
however hard she worked, but she was invaluable on all the
other fronts, smoothing your path by providing you with
manpower to keep your property maintained and someone at
Social Services to feed you clients. She idolized you, didn't
she? But all that has stopped because Malcolm and Edward
have told the police what they know, and Social Services have
withdrawn their support.'

'I am innocent of—'

'I know. You have nothing to hide, except that you have been
sheltering Hector. The time has come for you to tell the police
what you know about the man. so that they can see there is
someone beside Malcolm in the frame.'

She had been concentrating so hard on Ambrose that she
hadn't heard another van draw up outside, or footsteps in
the hall.

Ambrose's eyes shifted to look behind her. His neck
swelled.

Ellie half turned and saw Claire with the decorator, Hector.
Both were looking at her, and both were smiling. Not nicely.

It must have been Hector who had phoned through the
invitation for her to visit the Vision that afternoon, not
Ambrose.

So why had they wanted her to be there?

For revenge, because she'd thwarted all Claire's plans to
help Ambrose?

Ambrose hadn't known anything about Claire's blackmail, but Hector had known every little detail because
Hector had been the one she turned to after she'd lost her
own car, to give her lifts here and there . . . especially when
she wanted to collect her father's desk from her old home
. . . and then to check on what was happening there with
the girls . . . and afterwards she'd let him loose on those

very same girls, rather as one lets a pitbull dog off the leash.

Ellie said, 'Did you watch while he killed those girls, Claire?'

Claire's smile widened, and she sighed, remembering with pleasure. 'I watched everything he did to them. I encouraged you to take your time over killing them, didn't I, Hector? But you were always in a hurry to put your hands round their necks, weren't you?' A long, long, sigh. 'It was all over far too quickly for me.'

Ambrose's face was a mask of horror. 'Claire? You don't mean . . .? No, no!'

'Yes, yes,' said Claire, smiling. 'Didn't I do well? The police never guessed. The Vision could have gone on for ages with the work that Malcolm and Edward were giving us, until this stupid woman came along with her uppity ways, refusing us what we needed. So, Hector is going to deal with her, as is only right and proper—'

Ambrose gaped.

Ellie felt as if she'd been kicked in the stomach. She refused to show how frightened she was. She tried to steady her voice as she said, 'And how, may I ask, are you intending to get rid of my body?'

'We'll leave it here, with one of Malcolm's jackets beside you. Then the police will stop their dilly-dallying and have him for the three murders, while I will inherit the house I was born in and should have had all along, by rights. I shall sell it and give the Vision the money, to start all over again.'

Hector's big hands were opening and closing, clenching . . . eager to be put to work.

Claire smiled up at Ambrose. 'You see how much I can do for you?'

Ellie said, 'You, personally, killed those girls for Ambrose's sake?'

'No, of course not. *I* didn't do anything. Hector did it for me, right?'

Hector grinned. 'I did: yes, I did.' He growled and moved a step towards Ellie. 'And now I'll do you!'

Would Claire stop him?

No. Claire stepped aside to let him rush at Ellie with his big hands outstretched . . .

Big hands reaching for her neck . . .

With a roar, Ambrose leaped. He thrust Ellie aside and threw Hector backwards against the wall . . .

A confusion of blows and a thud.

Hector, eyes closing, slid down the wall and lay there like a broken doll.

Dead? No, he was still breathing. But knocked out, definitely unconscious. Thank the Lord.

Ambrose breathed heavily, fists clenched, glaring down at Hector.

No one spoke.

Someone giggled.

Claire.

The giggling turned to hysteria.

'Oh . . . what have you done!'

Ambrose continued to stare at Hector.

Claire wept and laughed.

Ellie reached, slowly and carefully, into her handbag for her phone.

Ambrose lifted his arms to heaven. 'Yes, what have I done?' He collapsed into a heap on the floor and wound his arms around his head.

A stir in the doorway, and Thomas came into view. 'Are you all right, Ellie? I didn't like your coming up here by yourself . . . Why . . . What?'

'I'm all right, thank you, Thomas,' said Ellie, in a voice that wobbled. 'But I must admit, it's all got a bit much for me. Hector tried to kill me, oh dear me, yes. Ambrose . . . he needs . . . He needs *you*, I think.' And into the phone: 'Ambulance and police, please.'

Thomas knelt down by Ambrose and lifted him into his arms.

Ambrose said, over and over, 'Why? What did I do wrong? Why, why, why?'

Thomas said, 'Pride, Ambrose.'

Ambrose said, 'Help me?'

A week later, over tea and cake

Lesley said, 'Hector's come out of his coma. The first thing he did was to ask for a solicitor so that he can sue Ambrose for assault.'

Ellie shook her head. 'Hector was aiming to kill me, and Ambrose stopped him. I'll testify to that in court, if necessary. I'm glad Hector's not dead . . . At least, I suppose I ought to be, but he did kill those girls.'

'Ambrose packs quite a punch.'

'It's fortunate for me that he does.' She sighed. 'This whole sorry situation was partly his fault. He didn't want to look too closely at all the help he was being offered, because it was making his life so much easier and forwarding his career. That was his big mistake. When he eventually realized how Claire and Hector had been propping up his project, he saw red. I'm sure he didn't intend to murder Hector, but he did want to hurt him as well as push me out of harm's way.'

Ambrose had clung to Thomas for the three long days in which he'd moved into Ellie's house. An uncomfortable guest; by turns spiky, weepy and full of rage. Thomas abandoned his own work to help Ambrose through a full-scale breakdown. Finally, he managed to persuade the broken man to see a consultant, who whisked Ambrose away to a quiet retreat house, where he could talk through his problems and decide what to do with the rest of his life. Much to Ellie's relief.

Claire had been sectioned. Unfit to plead. Claire had opted out of reality, as she'd opted out of taking responsibility for so much of her life.

Lesley ate more of the cake and allowed Midge on to her lap. Midge kept a beady eye on Lesley's plate. Perhaps, if he were very good, the woman would be so kind as to let him have a bit with cream on?

Ellie said, 'It's quite clear now that it was Hector, and not Malcolm, who killed the girls?'

'It is. Let's hope Malcolm doesn't start chatting up any more females before he comes up in court on the other, minor, charges.'

'I hope he gets a suspended sentence. Or community work. What a mess. They all started off with such high hopes . . .'

'Only to collide with real life. And if I don't get back to the station soon, reality will catch up with me, too.'

Later that week

Diana had brought little Evan round, purportedly to visit his granny, but really to see if Ellie would babysit that evening. Diana put Evan down and produced her smartphone. 'What time can you make it?'

Evan was a child who knew what he wanted out of life and usually got it. He was walking and talking, after a fashion. He said, 'Wose.' He still couldn't pronounce his 'r's properly yet, and so 'Rose' had turned into 'Wose'. He toddled straight out of the sitting room and into the hall.

Ellie said, 'Sorry, Diana. I can't tonight. Thomas and I are going out to friends for supper.' She started after Evan. 'Haven't you told him that Rose is dead?'

'Mm? I think I did. By the way, you might like the details of . . .'

Ellie hurried across the hall in Evan's wake. Susan was in the process of reorganizing the kitchen, and heaven only knew what havoc Evan could create if he was in there by himself. Where had the little rascal got to? He wasn't by the dishwasher, which was grounds for rejoicing. What Evan could do by way of emptying the dishwasher was nobody's business.

Diana followed her, looking at her smartphone. '. . . I went to see this wonderful woman, and I thought you might like to pay her a visit as well. Well, can you babysit tomorrow instead?'

'Um? No, sorry. Vera and Dan and Mikey are coming over for supper. What woman was that?' Where was Evan? In the broom cupboard? No. Had he got as far as the larder? No.

Diana was put out. 'Don't you want to look after your grandson? Oh, someone who took the curse off me.'

'Really?' Ellie could hardly believe that Diana had taken the curse seriously.

'Yes. She's amazing, if a bit pricey. Not that I believe in such things, of course.'

'Um? Oh. Yes, of course . . . There you are, Evan.'

He'd managed somehow or other to get up on to Rose's big old chair and was sitting there with an expression of amazement on his face. In his hand he held the silver bell which Rose and, before her, Miss Quicke had been accustomed to use when they needed attention.

He rang the bell. His mouth and eyes wide.

He looked up at the grown-ups, to check that they shared his surprise and delight in the sound he'd made.

'That's Rose's bell, isn't it?' said Diana. 'Is it clean enough for him to handle?'

'Wose.' Evan twisted in the chair, looking behind him. He'd sat on Rose's knee on that chair since he was so high, and before that she'd fed him in his high chair from it. That chair meant Rose to him.

'Wose,' he said again and held the bell high. And laughed.

Diana held out her hand. 'Give it to me, Evan. You don't know where it's been.'

Thunderclouds gathered on his brow. He might be young in years, but he knew what he wanted, and he wasn't about to give up his new toy.

Ellie got the biscuit tin out and tried for a distraction. She held out a biscuit in either hand. 'Here you are, Evan.' Thinking he'd drop the bell to take the biscuits. He didn't.

He considered her offer, took one biscuit off her and ate it, still holding on to the bell with his free hand. Then he took the other. And made the bell chime again.

Diana lifted him up and tickled him. That worked. He giggled and dropped the bell. Ellie replaced it on the ledge at the back of the chair, while Diana started walking back to the hall, allowing Evan to drop to the ground as she accessed information on her smartphone with one hand. 'Well, how about next week? Can you babysit on Monday?'

'I'm afraid he's getting too strong for me to handle.' Ellie watched, fascinated, as Evan made his way back to the kitchen, climbed on to Rose's chair and claimed the bell again.

'Wose's bell,' he said, nodding. 'Evan's, now.'

'Yes,' said Ellie. 'It's yours now. Look after it, won't you?' And to Diana, 'I think he might turn out to be musical.'

Diana's eyes lit up. Ellie could see her daughter was envisaging Evan striding on to the stage as a concert pianist or conducting one of the world's greatest orchestras.

Well, we all have dreams for our children, don't we?